This book should be returned to any branch of the Lancashire County Library on or before the date shown

WILD LILY

K. M. PEYTON

David Fickling Books

31 Beaumont Street
Oxford OX1 2NP, UK

Wild Lily
is a
DAVID FICKLING BOOK

First published in Great Britain by
David Fickling Books,
31 Beaumont Street,
Oxford, OX1 2NP

www.davidficklingbooks.com

Hardback edition published 2016
This edition published 2017

Text © K. M. Peyton

978-1-910989-28-9

1 3 5 7 9 10 8 6 4 2

Papers used by David Fickling Books are from well-managed
forests and other responsible sources.

DAVID FICKLING BOOKS Reg. No. 8340307

A CIP catalogue record for this book is available from the British Library.

Typeset in Adobe Garamond by Falcon Oast Graphic Art Ltd.
Printed and bound in Great Britain by Clays plc.

For Irene

THE 1920s

APRIL, 1921

1

'Pa, it's my birthday tomorrow.'

'Is it, by Jove!' His father lowered his newspaper and stared curiously at Antony over the top as if he had never seen him before, which he hadn't much. 'And how old will you be? Twelve?'

'Seventeen, Pa. I was born in 1904, if you remember.'

'Good God!' Mr Sylvester put the newspaper down. 'Seriously?'

'Yes, of course seriously.' Antony tried hard to believe his father was joking, but knew he wasn't. What was the use? 'I thought you might buy me a present.'

'Yes. Fine. What do you want?'

'An aeroplane.'

'An aeroplane? Hmm.'

His father went back behind his newspaper, and Antony waited. He wasn't too worried; his father always gave him what he asked for.

'Go over to Brooklands then and see my friend Tommy

3

Sopwith. He'll find you something sensible. You don't want to break your neck.'

'No, Pa. Thank you. I'll be careful.'

Which he wouldn't. Had he ever been? It wasn't in his nature.

His father didn't look up again and Antony left the breakfast table satisfied. His friends had scoffed and said the old man wouldn't go for it, but they didn't know the old man like he did. They had said try him with a racehorse, but Antony wasn't interested in racing. He could have got one, of course, even as well as the aeroplane quite possibly. But just for the sake of his friends . . . ? He often thought they were only his friends for what they could get. But all the same, he needed them, stranded in school holidays in this Godforsaken home. With an aeroplane they could travel. It must be a two-seater. He could get them to Paris one by one. They could all go up the Eiffel Tower . . .

Musing happily, Antony made his way out of the house. If he hadn't lived in Lockwood Hall all his life, finding the way outside from the breakfast room could have taken half the morning, the place was so large. It sat like a great frowning fortress on a wooded hilltop, looking down on its own lake, the farm, the grotto, the winding river . . . it just needed a row of cannons on the rooftop, Antony often thought, to dispel raiders – should they ever come. But nobody came much apart from the staff, an army of them: six gardeners under a head gardener, ten kitchen staff, myriad cleaning women, handymen, pantry boys, nurses for his sister, the garage men,

4

the forestry men, the charcoal workers, not to mention the farm workers scattered to the far horizons, only met in passing. One knew a few of them by name and joshed with the boys sometimes, and talked machinery in the garage, but of course none were friends. Antony was a law unto himself, with all these people to tend him, but at the back of his mind he often felt he was missing something. A mother? All his friends had mothers. He wasn't sure about it, knowing mothers could be a nuisance: fussy, bossy and demanding. Perhaps not. But an aeroplane . . . his heart lifted. He hadn't really doubted that his father would agree, but now the words had been spoken Antony felt an unusual frisson of excitement. For a boy who had everything, he now had a bit more than everything – an aeroplane!

I'm on my way, Mr Sopwith!

'Did you know, Squashy, that Mr Sylvester is buying Ant an aeroplane?'

'What's an aeroplane?'

'Those things in the sky, that men sit in.'

'Cor.'

Lily was kind to her brother Squashy who had little brain. None, said most of the village people. But he did no harm. Their father was Mr Sylvester's head gardener and they lived in a cottage on the estate. He often took them with him when he went to work, as his wife had died when Squashy was born

5

and he felt he had to keep an eye on them – Lily seemed to look for mischief and of course Squashy had no brain, so they slipped easily into trouble. Not that Antony was a good influence; as the lad had so little to do, he often came larking with Lily. The two were something of a pair, although Lily, at thirteen, was a good deal younger. But she had no conception of class where Antony was concerned, and treated him the same as she treated her village friends – that is, with her usual scorn, always the one who knew best.

'I don't know why he don't clip you one, the cheek of you,' her father said. 'You should remember he's the gaffer round here. A bit of respect would do no harm.'

'What, for Ant? He's only Ant.'

Her father, known by his surname Gabriel, as were all the workers on the estate, was not articulate enough to explain exactly what he meant. It was true that Antony was not the vicar or the doctor or the squire or Mrs Carruthers, or anybody to whom Lily was quite rightly in the habit of showing respect to, but all the same he was heir to one of the richest men in the county and therefore well up in the hierarchy of people to whom Gabriel touched his hat to and feared to look in the eye. Even if Antony was only a kid.

Gabriel called him Master Antony. If he got an aeroplane he might have to up it to Mister.

Mrs Carruthers was outraged. Her husband had told her the

news. He knew that she got very upset if she didn't know every detail of what was going on in the village or at the big house. Even if the news infuriated her it was easier for him to live with that than her outrage if she missed out on it. He braced himself.

'Sylvester's insane! The boy will kill himself!'

'The things are safer now than they used to be. The war advanced flying no end.'

'It advanced Sylvester too. How's he made all that money, I'd like to know? To buy his son an aeroplane, just for a toy! I ask you!'

'He's a very shrewd man, Mr Sylvester. A clever businessman. You always imply that he made his wealth dishonestly, but there's no evidence.'

She never called him Mr Sylvester, just Sylvester, because she ranked him as trade. She had scarcely ever met him for he was always in his Rolls-Royce when he passed through the village; he never came to church, nor to any of the village functions, but his lifestyle was widely described by his servants who were mostly local and only too willing to gossip.

Sadly, the gossip was very boring – no women, no parties, few visitors, no empty whisky bottles. The only items of interest concerned his daughter Helena, whom no one had ever seen save fleetingly, very occasionally, in the back seat of the Rolls-Royce on its way to London. She was twenty-one and very beautiful. But she was blind and deaf and lived in her own quarters in the vast house with her own staff to look after her. However those staff never came to the village. They had

7

their own staff to wait on them. This was really good fodder for gossip.

'Think they're royalty! Can you believe!'

'And she treated like a princess! Only a tradesman's daughter! That's what money can do!'

'But the poor mite – blind and deaf! Can you imagine it?'

Kinder souls spoke out:

'Why shouldn't she have the best? No mother to love her – it's tragic.'

'And the boy too. He could do with a mother to keep him out of bad ways. He runs quite wild.'

'Such a bad influence on those nice boys – the vicar's lad, John, and Cedric Butterworth – easily led, I'm afraid. Even that clever lad Simon, the one with his nose in the air, he's very much taken with Antony. They spend all their time up there when school's over.'

'Well, not surprising, considering there's the lake to swim in and tennis courts and servants to bring out lemonade—'

'And now an aeroplane! Can you believe it!'

'There'll be a death up there, you mark my words. Asking for it, a death for sure!'

Antony decided to invite his friend Simon to go to Brooklands with him to meet Mr Sopwith. He would want someone to talk it through with and Simon had more brain than the others – sometimes, Antony thought, more brain than was comfortable, by which he meant more than himself. Simon's father was a professor of some sort, much respected in the village, a real gentleman they said. Simon went to Eton, like Antony, but was given much extra tutoring by his father at home. He was said to be a brilliantly clever boy, unlike Antony.

Antony's father was out all the next day, as usual, so Antony ordered the Rolls and asked the chauffeur, Tom, to pick up Simon on his way out of the village.

'I say, I like this!' Simon waved to the unsurprised villagers as they purred away down the high street.

Tom was laughing. 'Two little squits like you in this motor! You don't know your luck, Master Antony.'

'I do, you idiot. You know I do.' Antony was not sure he wanted Tom's familiarity in front of Simon, but Tom was not one to take it too far. They got on well. 'You think you'll be able to service an aeroplane? We'll have to have some instructions,' he added.

'I managed to move from horses to motors, so I daresay I can move from motors to flying machines. They got an engine the same, haven't they?'

Tom, a young man who missed the Great War because of a history of tuberculosis, was obviously going to enjoy having an aeroplane on the premises, and Antony felt his excitement rising as the Rolls wound its way through the network of Surrey lanes towards Brooklands, not far from Lockwood. The area was graced by the homes of the rich; they flashed past in the shade of their private woodlands: so beautiful, like jewels set in emerald lawns – why on earth, with all these alternatives to hand, had his father chosen hideous Lockwood? Antony wondered. Presumably for its grounds, which were undeniably beautiful and very extensive. Good for landing an aeroplane, luckily, unlike these tree-girt mansions that saw them pass. Antony had already earmarked his airfield – a strip of land below the lake, beyond the grotto.

Perhaps Tom and some of his mates would be able to build him a hangar down there before next winter . . . he could not believe his luck, as the Rolls turned down the tarmac road marked Brooklands – his father saying yes.

He had visited Brooklands before, so was not surprised by the sight of the untidy conglomeration of huts and workshops that huddled on the edge of the famous racetrack, high-banked in a great ellipse all round them. It was hard to believe that during the war this place had been a hive of activity where the great designers and producers of military aircraft thrashed out their ideas: even then it had not looked impressive, but now it was decidedly down at heel, with dismantled aircraft, old cars and motorbikes scattered all over the place. The name SOPWITH appeared in large letters on a row of the sheds, but the great man, they were told, was not there.

'He's over at Kingston most of the time now, set up his works there. He a friend of yours?'

The man they spoke to was patronizing, but obviously impressed by the Rolls-Royce, uncertain.

'He's a friend of my father's.' Antony spoke with the assurance of the Eton boy. 'My father said he would find me a

10

suitable plane. That's why we're here, to buy one. My name is Antony Sylvester.'

The young man's attitude changed abruptly at the mention of the name Sylvester and thereafter the two boys – and Tom, hovering in the background – attracted a number of interested parties. They spent the afternoon in a blissful whirl of technical talk, pushed to see this one, that one, try this cockpit, what visibility eh? – this rudder is out on its own, handles like silk . . . get in and we'll give it a roll . . .

Rolling meant taxiing across the airfield without taking off. It was the beginning of learning to fly. Antony was given the controls and the chance to try it for himself, and he went zigzagging across the unkempt grass in hair-raising fashion, terrified he might take off by mistake – it easily happened, apparently: 'Suddenly the ground ain't there any more. So not too much throttle, be careful now.'

Be careful. Simon knew it wasn't in his friend's nature and was relieved that he himself wasn't offered the chance to try anything. He saw too how the name Sylvester carried weight. His father had told him several times 'to go carefully with the Sylvesters', but was unable to elaborate when questioned. Just a shrug and, 'I don't think I trust that man.' Simon pointed out that he rarely saw the father, only Antony, and with Antony came perks, like today.

The machines were mainly planes left over from the war, fighters being dismantled for parts. Several were two-seaters, carrying a pilot and a gunner, or a photographer; some still had a gun mounted. Some were monoplanes, some biplanes.

11

Antony realized there was no way he could choose in one afternoon, and decided the best thing would be to sign on for some lessons and choose to buy when he knew a bit more. A flying school was on the site, so he signed himself up, giving his age as eighteen. In spite of his father thinking he was twelve, he knew he passed for eighteen without much trouble. He wasn't questioned.

Going home in the Rolls they reckoned they had spent a very good day. Just before the car came into the village and approached Simon's house, a sprawling old place half-hidden back from the road in a tangle of trees, Simon said to Antony, 'What does your father do, that he carries such clout? When you said the name Sylvester their attitude changed in a trice.'

'*Do?* How should I know? He makes money.'

'Doing what?'

'I don't know. He goes up to London a lot, to see politicians and things. Manufacturers.'

'Manufacturers of what?'

'Money!' Antony laughed. 'What does *your* pa do? Does it matter?'

'He writes books. No, it doesn't matter. Just wondered, that's all.'

The Rolls stopped outside his gate and Simon got out. His mother was getting tea and a fire burned cheerily, sparks flying across the dog-worn hearth-rug; his father was writing at his desk and a smell of baking emanated from the kitchen. Simon thought of Antony driving on to godforsaken Lockwood Hall and grinned to himself, not feeling envious at all.

'How was it?' his father asked.

'Good. Very interesting. Ant looked at a lot, and has signed up for flying lessons.'

'Oh, showing some sense for once. Knowing him, I half thought he might be coming back in one.'

'It won't take long, I reckon.'

'Well, I might as well tell you now, you won't be going up in it. I forbid it.'

Simon laughed. His father was a cushy old thing and there was plenty of time for argument. Anyway, Simon thought he might not want to, after all, when it came to the point.

2

Antony told his father all about it over supper. For once he had something to talk about; they usually ate in near silence. When his father was home they ate together in the dining room at one end of a vast mahogany table that seated forty. It was too big to move out and had obviously been built on site. It was hideous, but neither Antony nor his father had ever really noticed. They ate at the end nearest the door that led, after a long walk, to the kitchen.

'Mr Sopwith wasn't there, but we had a great time. They showed us all sorts and I was allowed to drive one. "Roll it," they say – just along the ground, not taking off. It's how you learn. They're quite hard to control, strange. I signed up for lessons, so I can fly it home – when I've decided which one to have. If I have lessons, I can try them all, see what's best.'

'Very good.' Mr Sylvester was surprised at his son's sense for once, having half expected to find an aeroplane sitting on the drive when he came home.

They had an uneasy relationship, neither quite sure what

to make of the other. They did not meet very often, and there was no third party to ease the contact, no jolly wife or quarrelling siblings. Claude Sylvester's wife had died, quite suddenly, soon after they had moved to Lockwood. She had been excited about the vast prospect of turning the echoing rooms into a comfortable home, but perhaps the whole thing had been too much for her, for she died of a heart attack immediately after a meeting with a firm of interior designers who came down from London and exclaimed in horror at the task that faced them.

She had made a pretty flat upstairs for Helena – a prime consideration – but that was all she had managed. Antony had been eight when his mother died and Helena four years older. He had already learned at that early age to live his own life, as his mother – not unnaturally – was almost totally taken up with Helena. How could it be otherwise? Antony accepted the situation without rancour, but tended to avoid seeing too much of Helena – the atmosphere up in her quarters was not to his taste and he found it hard to please her, foundering in his own inadequacy to understand what on earth it was she was saying, or trying to say, or what she wanted, or how to please her. She laughed a lot and he thought she mocked him. He was sorry for her, of course, not to be able to see or hear. How did she imagine the world, he wondered, not ever having seen it?

His friends were always nosy about her, dying to meet her. He had been in the habit of bringing his Eton friends home in the holidays to stay – but none of them had ever wanted to come twice after they had found themselves banned from the freak upstairs, and only just managing to survive the discomfort of life in Lockwood Hall. Antony stopped asking them, but at the back of his mind he had always harboured the idea of a huge midsummer party by the lake, using the amazing grotto as a base. That would be quite something, especially if he got an aeroplane. That would impress them. They would come then.

The grotto was amazing, built a century ago by the master of the original Lockwood Hall – a very beautiful Queen Anne mansion which had been brutally destroyed to make way for the present monstrosity. Old engravings of the original house were displayed in the corridors, but were hard to make out in the ill-lit passages.

The new house was entirely panelled in dark oak, impressively expensive but also impressively gloomy. Cosy was a word that did not spring to the tongue. Many of the servants gave in their notice quite soon, especially in the winter when the great boilers in the cellar struggled to keep the chill out of the huge rooms. Antony was used to it, but was always surprised that his father seemed fond of the place and never considered moving. It must have sad memories for him, his wife dying so soon after they had moved in, but Mr Sylvester was not a sentimental nor sensitive man. Antony wondered sometimes if he took after him. He rather hoped not, for his father was not much liked, he noticed, not one to spread bonhomie and delight.

He spoke little, rarely smiled. He was not imposing to look

at, only of average height and build, with fading, disappearing brown hair, severely trimmed, and a large dark moustache that hid most of his lower face. He wore dark suits, impeccably tailored and obviously expensive, and used little round-framed spectacles for reading. Most of that reading was confined to the financial pages of the daily newspapers – Antony had never seen his father reading anything else. It was not surprising that they had little conversation when they did meet, and Antony guessed that his father was relieved when the holidays were over and his son went back to Eton.

For himself, he preferred being at home and mucking about with his village friends and the wild Lily when she came gardening with her father. He did not work hard at school, got into scrapes, got beaten and harangued that he did not use his intelligence for better things (than making stink bombs and writing rude riddles). He was popular and did not lack for friends, so had no complaints.

His father showed rather more interest in the impending flying lessons than anything his son usually had to tell him and actually said, 'I wouldn't mind trying it out myself if I had the time.'

'When I know how I'll teach you.'

Antony could in no way envisage this and knew it wouldn't happen, but his father gave one of his rare smiles in agreement. They ate and then went their separate ways, his father to his study and Antony to his own room. There was a sitting room, but it was never used. There was no family life in Lockwood Hall.

MAY, 1921

3

Lily was helping her father in the grounds of Lockwood Hall. When she didn't have other jobs to do – cleaning at the vicarage, running errands for Mrs Carruthers, washing pots in the Queen's Head or mucking out the livery horses – she helped her father. Squashy trailed along with his dog, Barky, as usual. Squashy was eleven, useless but cheerful. Barky, a small brown mongrel of countless crosses from a village litter, was also useless and cheerful and the two were never apart.

Gabriel had been instructed to make a smooth strip beyond the lake for Antony's aeroplane, when it came. 'I'm a ruddy gardener, not an aerodrome designer,' her father grumbled. 'It's a farm job, flattening and rolling.'

They stood in the spring sunshine on the side of the lake, looking out away from the house. The lake, clear and deep, ran like a wide river along the natural valley below the house. On two small islands on the far side from the house, someone a long time ago had made the once-fabulous but now decrepit grotto. Antony wanted to land his aeroplane 'somewhere near the grotto', on the far side. He was planning to build it a hangar, which would be hidden from the house by trees and the high mound of the grotto itself.

'We'll 'ave a look at it, and tell Mr Butterworth the state of it, and 'e can make it good,' Gabriel decided.

As they were standing outside the house, 'having a look at it' entailed a twenty-minute walk to the end of the lake where a bridge crossed it, and back down the other side. Where the bridge crossed over, near to the village road, there was a row of small workers' cottages that faced the lake, one of which was the home of Gabriel and his children.

Mr Butterworth was the man who farmed the estate. The estate staff tended to be closely related, descended from the estate workers before them, father to son. They had been severely decimated by the war and were still mainly the old and the young, only half a force, the strong middle contingent lost and buried in French soil. There had once been twelve strong young gardeners, but now there was only Gabriel and six what he called 'useless young dopes' from the village, just out of elementary school. He reckoned Lily was worth all six put together, although it wouldn't occur to him to tell her so.

They walked along what was to be the landing strip, up as far as the grotto, Gabriel marking the required distance as ordered by Master Antony, and deciding on the best site for the hangar. The space was certainly wide enough, bounded on the far side by the hedge that marked the estate boundary and a lane beyond.

While Gabriel was pacing out his plans, Lily and Squashy

went out to the grotto, attracted as always by this strange, creepy figment of the weird Georgian imagination. There were two islands quite close to the shore, and so close to each other that there was just a strip of water between them. They had been covered with great rocks, imported at great expense, built very high and now covered with a thick canopy of trees and undergrowth and swags of rampant ivy so the water between them was in a tunnel of verdancy.

On one of the islands the famous grotto had been built inside the rocks. Its entry was beside the water at its narrowest part, a yawning cave mouth, now blocked off with a securely locked iron gate. A landing had been built at the waterside outside the cave mouth for visitors who came by boat, but the island with the grotto in it was near enough to the shore to be connected by a rickety wooden bridge. Lily and Squashy used the bridge, although Lily always thought it would be very romantic to arrive by boat from the open lake, through the tunnel. The lake was supplied with various boats, kept near the house, which the boys used to lark about in, but it was forbidden to go to the grotto. 'Dangerous!' they all said on the estate. 'Horrible!' 'Do not go there!'

Of course they went. Antony knew where the key to the iron grille was kept, and once he had taken them right in there – but all Lily remembered was the awful smell of the underground, the enfolding chill like wings of death, the frightening echo of dropping water, the terrifying dark and Antony's scornful laugh ricocheting off distant walls. There had been narrow passages going off in all directions, lit only by Antony's

20

feeble torch. She had been petrified but, as ever, determined not to show weakness in front of Antony, her hero.

Going to the landing, as they did now, was nice, turning their backs on the grim cave mouth, sitting on the warm stones and dangling their feet in the water. Summer was coming and the water was warm.

'Fancy Antony buying an aeroplane,' Lily said. 'I wouldn't half like a go in it.'

'I don't want to go,' Squashy said.

'He'll take the others. I doubt he'll take me.'

Lily had no illusions as to where she stood in the group that made up Antony's gang: she was only a girl, after all. But she strung along, in spite of the insults, because she loved Antony and wanted to be with him for ever. She adored him. Everything about him: the way he spoke, (Etonian), the way he moved (like a mountain goat, bold and free), the way he looked (like a Greek god), the way he laughed (loudly), the way he swam (like an otter), the way he regarded her (kindly enough). When they were alone together he was really nice; when the others were around he mostly ignored her, but did not send her away. When she told him that she loved him he laughed and said he loved someone else.

'Who?'

'Melanie Marsden. I love Melanie Marsden.'

'Oh really, Antony.' What a disappointment! Mostly for his taste. Lily knew she was worth six of Melanie Marsden. 'You'll grow out of it,' she said.

'So will you then.'

21

'No. Not me, not ever, not till the day I die.'

'Blimey. That's a bit thick. What am I supposed to do?'

'Nothing, really. But later on we can get married.'

'I'm not sure about that. I've got to marry someone posh.'

'Who says so?'

'My dad would, if you asked him.'

'I won't ask him. You can make up your own mind when you're older, surely?'

'I daresay. Melanie Marsden.'

Lily hit him and they had a fight until Squashy started to cry and attacked Antony with a spade.

'Oh hush, Squashy. It's only for fun.' She hugged him. 'It's not real.'

But when she lay in bed at night she thought about it and knew it was for real. Antony could scoff as much as he liked but it made no difference. She was born with it. Whoever he might choose to love Lily would always love him better.

As she sat now with Squashy, kicking her feet in the water, she laughed, thinking of Antony arriving out of the sky in an aeroplane. How gloriously rich the Sylvesters were! Mr Sylvester went up to London in his white Rolls and saw politicians and investors and bankers and likewise men of power and fame, and obviously he acquired enormous amounts of money – but what for, nobody knew. If they knew they probably wouldn't understand! Antony himself had no idea how it came about. He took it for granted, being rich enough to have an aeroplane for his birthday.

Lily knew only too well the gulf that separated her from

Antony. He had never been inside her home, just as she had never been inside his, save for a few steps into the kitchen, to deliver flowers. Her home was a small cottage, built for the master workers. Most of the workers lived in the village, but as Gabriel was the head gardener he had been allocated a cottage. The cottage was well maintained, but the inside was Lily's department and something of a tip, housewifery not being one of her passions. She had to do all the shopping and cooking and do the fires, as well as work for various people in the village and for her father too in the summer, when the gardens needed so much attention. Sitting dangling her feet in the lake by the grotto was a rare moment of idleness, lasting as long as it took Gabriel to survey what was going to be the airfield.

Not very long.

'Crazy idea. The boy will kill himself for sure.'

Everyone in the village was saying the same thing. Lily disagreed. 'He won't. Aeroplanes are much safer now, since the war.' If he killed himself, she would die too, she thought.

'Come along. We've wasted enough time with this rubbish.'

And Lily spent the rest of the day on her knees in the herbaceous borders below the windows of the Hall, weeding, her large red hands expertly wrenching dandelions from their moorings, buttercups from their deep and wicked creeping roots, wandering ivy, chickweed, thistle and pernicious bindweed all consigned vigorously to the wheelbarrow, which Squashy trundled away to the rubbish heap. She was a cauldron of energy, her thin, childish body working its way through the hollyhocks, long yellow hair swinging – 'worth five boys at least' they said of her – and she laughed as she worked, and shouted at Squashy, and Squashy laughed at his dog who sat wagging his silly tail, and Gabriel told them not to be so damned silly and – at last – go home and get some food ready. The old man was starving.

A typical day in the life of Lily Gabriel, aged thirteen.

JUNE, 1921

4

The boys were sitting by the side of the lake beside what was now called grandly the airfield, waiting for Antony to arrive in his aeroplane. Nobody was pretending that they weren't excited: they were jabbering away and looking at their watches every few minutes.

Lily approached them dubiously. She was emboldened by knowing more than they did, Antony having told her what time to expect him – they were only guessing. Normally, without Antony being there, she would have avoided them. They tended to despise her when Antony wasn't there, as she did them.

It was a hot afternoon and the boys had been swimming to spin out the time. Lily was supposed to be picking beans in the kitchen garden, but her father had gone off to the farm and she knew he wouldn't be back till supper time so she was in the clear. She wanted to witness Antony's arrival as much as the boys. The whole village was waiting, she knew, for it was something of a local scandal, the young lad being so indulged as to be given an aeroplane for his birthday.

'What if he crashes?' Cedric was saying. 'I can't believe he's learned so quickly.'

'He's got more brain than you, dolt,' Simon informed him. 'It's not very difficult. Landing is the trickiest, of course, so who knows?'

'You can save him if it sets on fire,' John said. 'Be a hero. Count me out.'

Lily lay down in the grass near them, only half listening to their stupid conversation. Cedric, the farmer's son, always got dumped on by the others but, an amiable lad, he did not seem to notice. John Simmonds – also at Eton with Antony and Simon – was the vicar's son, rather hampered by his father's calling, but quite nice in Lily's opinion. She didn't like Simon. He mimicked Squashy and teased his dog till Squashy cried – Lily had had fights with him over it, but of course lost, until rescued by Antony. But sometimes she had given as good as she got by underhand means, scratching and biting, and knowing where to kick. Simon fought fairly, to his disadvantage. He was a gentleman, after all.

The lake lay still in the hot sun. Lily stretched out in the grass, loving a few moments of rest, so rare in her life. She was tall for her years and honed thin with physical work – stringy, the boys said. Her hands were large and capable. She wore old-fashioned flowery dresses left over from her mother's wardrobe, which she had cut about, made shorter, tighter and more becoming. She had an instinct for what looked right and was a clever seamstress, but she wore her clothes carelessly and they were often dirty and torn: she did not attempt to make the boys stare. Antony was the only boy she wanted to please and he liked her as she was, her long blonde hair unkempt, her face sunburnt, her bright blue eyes laughing with admiration for him.

'My little dandelion,' he said.

'That's a weed.' Lily was not flattered. 'What about rose?'

'You're no rose, save for the thorns. Sunflower, perhaps. Tall and gawky.'

Lily did not take offence. She liked sunflowers.

She lay watching the birds circling over the grotto island where they had their nests in the thick verdancy. There were blackcaps and woodpeckers as well as the sparrows and wrens and tits and blackbirds and thrushes, and at night she could hear the owls hooting. She loved this place, in spite of the horrid house.

Antony's friends were much intrigued by the beautiful Helena and were trying to get Antony to bring her out so they could talk to her. But Antony only said, 'When we have our party she will come.' Nobody was quite sure when or what this party was going to be, but Antony only said, 'When my father's away, of course.' He was planning to get his Etonian friends over and it would last all night. Lily wasn't sure if she would be invited, but supposed she could be a servant and get in that way. She didn't really think it would ever happen, but the boys were keen on the idea.

'Listen!'

The boys suddenly all sat up. Lily pretended not to be

bothered, but she felt a lurch in her stomach, a sudden sick feeling. It amazed her. She hadn't been at all nervous, perfectly cool, but suddenly she was. She lay still, trying to pretend nonchalance. The boys had got to their feet and were staring excitedly up towards the house, over the hill, from where now distinctly came the sound of an aeroplane engine.

The sun was so bright it was difficult to focus. A flock of jackdaws flew off the chimneys and a small un-birdlike thing scattered them, skimming alarmingly low over the roof of Lockwood Hall. The boys all screamed out and Lily, forgetting nonchalance, jumped to her feet.

'He's too far down for the runway, the idiot!' Simon shouted.

'He'll have to go round!'

'He's too low!'

The plane came towards them over the lake, its wheels skimming the trees of the grotto, and the birds flew in a great panic in all directions. The engine gave an anguished roar and the nose of the plane pitched up, the wings wobbling alarmingly.

'He's going to stall!' Simon screamed out.

The plane hung like a shot bird for a moment, then lurched sideways and came slanting down completely out of control, obviously set on crashing into the ground.

Lily screamed, terrified, and the boys were shouting too, and running towards the spot which seemed destined for what looked like Antony's disastrous arrival. But at the last moment, inches from the ground, the little aeroplane staggered onto an even keel, and with a great burst of throttle shot off down the lakeside. Its wheels were only inches from the ground and it raced towards a large stand of trees that marked the boundary of the estate as if intent on burying itself in their embrace.

'Oh, Jesus Christ!' said John the vicar's son.

Lily shut her eyes and thought she was going to pass out.

It seemed quite impossible for the plane to clear the boundary, but there was a fine gap in the middle of the stand and the plane made for it and managed to gain enough height to skim over it, its wheels brushing the topmost leaves so that they scattered as if in an autumn gale. Then it wheeled away like an eagle and its engine faded into the distance.

Lily joined the boys now, faint with fright. She saw that they were as stunned as she was, and she was now one of them in their combined concern for Antony.

'He'll make it next time,' Simon said confidently.

'He'll come at the right angle, surely? Not sideways.'

'He must start coming down at the end of the lake, not over the house.'

Lily was thinking bitterly, I could have done it better. She was deeply disappointed by her hero's performance and feeling quite faint in the aftermath of his near-death. Now she was as one with the boys in their exclamations of dismay and horror.

'You nearly lost him there, dandelion,' Simon said with a grin.

'And you your best friend. I don't see that it's anything to smile about. You won't laugh if he kills himself!'

'I don't suppose he's laughing now,' John put in. 'He's got

to come down, after all. I daresay that scared him more than it did us.'

'Not more scared than me,' Cedric said. 'I don't want to watch next time.'

The sentiments of them all, Lily thought, but of course their eyes were glued to the sky and their ears alert for the recurring sound of the engine. They stood like pointing greyhounds, faces turned upwards. The birds had all come back and the air was full of the singing of the skylarks. They would sing on, Lily thought, when Antony had crashed to his death right in front of them. She was shaking and felt the bile of fear in her throat.

Far away, they heard the sound again. In a better place this time, coming from the village end of the lake, in the proper place for descending onto the runway. But too fast, or too slow . . . how many times had he practised it, the clever bit of learning to fly, to land? Apparently any fool could take off. They were silent now, staring into the bright sky.

This time the aeroplane came into view at what looked the right height and in the right place. It seemed to be coming very fast. Did it have brakes? Lily wondered wildly. It seemed to waver about somewhat, its wings tipping one way and then the other (which was surely wrong?), but still high enough to clear the ground. Too high?

Lily cried out.

'Bloody hell!' breathed the vicar's son.

The plane sank suddenly and its wheels hit the ground. Too fast: it bounced up again, seemed to shudder like a wounded bird, and then dropped for the second time. Not quite so hard, another bounce, then another, and it slewed sideways nearly into the lake and came to an anguished halt half facing the way it had come. The engine stopped and there was a sweet silence, not even birdsong, for the birds had all been scared away.

The spectators let out a collective sigh of relief, and then they were all running towards the skewed plane, laughing and shouting, Lily as well. She wanted to scream to relieve her agony of fear, but she bit her lip and stifled the stupid words that came into her head, not to give herself away. It was just a lark; the boys were all laughing their heads off. Antony wasn't dead, after all.

He was still sitting in the cockpit, pushing up his goggles. He was as white as a sheet, but pretended nothing was untoward.

'Sorry if I scared you! Got it a bit wrong first time.'

'Yeah, and the second time too,' Simon said unkindly.

'Not perfect, no. But I will improve. Early days, you wait.'

If they had been scared, Lily could see that Antony, with reason, had been even more so. She wondered if it had put him off.

But he said, 'Piece of cake next time. You'll see. I landed properly plenty of times at Brooklands.'

'Nerves, that's all,' said John kindly. 'Are you going up again now? You know, like getting back on a horse after a fall.'

'No, why should I? I got it right the second time. Tomorrow I'll go for a spin, and one of you shall come with me. That's

31

what I got it for, for us all to have a bit of fun. Who wants to be first?'

There was a marked silence.

Then Cedric said, 'Not me.'

John cleared his throat awkwardly. 'Rather you got a bit more practice in first, old chap.'

'Simon?'

'No bloody fear.'

Antony stared at them, mortified. Disappointment and indignation mingled in his features. He pulled off his brand-new flying helmet and flung it down in disgust. Lily thought he looked as if he were going to cry, his triumph short-lived. 'I thought we were going to be in this together, get about and have a load of fun. I didn't think you were such a lily-livered bunch of old women. I went into it thinking of all of us, all of us having a lark . . .' His voice trailed off.

Lily stepped forward. 'I'll come, Antony. Take me. I'm not scared.'

'Lily!' They all gaped at her.

Antony's face broke into a great smile and Lily thought for a glorious moment he was going to hug her. But he rounded triumphantly to the others: 'You see, a girl! Lily's not scared! She's worth ten of you lot. You're a brick, Lily, I love you!'

If only, Lily thought. She stood, trembling.

Then Antony said, 'Tomorrow morning, Lily. Meet me here, and you will be my first passenger. I promise you, it will be great. My first real trip, all round Surrey. You will love it!'

The time lapse – tomorrow! – was balm to Lily's nerves.

She thought she would pass out with relief. All night to get used to the idea, to talk herself into believing in Antony's skill. Of course she had faith in him, there was nothing to be scared of, only a great treat to look forward to! She looked up and saw the three boys staring at her. Their expressions were hard to make out, but she had an uneasy instinct that pity was uppermost.

She felt her lips quiver, but she said, 'Fine, Antony, I'll be here in the morning.'

And walked home.

5

Lily did not sleep that night. She dozed, and her dreams were all of death. She dreamed of her dead mother. She saw her again, lying exhausted after Squashy's birth, and later with the life gone out of her, her beautiful blue eyes closed for ever and her cheeks marble white, sunk in disappointment. It was one of the neighbours who inadvertently christened Squashy: 'That baby's not right, you can tell – all sort of squashy-looking. The brain will be amiss, you mark my words. Poor little soul.'

But Lily took her baby brother under her wing and from his birth scarcely ever left him, trailing him behind her in a little cart their father made, playing with him, laughing. So Squashy grew up much loved by Lily and his dog Barky, and was happy. Their father was not a loving man, but he made sure the village boys didn't rag his son, nor the under-gardeners. He worked him very hard, but Squashy thrived on the work and was happy whatever the task.

He wouldn't be very happy seeing her fly away in Antony's

aeroplane, Lily knew that, and determined that he would go with his father in the morning, off to market. Then she would be in the clear. She could not convince herself that she had made a good decision, in spite of impressing the boys, but the admiration in Antony's eyes consoled her. If she hadn't seen his terrible landings she would have been more excited than terrified, and she tried to convince herself that of course, with her on board, he would take infinite care to get it right. He obviously didn't want to die either. She concentrated on thinking how amazing it would be up in the sky like a bird, looking down on all the woods and fields.

But it seemed a very long night, full of the sad cries of the owls and the lament of a distant cow with its calf lost and then the infinite silence with a half moon lying on its side in a sky full of stars where her mother's soul dwelt and all the souls of everyone who had gone before . . . how could one count the numbers? What matter if she and Antony were to join them? Who would miss them? Only Squashy and her father, and Mr Claude Sylvester, she thought. No wonder she could not sleep with such portentous rubbish floating around in her head.

In the morning her father departed with Squashy and Barky and she went down to the lake with her heart pounding. The awful fear had faded and now it was excitement that filled her. The worst imaginings always surfaced in the hours of the night, but with daylight and sunshine came optimism and hope. The water reflected the clear blue of the sky and the birds were all singing again. She made her way down to where the aeroplane stood, straightened out now and facing back the way it had come. It was a biplane, quite small and stumpy, with two seats one behind the other, a cocky little thing, Lily thought, and the right sort for Antony. Not too serious.

Quite soon Antony appeared on his bicycle, making round the head of the lake. He was wearing a long leather flying coat and a leather flying helmet, with goggles slung round his neck, and looked every inch the proficient pilot. The other boys were arriving too, agog, Lily thought, to see a bit of excitement.

Ghouls, she thought . . . they want to see us crash! But Antony won't crash – she willed it, a prayer to God. How she wished she could believe in God! It was so hard, after what he did to her mother. It would be a big help now.

'I thought you might have changed your mind,' Antony said when he arrived.

'No, why should I?' Very nonchalant.

'Lots of good reasons,' Simon said.

'Honestly, you haven't got to,' Antony said, rather unexpectedly.

'No, I want to come.' Big lie.

'Good. You're a brick.'

Her seat behind him had its own door, and the boys opened it and bunked her in.

'Do up the straps,' Antony called.

'Why? You're not going to loop the loop?' A flare of panic. Simon laughed.

'Coward!' Lily hissed at him.

'A live coward though!'

'It gets a bit bumpy up there sometimes, that's all.'

Lily could not conceive of air being bumpy, but conversation was cut off by the sudden roar of the engine as John swung the propeller to Antony's instructions. The noise was terrifying and the birds all left the grotto again in a great cloud of confusion, swirling high into the sky. And me too, Lily thought: here I go, and the little plane started to move off down the side of the lake, very sedate, like a car.

But instead of taking off, the plane stopped outside her cottage and Antony throttled down the engine and shouted, 'Go in and get a coat or something, and a hat – you'll freeze up there without.'

Lily struggled out of her straps and jumped out and ran indoors. Whatever did she have for such a trip? No smart leather coat and helmet like Antony's; she had seen pictures in smart magazines in the houses she sometimes cleaned of ladies in motor cars, or leaning on aeroplanes, with the most elegant suitable coats and hats. But as it was, after a quick scour in her mother's old wardrobe, she came out in a fur coat made of rabbits and moles, which her mother had once stitched from the gamekeeper's gifts, and a hat used for Squashy's christening, tied down with an old towel out of the kitchen. By then the boys had caught up with them and, after laughing themselves stupid at her get-up, they bunked her back in the plane and did up the straps again. Lily had a suspicion that their derision was a counter to the humiliation they were feeling at her having outdone them in courage. If it wasn't, it should have been.

She didn't show it, but her courage was fading fast as Antony turned the plane back on course down the side of the lake and revved up the engine. The terrible roar obliterated the boys' rude shouts of farewell. Perhaps I shall never see them again! Lily thought.

Antony turned, grinning, and gave her a thumbs-up, then the little plane went hurtling down the grass towards the far stand of trees that barred the open sky.

I am going to die! Lily thought. She knew she wasn't brave at all, only an idiot trying to gain Antony's admiration.

Then she remembered that taking off was easy; it was the landing she had to worry about. And it was true. They rose into the air so effortlessly that Lily did not feel the ground leaving them; only her eyes registered with amazement the grass receding, the lake opening out below, and what seemed the whole of Surrey gradually laid out like a map below, its beautiful trees and commons and tiny villages all spread about in summer abandon. It was so beautiful, the look of it, the feel of it, that Lily felt tears of pure delight springing into her eyes. (Or was it the lack of goggles?) Whatever, she laughed out loud, and vowed that even if she were to die, it would be worth it, this euphoria, never before experienced, at one with the birds, with the stars had it been night time, with God even: she thought she would burst with it.

And then higher and higher, and Antony was turning round and jabbing with his finger, pointing, and when she looked she saw what could only be the sea. Lily had never seen it before – a pale slender fingernail across the horizon, faintly curved, empty, the edge of the world. She screamed with delight, because no one could hear her, and she wanted to shout and sing and dance, it was so wonderful. If he killed her now, it would be worth it. What a blessing she sat behind him so that he could not witness her performance – lucky there were straps to hold her down.

Perhaps conscious of her excitement, Antony flew south towards the sea and she saw it properly, with steamers heading down the Channel, and a smattering of tiny sails, and the towns fronting themselves along its edge, close-roofed and tidy, and the yellow sand spotted with tiny tiny people, like ants.

How wonderful that she had volunteered for this wonderful outing out of pure bravado, not even guessing what she might see! Only the fear of dying had possessed her, and now even that, as the time for landing edged nearer, had faded into a mere unease. The flying had been so effortless, so easy, no wobbles, no bumps, that her faith in Antony had increased. As he turned and came lower over the more familiar boundaries of her home ground she settled in her seat and started to pray to the useless god that she didn't believe in.

'Please, God, I will believe in you if you get me down safely. I thank you for this wonderful flight.' She knew that God liked thanks and praise; he got fed up with only being asked for stuff.

The aeroplane came down lower and lower. Lily could almost feel Antony's concentration flowing out of his tense body into her face. She prayed for him. He was looking over the side to see how far up he was, and she could see the beginning of the lake over his shoulder. Someone on the lane below looked up and then ducked, so that Lily thought they were too close. She shut her eyes and felt a bile of fear rise in her throat. The engine was making stuttering noises. Oh no God – *Please!* She cried out; the aeroplane wobbled and bumped down, rose and bumped again, but not nearly as alarmingly as the day before, and then ran fast down beside the lake and it was as if they were in a car, driving fast round Brooklands.

They were down, but how did it stop, this flying bird? There were no brakes, but something held it because although they passed the grotto by quite a distance they came to a halt just where Lily's father had got tired of mowing the grass, marking the edge of the airfield. Antony then taxied it in a big circle and came back to the grotto where he turned the engine off. Lily saw his body slump with relief. He half turned to her, smiling, and the boys who had been waiting by the grotto came running up, all laughs and shouting.

'Great stuff, Ant! You didn't kill her, after all!'

'Very smooth! Brilliant!'

'Really good,' from Cedric, his red farmer's face shining with congratulation.

They both climbed out. Antony jumped down and then looked back into his cockpit and dragged out what looked a large canvas parcel. 'I'd forgotten this. It came with the plane – a parachute.'

'Only one for you? What about Lily?'

'It would be great, wouldn't it, jumping out and drifting down? I wouldn't half like to try it,' Antony said.

'You can't, idiot, if you're the pilot. You'd lose the plane.'

'No, but great to try it, eh? See if it works.'

'Not much fun if it doesn't.'

'Oh, it's in perfect order. They said so. You can trust it perfectly. Now you've seen how good I am at landing, one of you could try this. I only wish it could be me.' He offered it like a prize, a distinction, a present for the best boy.

No one offered.

'We're not stupid, Ant.'

Simon said, 'You'll have to ask Lily. She's daft enough.'

'Brave enough. You all make me puke.'

He didn't ask then, but Lily knew he would, later. She didn't want to know.

AUGUST, 1921

6

Antony's initial rapture with his new aeroplane faded quite quickly when he learned that the parents of both Simon and John forbade them to go up in it. Only the cheerful farmer Mr Butterworth and his equally cheerful wife thought it great for their Cedric to have a bit of fun.

But there was not much entertainment to be extorted from Cedric, whose greatest joy came in counting the cattle in the neighbouring farms and: 'Come a bit lower, Ant – I do believe old Harper's breeding red Devons – that's a bit weird, must tell Dad.' Antony knew what fun he would have had with Simon, skimming low over Bognor beach spotting bathing beauties. At least he managed to perfect his landings and amused himself by trying his hand at a few aerobatics, enough to frighten himself but not too much.

The parachute lay under his seat, untouched; one day he knew he was going to persuade Lily to try it, but not to mention it yet. He knew she would do anything for him, nut that she was. He privately thought it would be great fun to give the job to Squashy, who did anything you asked him, but he didn't think Lily would allow it.

The summer hols were nearly over and Simon and John kept reminding Antony about his planned party in the grotto, but there were problems.

'We can't do it unless my father's away, obviously, and he doesn't seem to be going anywhere soon. Next summer he's going to South America, I think, so we could plan it for then. This time next year. It'll take a bit of organizing, especially if Helena is to come.'

Antony knew that Helena's presence would be a great enticement for all his Eton friends, not to mention his home friends. She held a magical attraction for them, seen fleetingly, very beautiful, mysterious, locked away in her private rooms like the mad Mrs Rochester. When pressed, Antony had to admit that he didn't see much of his sister himself.

'Her keepers – nurses – are horrible. Two of them, they think they own her. They don't like me going in. She does, though, so we could have a bit of fun if they would let her out. They're terrified they'll lose their jobs if anything happens to her.'

'How do we get rid of them then?' John asked.

'I'm sure we can think of something. Get them drunk – I think they do drink, actually, I've seen sherry bottles – or bribe them, even. Or get them locked in somewhere. I'll think of something. But you can see what a lot of planning it will take.'

'We could start now – the planning. Let's have a look in the grotto and see how it could look for a party. You can get the key, can't you?'

'I'm not allowed.'

'What difference does that make?'

Antony laughed. 'Not a lot. I'll get it.'

Lily was determined not to miss out on this opportunity to view the grotto again. She knew it gave her the creeps, but it was worth it. Antony had not offered to take her flying again, although he kept promising, and she felt bitter when she knew she had been the only one brave enough to volunteer initially, but of course got no thanks for it. She was only the gardener's daughter after all, and only hung in there with the gang by dint of her own persistence and rhinoceros hide.

They were snobs, these Eton boys, she thought, but at least they suffered her, perhaps even respected her, although they wouldn't admit it. Cedric was a bit at the same level in the hierarchy as herself, but at least he was a male and useful in that his father had a fair bit of clout about what they could get up to on the estate. Lily could see that he was slightly outside the three others, who shared upper-class jokes that he missed out on.

She was quite familiar with the home lives of both Simon and John, the vicar's son, because she sometimes did cleaning there when their regular ladies were ill or having babies. It was amazing what one picked up. The vicar, the Rev Simmonds, John's father, was a pompous boring old codger and his wife twittered over her good works and ladies' circles and was disturbed by her son's friendship with the maverick Antony.

'I really don't trust that boy. I don't know what it is about him. Having no mother, I suppose, and the father letting him have an aeroplane, for heaven's sake! He has no guidance.'

'He's not got into trouble so far,' her husband pointed out. 'And without his father's largesse, the church tower would have fallen down by now, so we need the Sylvesters' goodwill, you must see that.'

'Yes, of course. Money talks. Where does it all come from, I should like to know?'

'It's politics and suchlike. He's up in Whitehall a lot of the time.'

'They say he's an arms dealer.'

Lily absorbed all this as she scrubbed and polished and cleaned out the grates. When she was in his house, John treated her like the servant she was. With parents like his he couldn't help being such a nitwit, but Antony seemed to bear with him quite amicably. She realized that Antony got on with everyone, however stupid or unsuitable. Squashy loved him too, but he only glowered at John.

Simon was a different kettle of fish, far more intelligent but hard to make out; unkind, but attractive in person. Lily was nervous of him. But his parents were very nice, wrapped up in their own lives, he with his writing and nature watching and she with her craftwork, embroidering curtains in wool as in the William Morris circle, or out in her shed throwing pots and fiddling with her kiln.

'She'll blow up the whole village one day,' they said of her.

But they liked her. There was a married sister somewhere, and a circle of intellectual friends who came to dinner and talked a lot. Lily was sometimes employed to wash up, and saw Simon in his best clothes behaving in an Etonish manner, very smooth. He ignored her as if he had never seen her before in his life.

Antony's father went up to London in his Rolls-Royce and Antony collected the grotto key from the drawer in his office. It was a hot summer day and the lake lay serene and inviting below the gardens where Lily and Squashy were supposed to be working. Lily saw the boys come down from the house laughing, Antony tossing the key, and approached them from the rose bed.

'Can we come with you? Please!'

Simon and John gave her their usual snobs' look and Simon said, 'No room in the boat, gel.'

Lily looked at Antony, who said carelessly, 'Yeah, there is. Why not?'

'We can come in a separate boat!'

'No. Come in ours. The more the merrier. We'll take the punt.'

'We'll sink it, all of us,' Simon said.

'You take another one, if you want.'

But Simon, put down, looking angry, got into the punt

46

where it lay against the jetty. There was an assortment of boats, some smart, some half-sunk, and a tangle of oars stacked up against an overhanging willow. Nobody looked after them. The boys always used the same one and haggled over who was to use the quant. Antony and Simon were very good at it and John and Cedric useless, but Antony didn't mind them trying. Farther out the water was too deep and they had to use the paddles that lay under the thwarts.

Lily lay nose down over the bows looking into the deep water, fascinated. She loved going on the lake, but didn't dare take a boat without asking, however idly they lay. Her father had a heavy old dinghy that he sometimes used for carrying heavy stuff across the lake, or down to the end, and both Lily and Squashy were confident rowers, but being in the punt with the boys was something quite different. Elegant! she thought. Like in the photos in the smart magazines. She imagined herself lying on cushions, with a parasol and a beautiful dress of chiffon and a straw hat.

She put her hand in the water and trailed it dreamily, watching the sun spearing down into the mysterious depths. They said it was very deep and dangerous. Not for a good swimmer, she thought. I would never drown, nor Squashy either, whom she had taught to swim almost before he could walk. *Never stand up in the boat* – she knew the mantra from her father's insistence – and had taught Squashy. Punting was different, of course, but then the water was shallow if the quant reached the bottom and so no danger of drowning if you tipped in. How lucky they were to have this beautiful lake to hand. And beautiful Antony to go with it . . . she laughed as he came forward and knelt beside her with the front paddle.

'Who are you? The Lady of Shalott?'

'Who's she?'

'A lady in a poem. "*Down she came and found a boat, beneath the willow left afloat . . . da di da, di da, di da . . . She loosed the chain and down she lay, The broad stream bore her far away*" and so on and so on. She was in love with a gorgeous knight whom she saw from her window.'

'The knight is you?'

'Of course. "*His broad clear brow in sunlight glowed, From underneath his helmet flowed, his coal-black curls as on he rode,*" et cetera, et cetera.'

Lily laughed. 'And she was very beautiful too, I hope?'

'Of course. That's what reminded me.'

'You are a nut. Is that what you learn at Eton?'

'I learned that at my mother's knee.'

'Lucky old you. I can't remember my mother.'

'No, I don't remember much of mine either. She was always with Helena.'

'Are you sure you're going to get Helena to this party?'

'It's for her, the party. Yes, I will. The whole point.'

'Why can't she come out with us sometimes? Doesn't she ever go out?'

'She has her own garden behind the house. She goes there. But she never meets anyone.'

Lily tried to imagine being blind and deaf, but couldn't. Neither to see nor to hear . . . how did you make contact with people? 'She would like to be in the punt, like us, wouldn't she?' she said. 'Feel it, smell the lake, put her hands in the water like I'm doing. And wouldn't she sense the other people, somehow? She could feel their faces, is that what they do?'

'She strokes my face when I go in there. And smiles. She knows me. She hugs me.'

'Can I come one day?'

'Why not? If the harridans will let you in.'

'They can't be so awful?'

'Not to her, I suppose. They are two sisters, living up there like royalty. My father gives them whatever they ask for. Salves his conscience, I suppose. But what can he do, otherwise? He's a useless dad, even to me.'

'He gave you an aeroplane!'

'Yes. That's his way. He thinks you can buy love.'

Lily wondered if that were true, and if so if it were true for other parents too. She wondered if her father loved her and Squashy. He never displayed any symptoms of loving, but on the other hand he never beat them. He never said please or thank you like Simon's parents, but then he never threw his dinner at her if her cooking went wrong. He ate it stoically just the same. No comment. He was very protective of Squashy, which surely meant he loved him, even if he must have longed to have had a strong and hearty son like Cedric.

'All my schoolfriends will come to the party and Helena will be queen. That's the idea.'

'Can I come?'

'Yes.'

'And Squashy?'

'Yes.'

If all his schoolfriends were coming, Lily thought that she and Squashy would melt into the crowd and not be noticed – what a relief! Her contact with Antony's Eton friends in the past had not endeared them to her. None of them had treated her like a human being. That's why she loved Antony so; in spite of all the teasing she knew he respected her.

'Will you ask Melanie Marsden?'

'Yes, of course.'

'I hate you.'

He laughed.

The punt approached the high rocks of the grotto and the boys paddled for the opening of the tunnel between them. The water was too deep for the quant and went dark as the punt drifted into the shadow of the overhanging trees. It was cold suddenly to Lily's hands, and she withdrew them and sat up with a shiver. It was creepy, this approach, no sun ever penetrating this entrance. She had never come by boat before. The sun shone on the other side.

The punt scrunched up against the landing and they all piled out. Squashy tied the mooring rope onto a tree trunk and Barky peed on it. They all laughed.

'Bags you cast off, Squashy!'

'I don't want to go in.'

'You needn't, Squashy,' Lily said quickly. 'You can wait here in the sun. Look after the boat.'

'Yes, we'd rather.' Squashy sat down on the landing with his arm round Barky, and Antony fished for the key in his pocket and unlocked the grille.

The boys had brought torches so the entrance was well lit by the stabbing beams, a large arched cave quite high at the front, lined entirely with silver shells that twinkled in the torchlight. From the roof stalactites hung down, spearlike, also glistening with that looked like pearls, and on one wall water ran down into a large basin where stone mermaids lay intertwined round the rim.

The sound of the dropping water was magnified by the acoustics and echoes, it seemed, from a far distance.

Antony's torch picked out the opening of a passage at the back of the cave. 'This is the way.'

Lily wished she was out in the sunshine with Squashy and Barky, but she hadn't the courage to back out in front of the boys who were pressing eagerly into what looked to Lily like the entrance into Hades. It did in fact run downhill. Are we under the lake, she wondered, where the water was so deep and dark and creepy? It was all she could do to force her steps to follow them. The gritty silver walls grazed her arms; she kept her eyes on the rays of the torchlight ahead of her.

The passage opened out into what was obviously the heart of the grotto, a large round room positively glittering with the silver shells that covered every bit of rock and all the ornate fountains and niches that lined the walls. Strange stone statues leered from the niches, half-saint, half-monster, with gargoyle faces, swathed in cloaks of coloured stones and with hollow eyes that stared unseeing at this crude invasion. More fountains played against the walls and fell into basins, again occupied by mermaids and grotesque fish. The torches flashed here and there making the figures seem to move, coming forwards and retreating into darkness, and the hollow noise of the falling water drowned their voices which – Lily was pleased to note – were stifled with unease.

Only Antony was his ebullient self. 'This will be the party room, lit by masses of candles. Just think of it – the look, all glittering and the food laid out and lots to drink, and then – a summer's night – swimming in the lake, lying in the punts looking at the stars. We'll choose the full moon nearest the longest day . . .'

'Does your father know your plans?'

'No, of course not. He's going to be in South America.'

'How will you pay for it?'

'On his account. He won't notice.'

'Crikey,' said John.

Lily noticed that Cedric had backed out, and guessed that he had been unsettled by the creepy atmosphere, the same as herself. She appreciated that the place would be quite different set for a party, full of lights and people laughing and talking and the food all laid out: she could see it quite plainly, but just now, the way it echoed and the clammy air in one's face almost like cobwebs – and the ghostly echoes from, it seemed, all directions – she could not wait to get out into the sunshine again.

On the landing Cedric was sitting with Squashy and Barky, chatting happily. Their feet hung in the water, splashing.

'Gives me the creeps,' Cedric said to Antony.

'Yeah, well, it's been neglected. But it won't be like that for the party. It'll be all lights and sparkle and fun.'

'Does the water run in the fountains all the time?'

'No. You switch it on in my father's office.'

'Really weird! Who built it? All that work! Must have cost a fortune.'

'It was a fashion a long time ago, to make grottoes. Just a fashion. You can't imagine anyone doing it now. That's why I think it's a shame not to make use of it. Such a waste. It cries out to be used.'

The others obviously thought Antony was biting off more than he could chew, but any chap who could get an aeroplane for his birthday had to be respected. They were happy to follow where he led.

'By the way, no word of this to anyone. It's got to be a secret, else it won't happen. Not to the vicar, John, for God's sake.'

'No, of course not.'

John, without adventure in his soul, didn't look too happy about it and Lily guessed he would cry off when the time came. Not a party animal. They all got back in the punt and Squashy cast off. Barky jumped in as he pushed off. As they paddled out through the dark tunnel of trees, heading for the glorious light, Simon said to Antony, 'You know, you can't just bring Helena to the party out of the blue. She hardly ever goes out – it'll terrify her, plunged into what you're planning.'

'No, I've thought of that. I'll have to work on it. I thought

Lily might take on the job. Better to have another girl, tame the harridans, take Helena out and all that. You'd do that, wouldn't you, Lily? Start giving her a life.'

He smiled at her, as Lily's heart stopped in mid-beat. She stared at him and her mouth dropped open. The words came back into her head: '*His broad clear brow in sunlight glowed . . .*'

'Yes,' she said, wanting to die.

'Good, that's settled then.'

7

Lily knocked on the door at the tradesmen's entrance to Lockwood Hall. Antony had said to come at eleven o'clock, but he wasn't waiting for her outside and she felt it wasn't her place to use the front door. She was excited and very nervous. She had told her father about the invitation and, to her surprise, he had been sympathetic towards the proposal.

'The poor lass has no friends, the life she leads. Maybe you could help her.'

She had dressed carefully, to try and look like a lady. Not that the Lockwood servants would respect her, although several were friendly, mostly the younger ones. Antony was a pig not to be meeting her.

A manservant opened the door and looked down his nose at her.

'Mister Antony is expecting me.' She lifted her chin.

'Come in.' He led the way into a gloomy room full of boots and muddy coats and unused dog baskets. 'Mister Antony receives at the front door as a rule.'

'Well, how am I to know? He didn't say.'

'Follow me.'

The room opened into a scullery. In the kitchen beyond, the cook and kitchen maids stared at her as she passed by, but Lily kept her head down. Through a maze of gloomy corridors they emerged eventually into the main hall where she should have been received at the front door.

'Wait here, miss.' The man indicated a dusty sofa by an empty fireplace and disappeared.

The hall was huge, bleak and terribly empty. An enormous stone staircase led out of it to a gallery above, punctuated by closed doors. If ever the place had received a woman's touch, Lockwood Hall had long forgotten it. Lily dreaded to think what she was going to find in Helena's apartments.

Antony came, unapologetic. 'Good, let's go visiting then. Hey, you look smart. Waste of time, Helena can't see you.'

'It's to impress the harridans.'

'Oh, they'll be as nice as ninepence, don't worry. They won't show their harridan side to you. They'll be all charm – until we suggest we take Helena for a row on the lake. Then it's *shock, horror, hands off! How dare you suggest such a thing!* You'll see. This way.' He indicated the staircase and bounded up.

Lily hurried after him. Then she lost track of the rooms they passed through, more passages, some with high windows looking over the parkland, another staircase, up, down, until there was a pair of double doors facing them in what Lily reckoned must be the very far end of the house.

Antony knocked loudly.

The door opened and a mousy-looking middle-aged woman peered out. 'Oh, you've come, Mr Antony. We thought you wouldn't.'

'I told you. I've brought a visitor. This is Lily. She lives on the estate.'

'Pleased to meet you, miss. Come in.'

Amazingly, Helena's quarters were as inviting and beautiful as the rest of the house was hideous. High windows gave on to the lake and filled the room with sunshine. Comfortable armchairs were smothered with colourful cushions and beautifully embroidered antimacassars and a gorgeous Persian carpet patterned the floor in rich reds and pink and purple. Matching curtains fell in swags beside the windows and lots of bright paintings hung on the white walls – yellow sunflowers, landscapes of hot, wild places, and one of boats pulled on a beach beside an impossibly turquoise sea. As well as the sunshine the room was warmed by a bright fire and a small table was laid with scones and cream and a coffee pot gave off a lovely aroma.

Lily was so enraptured by the sight – even Simon's mother had not risen to such heights in her beautiful home – that she quite forgot what she had come for and just stood there with her mouth open. Why ever was the rest of the house so bleak when someone had made this paradise?

'My mother did it all,' Antony said, although she hadn't asked. 'Bought the pictures and everything, Van Gogh and all.

"Just because Helena can't see them," she said, "she can be surrounded by beauty just the same." Bit daft really. Pity she didn't do the same for her old man. And me.'

Lily had never guessed that Antony's mother had been anything but a disappointed invalid, keening over her poor daughter, but she now took on a completely different guise with her eye for beauty and elegance. Oh, why had she died! Just like her own mother. But mothers were needed . . .

'Here's Helena.'

Helena was another embellishment to this beautiful room, outdoing all else. No wonder the Eton boys thirsted after invitations, having set eyes on her. She was as fair as Antony was dark, with corn-gold hair loose in thick curls over her shoulders, a porcelain, creamy complexion, and full curving lips. Her cornflower blue eyes gave no hint of their uselessness. She was slender, tall and full of grace, and she smiled as she was guided towards Lily by the other harridan, who was a carbon copy of her sister.

Antony stepped forward and hugged her and kissed her and laughed and ran her hands over his face. He kissed her fingers one by one and Helena laughed again. He laid his cheek on hers, both sides, and caressed her hair.

Watching them, Lily was filled by an overwhelming awareness of her love for Antony, as if it were her face he was kissing, her hair he was running his fingers through, his cheek against hers. Why was she so stupid, so hopeless? It wasn't as if he was terribly nice, after all, the maverick Sylvester whom nobody could quite put a finger on. You knew where you were with Simon, and dreary old John and even dull Cedric, but you never knew where you were with Antony. This lark about the party was, after all, quite mad – in that creepy grotto, and having Helena there among all those crazy Eton boys . . . and where did she stand in such a gathering? Was she to be Antony's guest or the serving maid? She did not think he would enlighten her, and how could she ask, when he dismissed her doubts with an off-hand, 'Of course you'll come, idiot.'

While all this confusion was making an upheaval in her brain, Antony reached out for Helena's hands and placed them on Lily's shoulders. 'Stay still,' he said softly, 'and she will feel your face, get to know you.'

The hands were cool and delicate, so soft, slow, into her rough hair, gently down her cheeks.

Lily felt herself trembling, looking into the blank blue eyes so close to her, feeling her own eyes smarting with tears at the emotions that were almost overcoming her.

Antony, noticing, said quietly, 'It's all right.'

But it wasn't – how could it be? Only to forget Antony, which wasn't possible.

Helena was smiling. She reached for Lily's hands and kissed the palms.

'There, she likes you.'

Lily instinctively put her arms round Helena and hugged her and Helena hugged her back, and laughed. And then Lily felt all right again, back on balance.

Antony argued with Helena's two keepers for permission to

take his sister for a walk, which they granted with great reluctance. Lily could see how they thought they owned her, and how bad it must be for Helena to be in the hands of such – if not harridans – inward-looking, timid people.

Antony said they only took her for walks in the grounds, never down to the village, and rarely down to the lake. She had her own garden on the other side of the house.

'We'll go there, don't worry,' Antony said sharply, not wanting an argument.

Lily knew he would do what he wanted, as usual. Strangely, she had never worked on the other side of the house and her father, in fact, had rarely gone there. It was nearly all gravel drive and grass – which the farmer kept cut. The drive, after sweeping grandly up to the rarely opened front door departed towards the farm. The nearest buildings were a rather grand stable block, which now housed the Rolls-Royce and a more modest 'shopping' car, as well as the farm machinery and ten carthorses. Beyond was the farm proper, the threshing barn and the haystacks and the farmhouse, mostly hidden behind a clump of trees. Helena's garden was at the side of the house and had once been the kitchen garden for the house, enclosed by a wall, but it no longer produced vegetables, only a lot of weeds, some tangled roses and ancient fruit trees. It was, in its disarray, quite pretty, even the broken glasshouses sprouting rampant vines, and there was a seat amongst the unpruned roses whose scent still graced the air. Helena made for this seat unaided. She obviously knew every footstep of the way.

'My mother took her here, when it was a proper garden. It was beautifully kept when my mother was alive. She spent all her time up this end of the house. She hated the rest of it, not surprisingly. If I wanted to see her I used to come up here, but she didn't want me, I could tell.'

Antony spoke quite plainly, without a hint of self-pity, but Lily found his words excruciating. This awful bleak house and not wanted by his mother in the only place where there was comfort and beauty . . . and not much rapport with his largely absent father: it was amazing that he was still a mostly cheerful soul.

'Since she died, those women have taken Helena over. Before, they looked after her, but only did whatever my mother said. They came from the village, live in now, and I can see that this job is their meal ticket, and I suppose they do it well. But they think they have taken my mother's place, and of course they are wrong. Nobody could. They are called after flowers, would you believe, Rose and Violet. More like Hemlock and Deadly Nightshade, I'd say.' He laughed. Then he took Helena's hand. 'We'll go down to the lake. Take her other hand, she will like that.'

They walked with Helena between them, and Helena swung their arms and laughed, and wanted to run when the lawn started to slope downhill to the water. They ran with her, and when they got there they put her hands in the water and splashed, and took their shoes off and paddled where there was a strip of sandy beach. They showed her how the water deepened, took her out until it was up to her knees, and she understood to go no further, and stood wriggling her toes in the sand, laughing. It wasn't difficult to give her pleasure.

When they took her back, her keepers were dismayed by her splashed dress but Antony was short with them. 'She loves the lake. Why don't you take her there? It's your job to make her happy.'

'We do our best, Mister Antony.'

'She needs to go out more.'

'Yes, Mister Antony.'

That evening, when Lily was back home and was sitting at the supper table with Squashy and her father, having scraped out the last of the rabbit stew she had concocted with the limp carcass her father had brought home from the harvesting, she asked Gabriel about Antony's mother. Her father had been in the pub and she knew he was more talkative with the beer inside him.

'Did you know her?'

'Yes, she was always in the garden. She loved the garden and the flowers. I was a proper gardener in them days, not just a maintenance man like I am today. There was more of us, for a start. And the herbaceous beds – they was a picture. She loved them so. And the walled garden where she went with Helena – it was all beautiful. And she was beautiful too, a real lady. It was all different in those days.'

'Antony said she spent all her time with Helena, and didn't want him.'

'I think that was true. He spent more time with us servants than with his mother, poor kid. But you could understand it, I suppose, the girl needing all that care. It don't seem to have done him no harm though, not as I can see. Cocky young bastard.'

'What did his mother die of?'

'Oh, it was sudden, very unexpected. We was all shocked. It was one of them illnesses – her heart, I think, or summat like that. Meningitis? I dunno. Here one minute and gone the next. She had a lovely funeral, though, and all the flowers from our gardens – I was right proud, and she would have loved it, so pretty. They dressed Helena all in black – just a young girl she was then, your sort of age I suppose, or even a bit younger – and she stood by the coffin with all the white lilies, and then she lifted them up, a great bunch, and held them and started to sing – did you know she could sing? Such a weird sound, like a bird in the night time, standing there, and no one moved – made me think, what they say about swans singing before they die, not that I've ever heard it like, but it was like she was singing for her mother and she knew all about death and she just stood singing for her mother, not really sad but sort of triumphant – I don't know how to explain it, but we was all dumbstruck. Not just us servants, but the old man as well. I thought he were going to pass out.'

'Was this in the church?'

'No. Outside the front door when they lifted the coffin

into the hearse. It was an open cart from the farm, all covered in flowers and ribbons, with our own horses to pull it, and we was all going to walk behind it, even the old man with young Antony holding his hand, and that Aunt Maud, the old battle-axe, Mr Sylvester's sister. Only half a mile to the church, but with that weird singing we was all sort of paralysed like and no one moved, until that Aunt Maud called out in a loud voice to the coachman, "*Drive on! Drive on!*" and that sort of broke the spell. Helena stopped singing and old Maud got hold of her and brought her back to her father and they held her hands between them, and Antony had to drop back out of the way. I remember then feeling right sorry for him, pushed back, and no one to hold his hand when he were crying like. Weird it was, I can tell you.'

'Antony's never told me this.'

'Reckon he's tried to forget it, the way it was for him.'

Lily was stunned, picturing the scene, after having been so close to Helena and Antony that afternoon. And the lilies. And the coffin cart, all covered in flowers. What else did her father know, his link to this strange family going back so far . . . or, perhaps, not so far, in reality, twenty years or so? He had had a wife then. Was her mother alive then, to attend this funeral?

'She stayed at home, to look after you. And she were big in her pregnancy then with Squashy. A couple o' months after, she were gone too. And another funeral.'

Lily's mother was buried in the village churchyard under a simple stone, not far from the grand, angel-embellished tomb of Antony's mother. Lily went there often, with wild flowers for her mother, crushed into a jam jar. Poor Mrs Sylvester, after the first few months, no longer had flowers. Antony said she didn't need them: 'She's got angels, much better than flowers.' But Lily didn't think so. Flowers, often, meant you remembered. Not that Lily could recall her mother very well now, save as a quiet, comfortable sort of person and a good cook, nice for her father to come home to. Perhaps, if she had lived, she – Lily – might have been pushed to one side, like Antony, in favour of the more needy sibling.

'Did she have the farm cart and the farm horses too?'

'Yes, she did. Mr Sylvester was very kind, and also paid for the food and drink.'

Lily was sad that she had not been able to provide her father with such good care as her mother had. She did her best, but she couldn't help being a rowdy, untidy, slap-dash sort of girl. At least she had a lot of energy and managed to keep things going, as well as work quite hard for a living. She wasn't a droopy useless thing like some of the girls, Melanie Marsden for example. And her father rarely complained and actually, every now and then, called her a good girl. He was very forbearing.

'Is Mummy coming back?' Squashy asked.

'No, not ever. She's gone to heaven,' Lily said.

'What's it like up there?'

'Very nice. She's very happy. If you're good you'll go there one day.'

65

Squashy wasn't impressed. 'I'd rather go to Guildford.'

Lily cleared away the dishes and took hot water from the range to wash up. Her father went out to water the young cabbages and Squashy went out with his catapult to try and kill something. So far he had had no success.

SEPTEMBER, 1921

8

Just before he went back to school Antony talked to Lily about the parachute he had acquired along with his aeroplane. He seemed to be fascinated by the thought of flying high and jumping out to float serenely down to earth.

'It must be a terrific feeling. I would love to do it. I've asked around at Brooklands if someone would take me up so that I can try it, but no one would. They all say these chutes work so well it's as safe as houses, but they won't let me try. I think they're scared of my father. I tell them he need never know, but they won't.'

He had never taken Lily up again, much to her disappointment. Simon and John were forbidden, but Cedric enjoyed it and went up a few times. Lily knew though that Antony found Cedric boring with his obsession of spying on all the neighbouring farms. If he had taught her to fly too she could take him up and he could jump out with his parachute. She pointed this out to him, but he laughed her to scorn.

'Teach you to fly! You're mad, Lily! That's why I like you so.

But, for a treat, I could take you up and you could jump out with the parachute – how would you like that?'

Lily tried not to show how the idea frightened her. The awful thing about her relationship with Antony, she recognized, was what a puppet she was: if he said dance, she danced. Anything to please him. But to jump out of the aeroplane . . . the idea was terrifying.

'I'll think about it,' she said tightly.

'You're such a good sport, Lily. It would be great. Just us two. No one need ever know. We can find a nice airstrip, a private one where you can land safely, and I can come down after to pick you up. What a lark, eh? Until I can find someone to take me up, that is.'

Lily prayed that this might happen. But she doubted it. And, strangely enough, after the first shock, the idea that Antony had voiced was not completely unappealing. If she could really believe it was safe, the thought of swinging down through the sky from a great height had a fascination she could not deny. The more she thought about it the more the strangeness and the beauty of it took hold in her imagination. After all, she had been terrified with her flight, but it had turned out to be magic, something she would never forget. Her life was so boring and, as far as she could see, would always be so, without an education to take her out into the world, her father and Squashy to look after all her life and the unrelenting hard work – perhaps these moments that Antony offered, when her muddy heart took flight into realms she would never ordinarily reach, should be taken willingly, greedily, to feed great memories into her dull future. All this only came to her long after Antony first broached the idea.

He said, 'I'll try and find the right place, and we'll do it, if you're not afraid. I suppose we'll have to wait until the spring, because of the weather. Not much good at Christmas. Aunt Maud is coming at Christmas, God help us, but after that, in the summer, we've got the party to arrange – that'll be fun, and your jump – great stuff.'

'I thought you were supposed to be thinking about your career. You'll be leaving school soon. What are you going to do?'

The ever-present thought of Antony's departure from her life haunted Lily more and more these days. However long did these boys take to be educated? He never spoke about going to university, like Simon and John.

'Do? Enjoy myself, of course,' was the flippant answer.

If he went, Lily thought she might as well die.

When Antony went back to school Lily counted the days until Christmas. If he wanted her to jump, she knew she would. Strangely, she started to look forward to it. She wondered if she was capable of actually doing it when the moment came – she might be too petrified and seize up, unable to move. It occupied her thoughts all the time she was working at the mindless tasks she spent her days with: cleaning, digging, shopping, cooking, weeding, washing, running errands. Although she had thought she might spend more time with Helena, Rose and Violet thought differently and turned her away if she tried to visit. She hated going into the big house on her own and decided she couldn't persevere with it, in spite of Antony's wish that she should. He didn't own her, after all.

'What's this Aunt Maud like, that's coming at Christmas?' she asked her father. 'Is she nice?'

'Battle-axe. Old battle-axe.'

Just Antony's luck, Lily thought.

'Funny a brother and sister being called Claude and Maud. I suppose if you called one they both came. Save breath.'

'They were orphaned quite early on, left a packet. There's only money in that family, no love.'

Antony's got me, Lily thought, feeling warm and devout. He will always have me.

She didn't tell her father about the parachute jump.

DECEMBER, 1921

Aunt Maud arrived before Antony came home and made her presence known at once. She had a very large dog with her which needed exercising.

'Hey, you, girl!' she shouted, as Lily trundled a barrow of weeds towards the compost heap for her father. 'Come here!'

Lily came.

'This dog needs about two miles at least, every day. If you

do it for me, I'll give you twopence. That's generous, for just enjoying yourself. Suit you?'

Lily considered saying that no, it didn't, but a close look at Aunt Maud persuaded her that it would not be wise. She had an aggressive, masculine stance, foursquare on the drive in her long, belted leather overcoat, felt hat pulled firmly down on her big grim head, little grey eyes beadily taking in Lily's inadequate presence. She was not a kind smiling auntie as in children's books but, as Gabriel had predicted, a battle-axe.

'What's his name?'

'Ludo. Be firm with him.'

'What is he?'

'A dog.'

'I mean—'

'A dog of no pedigree. It's of no consequence. Here, take the lead.'

The dog of no pedigree was a good deal more amiable than his mistress and Squashy and Barky both took to him with delight. Lily's heart lifted, seeing that walking the dog, to obey a demand from above, was something her father could scarcely condemn given as Aunt Maud was in lieu of his employer. Ludo was large and brown and sweetly obedient, like a larger Barky. The two dogs of no consequence quickly became like brothers. Seeing them together gave Squashy such delight that their father grudgingly permitted him to do the dog-walking together with Lily.

'Interfering old bitch,' he muttered though, as Lily and Squashy danced away across the park.

'Can I have him?' Squashy asked Lily. 'For my own? Like Barky.'

'No. He belongs to Miss Sylvester.'

'I shall steal him.'

'She will know where he is. She will come for him and have you put in prison.'

Squashy started to cry.

'Don't be silly. Of course you won't go to prison. You can take Ludo for walks all the while she's here and that's good enough.'

Sometimes Squashy drove her mad. But walking the dogs every morning was more fun than most of the things she had to do, so bully for Aunt Maud, Lily thought. If the dog loved her she couldn't be that bad.

Mr Sylvester was generous to all his staff at Christmas and gave them big joints of meat and branches of holly, and delicacies for the old and sick. At home he didn't bother much but Aunt Maud took over, stoking up the fires in the gaunt rooms and organizing the festive dinner. The kitchen staff and the housemaids were all terrified of her and complained to Antony, but he told them he was terrified of her as well and there was nothing he could do about it. He kept well out of her way.

Rose and Violet complained that she was upsetting Helena, but there was nothing Antony could do about that either.

'That girl should get out more,' Aunt Maud declared.

'There must be some way of educating her, this day and age. Claude does nothing to improve her life, shutting her away with those two demented women.'

Antony agreed with her, but what could he do? 'Talk to Father about it.'

'He's so wrapped up in his work, thinks money solves everything. Throws it at you two – Eton for you, a mindless paradise for Helena – solved, as far as he is concerned. Useless. Eton's done nothing for you save keep you out of his way. Not that I've noticed, at least. Bored? Buy you an aeroplane. Problem solved. So what are you going to do, Antony, when you leave school next year?'

'I'm not going to university.'

'I said, what are you going to do? Not, what are you *not* going to do?'

Antony realized that his flippant answer to the same question from Lily – '*enjoy myself*' – would not go down very well with his aunt. His latest, vague idea had been to hang around Brooklands, although not actually to work. He didn't think that would impress his aunt. A bit of motor racing appealed, if his father would finance it. Somehow he didn't think Aunt Maud would be impressed.

'I haven't really thought about it much.'

'That seems to me to be your whole attitude to life. You've got a brain, haven't you? Good heavens, Antony, you're a man now. Are you so spineless that you are going to trail along in your father's wake, spending his money, being quite useless? You could come and live with me in Hampstead if you want

73

and get a job in the City. Start a business. Or go abroad and see the world. I'm sure your father would finance that.'

The idea frightened Antony. He had never thought much about going abroad: it did not interest him. He had a very parochial outlook. He knew his limits: a fair amount of brain, but little initiative, indolent, lacking ambition. He had no core. He wasn't brave: flying the aeroplane had proved that. He knew himself quite well, and sometimes it filled him with despair. He wasn't even mad on girls like most of his friends. The adoring Lily pleased him, but he wanted no more of her. What was wrong with him? He only teased her with Melanie Marsden to see her spark up. The fun he had with the boys in Eton was more to his taste, but where did that get you? In prison, if the worst happened. The only idea he had with what to do with his life was very short term, as far as the great party he planned in the summer, in the grotto, but he would hardly tell that to Aunt Maud.

'I will talk to your father about it.'

This did not frighten Antony, for his father would just take the easy way out, whatever it was. Perhaps he was more like his father than he had realized? He had never thought of this before. He was not responsible for his deficiencies, he couldn't help it! This thought cheered him considerably. He was just like his father! With luck he might have inherited his father's genius for making money.

For the time being he turned to making plans for Lily to do the parachute jump and to making arrangements for his big party. Lily's jump first. He was convinced there was no danger in it, but not convinced when the moment came she would be brave enough to jump. He wouldn't be able to make her, after all. But she was a very spunky girl and he had hopes. If only he could do it himself! He determined, after Lily had had her go, to get a pilot at Brooklands to take him up. When his father was away in the summer would be a good time. His father need never know. For enough money, someone would oblige him, especially as they all told him it was as safe as houses.

His father was going to South America in June or July, so that was when he would have his party. At the time of a full moon.

His Eton friends were all to camp by the lake, or bed down in the house with their own gear if they wanted, and they could have the run of the kitchen as he was going to give all the staff time off. Getting rid of Violet and Rose was his biggest problem, for the party was for Helena. She would be dressed in her most beautiful clothes and come to the grotto in a punt. Of course Violet and Rose would not allow it, so they would have to be locked in somewhere out of the way. He wasn't sure yet how he would manage this, but it could be worked out easily enough he was sure. Alcohol might come into it. He was sure they were secret drinkers. Then the party would take place in the grotto, which would be lit with hundreds of candles and the food and drink would all be spread in the great interior cave with the fountains playing, and everyone would come by water and music would be played and there would be dancing and swimming under the light of a full moon. He had the invitations already given out, only the date to be finalized.

'You haven't given me one,' Lily said.

'I don't need to. I know you'll be there.'

'You will need me.'

'Yes, I'll need you.'

It was so exciting just talking about it, and with Simon and John and Cedric helping to work out the sequence of events, the parking, the ordering of the food, the hiring of the table-ware – 'No, forget that. We've got mountains of plates in the dining-room cupboards – we can use those.' Mountains of incredibly valuable china, Spode and Minton and Crown Derby, Lily thought, but she knew better than to protest.

'We can punt it all across the day before, and everything we need. The food can be delivered straight there, we can carry it across the bridge ourselves. It will be ready-cooked, the joints and hams, and the desserts all made up, I've worked it all out, what to order.'

'And the drink of course,' said Simon.

'Yes, from Father's wine merchant. He knows.'

'What, your father?'

'No, the wine merchant, ass. I'm tipping him to keep it under his hat.'

'Your father's bound to find out.'

'Yes, but it'll be long over when he comes home. And he won't mind. He's never given me a party in my life before so I'll say it's a birthday party really, a bit late. That's all. He owes it me.'

Lily was pretty sure it was not going to be the sort of birthday party Antony's father would approve of, but nobody mentioned the obvious. It was too much fun doing it their own way. Lily had been told not to tell her father, but she knew that he was already aware of something going on, and so was probably most of the village. He didn't ask her, saying only, obscurely, 'Know nought, say nought, that's my motto.'

'Maybe you could do your jump at the party, Lily, when we've practised it first. It would be fantastic—'

'What, into the lake, to amuse your friends? I don't love you that much, Antony. I'm only doing it once, without anyone seeing, somewhere private. And even then I might not, when the moment comes.'

'Soon, Lily. The next time I'm here when the weather's right. No wind. In the dawn, just when it's light but everyone is still asleep. It will be wonderful.'

Will it? Lily wondered. Her insides tingled at the thought. It was big in her head now, this thing she had to do, and it filled her with excitement, misgiving, downright panic. But she knew if she refused it, she would never forgive herself.

Aunt Maud went home, taking the dog, and Squashy cried inconsolably, driving Lily mad.

'Barky loved him too. We both want him!'

'He'll come back when Aunt Maud comes again. Not long, I expect.' Not in the middle of Antony's party, she prayed. Aunt Maud had intimated that with her brother expected to be in South America for a few weeks over the summer, she might 'drop in' to keep an eye on Antony. Antony had lied to her and told her he was going to be staying with friends in the early summer, and she said she would come later, though she also needed to check her itinerary for her annual trip to the French Riviera. One could only pray.

'The old bat! She thinks I'm not to be trusted.'

A wise old bat, Lily thought, but did not say. 'Forget about her. She's a pain. Nice dog though.'

'Yes, nice dog.'

Squashy started to cry again.

'I want Ludo!'

Lily wanted to hit him, but knew she couldn't. Oh, to be up in the sky, floating slowly down with the clouds all round and the sun shining on her and her soul free like a bird . . . she longed for it suddenly: a rare, rare brightness beckoning, which she would remember for ever. Antony said it was as safe as houses, and no one else knew they were going to do it.

APRIL, 1922

9

'Now the weather's warmer, the first Sunday with no wind. Early in the morning, so no one will see,' Antony had said on a Long Leave at home in the spring.

Already Lily could feel the excitement mounting.

'If I come home specially, you won't funk out, will you? You won't let me down? I trust you.' His eyes had been challenging.

'I might at the last moment. How can I tell? I might not be able to make myself—'

'I shall never forgive you.'

'How can I tell though? If it was you – it's not as if the plane's on fire or anything so's you've got to get out. Only a bit of fun.'

'I know you can, Lily. That's why I love you so.'

That clinched it. She said no more. But the fear bubbled inside her. She tried not to think about it. But it was like those volcanoes they had been taught about at school, always ticking away beneath the surface, to erupt in flames without warning (not in England fortunately) – the fear leaped into her throat without warning when she was cooking or pulling up a cabbage or just lying in bed nearly asleep. Fear or excitement, she could not tell, just the feeling of bursting with an uncontainable emotion, indefinable . . . when it was over, if she were still alive, how dull life would be without it . . . although there would still be the party to anticipate . . .

Her father thought she was sickening for something. 'What's wrong with you, gel? You're like a cat on hot bricks.'

She tried to play it down, contain it. But she didn't have long to wait. Antony arrived unexpectedly, saying he had been suspended, whatever that meant, for a couple of weeks. Not to come back till after the Easter hols. His father gave him a thrashing, then was quite nice to him, forgetting all about it.

'A fortnight off is a waste of his money, that's all he thinks of. He doesn't really care about what I did.'

'What did you do?'

'Oh, a bit of larking about. Bit of a birthday celebration – I *am* eighteen now, don't you see! Someone got hurt though, so we got into trouble. Nothing really.'

It sounded like her parachute jump.

'Tomorrow, eh, Lily? The weather's just right, no wind, clear visibility. We can go off early and be back for breakfast. No one need know.'

'Yes, all right.'

In a way, it was a blessing to get it over. No more agonising. Dead or alive, it would be decided. To be dead would be so peaceful.

'Piece of cake,' Antony said.

From that moment, through the evening and all through the night, Lily's brain wrestled with emotions she could scarcely contain, ranging from a pitiful fear of death to euphoria of a blazing intensity. Sleep was impossible. It was a calm spring night, the sky glittering with stars. She felt she was to become part of the sky like the stars themselves, a magical being at one with the clouds and the raindrops and the highest flying eagles, pitched from a prosaic little aeroplane into a sphere unknown to human beings: the great canopy of the sky, all alone. She did not think her mind would work in such conditions, to instruct her to do all the things Antony had taught her, to save her life. To walk out on the wing and jump off backwards, not to pull the ripcord until she was well free, not to panic . . . impossible . . .

They do it all the time in America . . . Lindbergh's done it four times . . .

Then to think: it's all a dream, Antony just said it for a joke and it's not going to happen. And then the hollow disappointment worse than the fear, the falling into a black pit of misery to think her boring life was not to be illuminated by this wonderful intimacy with the clouds and the sky, out there alone in inestimable space . . . I am going batty, she said to herself. I might never recover my brains after this. They say a great shock sends you loopy. Antony is doing this to me. She told herself that hundreds of men had jumped out with parachutes and lived to tell the tale, and Antony had bought her the latest design by Mr Irvin, unimaginable that it would

81

not work, a piece of cake indeed, go to sleep. Impossible.

The stars began to fade and the grey light of dawn filtered into her bedroom under the eaves. She crept out of bed, dressed rapidly and went downstairs. She had put out her warmest clothes and a scarf to contain her hair in case it should get caught in the rigging. What hadn't she thought of? Absolutely nothing. Her brain had now cooled and she felt calm and slightly sick. It was impossible to think of eating, so she unlatched the door quietly and went outside. The sharp fresh air was wonderful, a slap in the face to shift her stupid imaginings. She drank in deep breaths and started to walk firmly away from the cottage. Would it be the last time? Don't be so stupid! The lake with its familiar blurring of mist hiding the far trees lay silent and mysterious as always. Would the sight of it be her last? Don't be so stupid!

'Lily!'

'Oh, Antony!' The relief at seeing him, all the ridiculous clutter in her head dropped into oblivion. She did not notice that he too was pale, and frightened, yet seeing her he also laughed, and they hugged each other.

'I didn't think you'd come!'

It had been a hope, in reality, his night having been spent sleepless in a terrible fear at what he was asking of her. But seeing her so game, laughing, changed his mood.

All the same, he said, 'You don't have to, Lily.'

'Oh yes, I do,' she replied. 'I must do it.'

She had not suffered those weeks of doubt to fail at the last moment. She did not know the thoughts that were going through Antony's head: that if she were to be killed, then he too would crash the plane and die. It was a wild and impulsive resolution. He could not believe, in the cold light of dawn, that he had been so stupid to ask her to do this thing. It had been in the nature of a joke initially. He had not expected her to agree.

'You are wild, Lily!'

'Hark who's talking!'

They walked down the side of the lake together towards where the little plane stood waiting. Antony had had the tank filled, and the brand-new parachute was sitting waiting in the passenger seat. It looked to Lily cumbersome and grim, a rucksack thing with heavy straps. Antony arranged it on her and gave her instructions.

'When I give the word you climb out onto the wing. You can see that's quite easy, holding onto the strut. The wind will try and blow you off so to jump is quite easy. You just let go and go off backwards, the wind will take you. But don't pull the cord until you're well clear. You've got to fall clear first, else the chute might open and get caught in the tail. Fall clear first and then pull the cord to open it. It's very simple.'

'Yes.'

'I've picked an airfield about twenty minutes away, not near anywhere and no one will be about at this time of day, so with luck we'll have the place to ourselves.'

God, if her father found out! Lily thought. But it was scarcely daylight, and little stirred. The sky was steely grey, with just a faint streak of a greenish dawn beginning to stir behind the trees. Even the farmers were still asleep. If they were not back before her father was up she could say she went out for . . . what? She would think of something before they got home. She shivered.

Antony tightened up the straps and showed her the red ribbon of the ripcord. 'That's it then. We'll be off.'

He fastened up his helmet, pulled down his goggles and went to start the engine. Its crackle sent the birds spinning out of the trees, shattering the peace of the morning and setting Lily's blood racing. Now there was no going back: the little plane careered down its strip of mown grass and rose gracefully over the roof of the cottage where Gabriel and Squashy no doubt were coming to swearing life, cursing the young Sylvester and his new-fangled idiot contraption – Gabriel did not mince his words in his contempt for Antony and his way of life.

If only he knew – Lily laughed out loud. Twenty minutes and already her blood was throbbing with excitement and her hands trembled; she twitched and shivered in her seat, free of any straps holding her in, aware only of the weight of the parachute and wondering how it would feel when she made her move. It was a cumbersome thing, this giver of life. Climbing out might be quite difficult, dragging it with her. She would fall off the wing with no trouble.

Antony was making height, higher and higher. Usually he flew quite low, enjoying frightening what he called the peasants, not to mention the cows, the horses, the hens and the pigs, but now the fair earth was falling away at an alarming

84

rate. Peering over the side Lily was terrified afresh at how far she had to fall. But the further up they were, the safer, so she understood, and – if all went well – she would enjoy it more. As it was, she could not even think of enjoying it, as the fear swelled inside her.

Antony turned his head and grinned at her and mouthed, 'Nearly there!'

At last he levelled off and the plane flew smoothly on its way. Lily could see half of England and the sea that bounded it away to port, and tiny puffs of cloud below them, inviting, as if you could lie on them as on a gigantic cushion. Would they come to meet her, clammy and full of raindrops? She was shaking all over, half crying.

Antony's head turned again and he made a gesture for her to start moving.

She lurched to her feet, reaching out for the wing strut to haul herself out. As she put her leg over the side of the cockpit she felt the wind tearing at it, and as she pulled herself after it the wind grabbed her like a human hand and pushed her backwards. She managed to crawl against it for a fleeting moment, then her hand on the strut gave way and without even willing it she was falling through space, head down. She had not decided to jump: the decision was made for her and afterwards she thought 'how lucky', so strong had been her instinct to stay with the plane.

Without even considering how clear she was of the plane she jerked desperately at the red ribbon of the ripcord and immediately felt a great lurch, her body coming upright and swinging violently at the same time so that she thought her stomach would fly out of her of its own accord. She looked up and saw the great flower of the silken chute billowing out against the pale, thin sky, as beautiful a thing as she had ever seen, holding her, comforting her: '*You're not going to die, dear thing.*' The words sung in her head. She was in love with her parachute, holding her so sweetly high above the amazing earth that seemed no nearer than when she had looked at it minutes before. So slowly, slowly she sank towards it, the amazement and the beauty of it making the tears spring into her eyes – or perhaps it was just the wind – she could not tell: the emotion was almost uncontainable. So she wept at the most heavenly thing she had ever done in her life, and through the tears watched the little fields grow into bigger fields and the little roads grow into cracks across the earth, higgledy-piggledy, and the white spots turn into sheep and the dark lines become the shadows of elms around the fields, long morning shadows cast by the morning sun that she was high enough to see, poking over the trees, making her blink.

Softly, softly she swung, as if for ever, and then, suddenly the field was no longer a sweet vision below, but a hard landing coming at her very fast. Antony had not said a thing about landing and she had thought it would be just a caress of her feet in the grass and a gentle subsidence of the body onto the dear earth. But actually it was a very sudden crash which jerked all her lovely thoughts into oblivion as the great folds of silk above her turned into a sort of flogging train dragging her willy-nilly across the field. For some moments she could not make sense of it and then, as it started to hurt, she managed to turn herself over and start to fight with the billowing silk. Or was there some release mechanism to cut her free? If there was she had no time to search for it.

An innate sense of self-preservation gave her the strength to overpower the now capricious chute, throwing her body onto it and stuffing its surges underneath her until all the wind was knocked out of it. Then she lay still, wondering where to find the release mechanism, but not caring very much, her thoughts more intent on realizing that the great adventure was now over. It was hard to believe what had happened, that all those weeks of fear and indecision, excitement and horror, were now behind her. She had done it. She was still alive. She had with her now a memory – what a memory! – to take with her till her dying day.

Dear God! She kissed the dew-wet grass and stopped crying.

And then Antony was beside her, holding her in his arms, hugging her and kissing her and finding the release without any trouble and pulling her free, gathering up the great heap of silk and telling her she was marvellous. 'I love you, Lily! What a day! Here, drink this. You're frozen. Sit up!' Something from a flask that he held to her lips and a wonderful fire filled her trembling body so that in a little while her senses came back.

She started to laugh. 'It was—' But there were no words to describe it.

The parachute safely contained, Antony pulled her to her

feet. 'You're a corker, Lily. There's no one like you. Absolutely brilliant! What a pity the boys weren't here to see it. They'd have died!'

'You're not going to tell them! No one must know!'

'No, I know that. My father would flay me and so would yours, I daresay. No one must ever know. Just us.'

'No. Just us.'

Flying home, Lily could not believe it had happened.

10

Neither of them said a word, yet Lily was aware of a strange reserve in the people around her, not saying anything, but just looking, or not saying and not even looking, eyes down, suddenly shy of her. She thought it was her imagination. Even her father, who did not ask, was strangely distant; his adage 'see nowt, say nowt' seemed to take on an extra tag: 'know nowt'. He did not even mention being awakened by the plane so early, which he must have been, despite a growing deafness these days, nor curse as he usually did about 'that idiot boy'. Lily kept out of his way, scared of his reaction should he find out.

But the days passed, and everything settled into normality. A month later Lily was sent up to the Butterworths' farm with a message from her father and she met Cedric on her way back. He had stopped to water two carthorses at a pond and was waiting for them, chewing on a grass and looking very yokellish.

'Hey, Cedric.' Lily stopped, admiring the horses. The Butterworths kept their horses beautifully, turned out for work as shining and polished as if they were going to a show. 'Which ones are these?'

'Hector and Olly.'

'They're gorgeous. Do you do them?'

'No. The men do them.'

Stupid. Of course, he was the farmer's son, not a stable boy, although he worked as hard. Lily found him a relief from the other boys, easier to understand. She knew he was attracted to them for the same reason as she was: for their larks and the carefree world they represented. Like herself, Cedric was tied to the earth and its drudgery and, like herself, he had a severe father so there was little escape, but he had a patient nature and rarely complained.

'Are you looking forward to this party of Antony's?' It was the only thing she could think of that might engage him. For herself, now the parachute jump was over, it was the only thing she had to look forward to.

'No, not very much. It'll get out of hand, if all his friends are like he is.'

'That'll be part of the fun, won't it?' How stuffy he was.

'All right, as long as Helena isn't involved.'

'But the party's for her, isn't it? She will be the star.'

'You say so. But how will she know what's happening? She might be terrified.'

'She loves the lake. We've taken her.'

'Quietly, just you and Ant. But imagine all those idiots, shouting and screaming around her, and she out where she's never been, doing what she's never done.'

'But she's deaf, she won't hear a thing. Or see.'

'But feel and sense, Lily – imagine it. She never goes out. It's wicked the way they keep her.'

'But this is to give her an outing, surely? To give her some fun.'

'Yes, as long as they are gentle.'

'Gentle' was not a word Lily thought applied to Antony's friends.

'Well, I don't know . . .' She didn't; she had never thought about it. A bit of fun for Helena, as Antony had said. She was puzzled by what Cedric was saying.

'Anything might happen.'

'But—'

'For example – with Antony and you. Did you agree to do that thing with him, or did he trick you into it?'

'What thing?'

'You know what I'm talking about. He borrowed the Rolls to drive to Brooklands, to take the parachute back to be repacked. Tom told me. He said he saw what Antony was doing and Antony swore him to secrecy, but he couldn't help telling me. And God knows how many other people he told.'

'I wanted to do it. Antony didn't make me do it.'

'I bet it was his idea. He knows you'll do anything he asks, even kill yourself.'

'It was perfectly safe. I'm not so stupid. And besides, it was amazing, and wonderful, and the most glorious thing I've ever done, and I've Antony to thank for it.'

'He should never have asked you. It was wicked. He knew none of us others would have agreed. He just uses you, to dance to his tune.'

'Well—' It was difficult to argue, for she knew what he said was the truth. The agony of thinking about it before it happened, the nightmares and the horrors of what her imagination had thrown up, were easily forgotten in the memory of the jump itself.

'Don't waste yourself on Antony. He's not worth it.'

'Oh, Cedric!' She could not begin to tell him what part Antony took in her life. Cedric had no imagination, else why would he question what she had done? If Antony had asked him to do the jump he would have refused. How boring he was! Nice, but boring.

'You're brave,' he said. 'I'll give you that. Brave, but stupid.'

She laughed. That was the two of them, brave but stupid, nice but boring. A good pair.

'You'll not be a wet blanket about the party though? There's no danger there. Just a bit of fun. You'll go along with that?'

'Yes, as long as I can get away. It's hay time.'

'The party's all night, Antony says.'

'Yeah, good. But sometimes hay-making is almost all night too.'

Lily went on her way, thinking Cedric was not so bad really. He was a bit like a bale of hay or straw himself, golden brown and slightly gingery, slow-growing and inevitable. He would never take flight, move from the farm. He had never even been to London. (Nor had Lily, but that was different.)

The months passed, spring was burgeoning into midsummer and Mr Sylvester was packing his bags to go to South America. Antony was finalizing his date for the party. He wanted a full moon, and surety that Aunt Maud would not be around, which meant finding out the date when she made her annual trip to the French Riviera. By rashly inviting her for a later date – she had, after all, made noises about visiting while his father was away – he found the crucial dates of her French visit, and by these roundabout means fixed a date that, with Aunt Maud guaranteed to be away, agreed with most of his school mates' itineraries: soon after they broke up from school at the beginning of July, and before they all went off with their maters and paters to their second homes in Monte Carlo, Lake Como, Montreux, Baden-Baden, etc.

Simon, John and Cedric were certainties and Lily was reassured that there was a place for her. Lily suspected that it was as a servant, but didn't care, as long as she was there. She doubted if Antony dare ask any of the house servants to help. He said he was going to send them all off on holiday as soon as his father left so that the house would be clear of staff save for Rose and Violet, who were so far away in Helena's rooms that they might not even notice. Getting Helena away from them, out for the night, promised to be the biggest problem and Antony was not ruling out force.

'Lock 'em in 'ld be best, give them a bottle of gin each, that should fix 'em.'

Planning this outrageous escapade was obviously giving him a great deal to think about. There was little he could do until his father actually departed, and he was terrified that this departure might be delayed, for his father seemed to be in a nervous state of mind about it, spending much time humming and hawing on the telephone and rushing up to London at odd hours. It was not until his trunk was actually packed and carried out to the Rolls-Royce where Tom was waiting to take him to Southampton that Antony felt his heart lifting.

His father shook his hand formally and said, 'Be a good man now, I'm trusting you.'

'Yes, sir.'

Antony contrived to look trustworthy, knowing he was acting out a lie. But with luck his father would never hear about it. It was going to be impossible to keep the party secret from the village, but his father never had much to do with the village fortunately, save through the window of his Rolls-Royce.

'Goodbye then.'

By the time he returned the party would be old hat. What was he going to do when it was over? Antony wondered. He stood with his hands in his pockets watching the car disappear round the bend in the drive, wishing suddenly that he was going too. To cross the Atlantic was quite something: it had never crossed his mind to ask his father to take him with him. There was little companionship between them, but seeing the world was something that surely a rich man should be offering his son? Pals at Eton were off all over the place. He had been offered trips with several, but it had never crossed his mind to accept, fixated on the amazing party.

When it was over . . . Antony felt the familiar abyss open before him. What was a mere party, after all, compared with the great void that lay ahead? He knew he had flunked all his exams, would never go to university, would never be part of whatever nefarious business his father was mixed up in. His father had never suggested that he should follow in his foot- steps, learning how to make money, and Antony had a deep suspicion that it was because his father did not want him to know how he made his money, nor did he seem to want anyone else to know. Where were the congenial parties of fellow businessmen that other chaps' fathers seemed to have, where the father-to-son conversations about his beginning to learn the ropes, why the secrecy, the long telephone conversa- tions into the night, the nervous twitch that had started to operate at the corner of his father's mouth? It was all very well for his father to say that he was trusting his son, but Antony did not trust his father.

Simon was going to Oxford to study classics; John was going (rather reluctantly) to theological college to see if he was cut out for the religious life, and Cedric was just working on the farm as usual, all perfectly straightforward. Friendly old people in the village who had only just stopped remarking, 'My, how you've grown!' were now asking him, 'And what are you going to do now, dear, that you're leaving school?' and he had no answer. He made things up. 'I'm going abroad for a bit'; or, 'I've been invited to join an Everest expedition'; or,

'I'm going to Newmarket to train racehorses.' He liked seeing the surprise on their faces. If he'd stated the truth: 'I'm going to die of boredom; I might kill myself,' they would probably be more surprised still.

Thank goodness the idiot child Lily still had faith in him. Her adoration always cheered him. She was a real nut, sharp as a needle in spite of having scarcely any education. She read and wrote with difficulty, but could add up the cost of a load of groceries in her head, in a trice, while he was still wondering whether to tender a note or would coins do? If she'd gone to Eton she could have been the first woman prime minister.

She was brilliant at planning the amount of food to order too, remembering all the basics while he was thinking caviar, foie gras, champagne . . . 'Fresh bread – you must order it. Glasses – are there enough in the house or can we get some from the church hall? Meat pies from Fortnum and Mason – you've got to think ahead, get the order in, and the delivery. You can't sack all the staff, we'll need help to get it down to the grotto.'

'The chaps'll do that, if everything is delivered to the house. They'll row it out to the grotto.'

'It'll be pandemonium.'

'I'll put you in charge, Lily. You can give the orders.'

'But we have to get the grotto ready first. Tables, candles, all the drink down there. The food out of the kitchen will go last.'

'We can get it ready before the chaps arrive.'

The date of the party was just a week after Mr Sylvester departed. It was early July, and the weather seemed set fair, but Lily could hardly take time off from her father's bidding, as Antony required, just to set up the party.

Her father already had a premonition of what was going on. 'Just keep that idiot lad from making a fool of himself, if you're involved. Keep your nose clean, Lily. You owe it to Mr Sylvester, he's your employer.'

'It's only a party, nothing out of the way.'

'Those public school boys – a bit of drink and it will get out of hand, you mark my words. You just keep clear of trouble. And Squashy – I won't forbid you to go, God knows you don't get much fun in your life – but those sort, make sure you keep them from Squashy. He's a prime target for those sort of arrogant bastards. I can't stop him going, he's full of it already, but I'm relying on you to keep him away from trouble.'

It was lucky her father didn't know that Helena was destined to be the star of the party. Lily knew that he would be appalled at the idea. He mustn't find out. Luckily Squashy didn't know about Helena, so would not give the game away. But as the days went past Lily felt her father's forebodings begin to weigh. Antony's plans were getting wilder and Simon and John and Tom the chauffeur, and Cedric when he could get away, did little to calm him down. The absence of Mr Sylvester's heavy hand on the estate seemed to have released a common geniality into the atmosphere and even Gabriel himself seemed to have taken to whistling and even laughing with the under-gardeners amongst the vegetables. The house staff, looking forward to their weekend holiday as the date of the party approached, were mostly partying themselves in the kitchen and could be heard shrieking and giggling at all hours in a most unseemly manner.

Antony had made a plan to get Helena released from her carers. He told Rose and Violet that she was to appear at his party and they must dress her and set off her beauty as well as only they knew how, and that they were to bring her down to the garden when dusk set in. They did not know that the party was being held in the grotto; they knew nothing about the punt that was being painted up and dressed with silken cushions and cloth of gold (out of an old trunk of Antony's dead mother's), nor of the journey she would make across the lake to the grotto to the accompaniment of beautiful music that Simon was having great difficulty in trying to pipe amongst the willow trees from the old gramophone in Mr Sylvester's study: they would not see her board her vessel, because as soon as they had brought her onto the floodlit lawn they would be hijacked by Eton's rugger team and manhandled back to their quarters and securely locked in.

'It's in the bag,' Antony breathed. 'Just let the moon shine down upon her! What a party it will be!'

'Dear God, I wish!' prayed Lily.

JULY, 1922
FULL MOON
11

In league with Antony's desires, the days and nights were hot and still and the moon grew towards its zenith on the night of the party. The air was filled with the scents of the flower gardens and the smell of mown grass from the hay meadows. The hay-making had proceeded at a record pace and Cedric was in the clear for the party, the last load stacked three days before the eventful night. The horses were turned out for a short rest and grazed under the stars, and in the bright light of the full moon Lily, unable to sleep, slipped out of bed and crept outside and walked down beside the lake to calm her nerves, absorbing the silence and the radiance of the park under the moon and thinking how amazing it would be the following night, impossible to imagine.

She felt burdened with responsibilities, knowing how Antony depended on her, for she had taken on nearly all the difficulties of organizing the food, how to keep it fresh and get it to the grotto safely, how to arrange it in the candlelight, how to serve it without the boys turning it into a scrum; and to keep Squashy safe, and see that Helena was treated with the care she demanded, that was her duty too. She was exhausted before it started.

How beautiful the night was! How strange that she lived in this heavenly place and rarely stopped to appreciate it. A pair of swans drifted on the water down the path of the moonlight, silent, scarcely moving, unaware, serene.

Tomorrow night they would fly away.

She went down the length of Antony's airstrip and came to the fence that marked the boundary between the park and the farm. The horses grazed with long shadows from the moon following them across the sweet-smelling grass. She leaned over the gate, and two of them came to her, to lip at her fingers, so gentle for such great strong creatures: she was filled with love for them, that they worked so hard and never gave up, however tired and belaboured they were. She put her cheek against the hard muscle of the neck, loving the smell of them, the feel. I am going batty, she thought. Antony's demands are turning me mad. She wanted to be at peace, for tomorrow to be over, yet she wanted tomorrow with longing: the glamour, the high spirits, the excitement.

How strange and utterly empty life would be without Antony in it, and yet he was hopeless: she saw now as she grew older how competent she was compared with Antony, what a load of hopeless dreams he was, with no stuffing, no ambition, someone only to be loved without return. It was Simon and John and Tom the chauffeur who had done the hard work, besides herself: the mending and painting and preparing of the boats, the complications of wiring the grotto, the repair of the machinery that turned on the cascades, of clearing the overgrowth so that there would be safe landing, and cleaning the grotto walls with a magic potion ordered from London.

'But it was my idea,' Antony said truly.

They all worked willingly for the consummation of the terrific idea: the party to outdo all parties. When it was over the magic would die: Claude Sylvester would return and the staff would all come back to toe the line. They would go back to work; her father would clamp down again, Simon and John would go away, and Antony . . . who knew? Not even Antony.

She walked slowly back along the lakeside, absorbing the peace and the beauty. It will never be like this again, she thought, not like this moment, on the brink, her heart so filled with hopeless desires, trembling with premonitions. Stop my brain, close down . . . I will never sleep.

Surprisingly Lily slept, overslept, and awoke with a jolt when her father shouted for her. Her head was perfectly clear, not a shred of the sentimental rubbish she recalled from only a few hours previously cluttering its clear conception of the tasks that lay before her.

'So this is the great day, eh? You're worn out before you're started,' her father commented, not entirely without sympathy. 'Perhaps we'll get some sense out of you all when it's over. Just remember what I said, that's all—'

He nodded his head towards Squashy who was getting Barky onto his hind legs and shouting at him, 'We're going to a party! We're going to a party!'

'Barky might be better left here with me,' Gabriel added.

'No! No! No!' screamed Squashy. 'Barky loves parties. Barky must come!' He burst into tears and lay on the floor hugging poor Barky tightly to his chest. The popping eyes of the little dog pleaded deliverance.

'Of course he'll come,' Lily said, prising him free. 'You can make him a party collar with that bit of red stuff in my bedroom, like a little scarf.'

She had been trying to work out something pretty to wear from the minimal contents of her cupboard. Modern dresses just seemed to hang down straight from what she had seen of them, not very complicated, but most smart girls now had short hair and there was no chance of her getting hers cut, not without incurring her father's wrath. She had been practising tying it up in some way, but it slithered all over the place; she was not a natural lady's maid. Anyway, she reminded herself, she was only a servant. Her hair was clean and shining and would hang free as it always did. The worst thing was that she had no shoes, only work boots, and broken slippers for the house. She should have asked Cedric to borrow a pair for her from his sisters: he had two sisters, as well as several younger brothers. It wasn't too late; she must ask him this morning. The rest she could manage. There were so many things to do!

The weather was perfect, as Antony had commanded. Some of his friends had arrived the night before and were making breakfast in the kitchen. Lily went there to start seeing to the food, but stopped in the doorway as she saw the strangers who had taken over, some six or seven lanky youths pinging bread pellets at each other. The table was strewn with dirty plates and cups and saucers and the boys sprawled in their chairs, two with their feet on the table. Antony wasn't there.

Lily froze with embarrassment. Squashy was right behind her with Barky, who lived up to his name, taking immediate exception to the strangers. Lily felt the same. She obviously did not impress them for none of them got to their feet as she knew gentlemen should when a lady entered the room.

'Sorry, I'll come back later.'

'No, stay, sweetheart. Have a cup of tea.'

'I'm here to work, but obviously the kitchen is still in use. I'll come back later.'

She turned abruptly and swept Squashy before her. Barky stayed behind yapping, and one of the boys threw an egg at him. Barky fled. Squashy tried to turn back to punch the aggressor but Lily marched him firmly out, down the corridor and out into the yard.

'Pigs!'

Surely not all Antony's friends were like this? Of course, having the run of a stately home with no adults on hand was going to prove very attractive: she feared the worst. But that was not her department. Thank goodness Simon and Cedric were down by the lake, testing the electrics in the trees, and she went to them with relief.

'There's some beastly boys in the kitchen. I came away.'

Simon said, 'Those beastly boys are going to get jobs to do, don't worry. You've done your bit, Lily. All the food will get carried out to the grotto – not your responsibility any more. There'll be plenty of manpower around today. You enjoy it all now, and stop worrying.'

'I can't help it. It's been—' Everything had led up to this, for so long; when it was over, how strange . . . 'I've got no shoes to wear. I wondered if one of your sisters could lend me a pair, Cedric?'

'Yeah, why not? Go and ask. Did you see Ant in the house?'

'No.'

Simon said, 'You know he's promised to take his pals up for joyrides today if they want it? So we're not going to get much sense out of him. If you see him, tell he's got to organize getting everything down to the grotto for tonight. That's not our job. We're boats and lights and things electric.'

'And Helena?'

'He's doing Helena. He's the boss there. We just wish that wasn't happening.'

'What? Helena coming?'

'Yes. Anything could happen. She won't know what on earth is going on.'

'She'll have lots of people to look after her.'

'Hmm.' Simon obviously wasn't convinced.

Having seen the crowd in the kitchen, Lily understood his doubts. 'We can always bring her back if she's frightened.'

'Some of us will stay sober, don't worry,' Cedric said.

Lily realized how totally ignorant she was of party behaviour. The nearest she had ever come to a party before was the annual harvest gathering up at the farm, which was a jolly and simple affair where she fitted in. Certainly there was a lot of drinking, and even her father fell over on the way home but that was only funny. It didn't compare with the lavish expectations that she felt were overcoming her now.

She went up to the farm to see about the shoes. She didn't know Cedric's sisters very well, but his mother was a homely old thing and always friendly and happy to help.

'Just an old pair of sandals, nothing special. I'm not really a guest, just helping out.'

'Make the most of it, my dear. Don't let that boy put on you, you're not his servant.' Mrs Butterworth brought her a selection, mostly quite plain. She tried to make her take the smartest, but Lily chose the oldest and most comfortable.

'I'll bring them back tomorrow. It's very kind of you.'

'You can keep that pair. Amelia never wears them now.'

'No. I'll bring them back.'

'Well, enjoy yourself, and be careful.'

What did that mean? Lily wondered as she made her way back. The shoes were gloriously light and comfortable. She often went barefoot in the summer, depending where she was working, but these were so lovely that by the time she got back to the grotto she had decided that no, she wouldn't take them back, not after she had been invited to keep them.

It was getting hot, not a cloud in the sky. Up at the house, across the lake, she could see that more cars were arriving and

105

figures were idling on the terrace, some putting up tents in the gardens. Squashy was still over by the boats with Simon and John, whom she knew would take care of him, so she decided to have a last look at the grotto while it was still empty. Tonight it would be very different.

They had spent so much time bringing it back to its former glory and this was the first time she had stepped into it alone without a bucket and scrubbing brush in her hand. The usual cold hand reached out as she walked along the narrow entrance towards the inner sanctum, but the walls even in the darkness seemed to sparkle as they never had before, and as the great inner cave opened up over her head she gasped at the sight: thousands of little coloured lights had been threaded through the stalactites and were shining now as if they were the stars themselves in the night sky. And the reflections of the lights doubled and trebled through all the convoluted surfaces of the grotto and in the spray of the cascades that tumbled down into great troughs where the stone mermaids and fabled monsters and fishes gambolled, scrubbed clean of green mould by her own hands over several weeks. She had never seen it with the lights turned on, although she had spent many hours there watching Simon and John at work on high ladders borrowed from the farm. A certain amount of daylight came in through cleverly concealed orifices amongst the leaves and verdancy that grew over the roof, but it had only served to fill the haunting space with a grey twilight. Lily had always found the place austere; she could never have imagined how glorious it might be now the lights seemed to laugh and twinkle like a million friendly eyes: the place was quite transformed. She knew too that later there would be masses of candles, high up on the walls where the boys had made special sconces; they were in place, ready to be lit. Antony said they would warm the place as well as add scent and more light. The long tables were in place, covered in gold cloths, empty as yet, but soon to be filled with all the delights from Fortnum and Mason and with the ranks of champagne bottles: all the food that they had dreamed up between them, even including Squashy's favourite lemonade and a bone for Barky.

Simon was obviously testing the electrics, for even as she stood there the lights went out and the cascades fell quiet and the eerie silence of the grotto's normal demeanour took over, broken only by distant birdsong from outside. Lily stood absorbing the space and the astonishing sight that had quite overwhelmed her. For several moments she felt she was not in the real world at all, and then the usual echoes of cheerful birdsong filtered in along the corridor and she followed the familiar sound until it led her to the bright landing where the water lapped softly against the stones: out in the everyday again.

Then she laughed, enchanted by her visit, amazed by her own surprise, that she had never envisaged the finished product all the while she had worked there with the boys. She sat then on the stones, kicking off her lovely sandals as her feet dipped into the water, and let herself enjoy the moment. Never in her life had something so sweet and lovely appeared to her. In quite a different department from the parachute jump, it was just as valuable: a memory to be stored for the future, to recall when things got bleak. For her future was not bright, she knew. Like Antony she put off thinking about it.

It was so quiet here now, on the familiar spot where they so often played. Tonight the boats would land here, one by one, bringing the guests from the far shore, and Squashy was going to help Cedric take the empty boats away and park them. He was very at home on the water and with the boats and it would keep him nicely occupied. Helena was going to arrive with an escort, in the best punt, which Lily had seen cushioned and padded and made to look like a royal barge. Antony and Simon were going to punt her, and then change to rowing nearer the grotto where the water became deep. Lily had been told to be ready to receive her and help her disembark. 'Nothing must go wrong,' Antony had said several times. 'It must all be perfect for her.'

While Lily sat there, she saw Antony come roaring down the airfield in his father's Rolls-Royce with a full complement of friends arranged over the seats and the bonnet. He was going to take them up one by one for what he called a spin, and Lily decided to disappear, to nurse her happy thoughts back home where she needed to spend time working out what she was going to wear. Her wardrobe was so hopeless it wouldn't take long. If only she had thought ahead and arranged something with the few girls in the village she still called her friends! But too late now, even if she could be bothered. Thank goodness it was going to be very hot, so her mother's nicest

108

summer dress would do. And Squashy must have a clean shirt if she could find one.

Her father was working on their own vegetable patch behind the cottage, complaining that there was no getting to work at the big house for all the idiots roaming over the place. Honest as he was, Lily had noticed that he had not worked quite so hard since Mr Sylvester had departed. Antony was taxiing out with his first volunteer and shouting and laughing echoed across the lake from the gathering guests outside the house. Lily lay on the bed to think about things, and fell fast asleep.

The party was not to start until dusk.

12

Rose and Violet were thrilled at Antony's request to bring Helena out, looking her most beautiful, for the admiration of all his friends.

'Our little duck, she will love this! She knows, doesn't she, that something is going on? She senses it. See her face, all alight – oh, what a beautiful evening for her, and those beautiful lights across the lawn! She will feel it even if she cannot see it, how she will love it!'

Helena did not lack for gorgeous clothes and brilliant jewellery, once her mother's, and the two women knew how to make the most of her golden colouring, bringing out her best long dress of turquoise silk and a shawl of white silk shot with gold and silver threads. Her hair was loose and fell in shining curls over her shoulders and a diamond necklace glittered at her throat. At the age of twenty-two, she had a sweet childish face untouched by sadness or worry, which gave her natural beauty an extra dimension, a purity that seemed to shine from her strange, sightless blue eyes. Lily, used to her, was stunned when she saw her emerge from the house.

Some thirty or forty young people had congregated to greet her, now all in their party clothes and on their best behaviour. Antony led Helena out onto the lawn and announced: 'This is my sister Helena. This is her party. This evening is for her. No one must do her any harm.'

That was plain enough, Lily thought, her eyes now only on Antony, on whom a matching radiance seemed to have fallen: to Lily he had never appeared more handsome and desirable, so dark to Helena's golden brilliance, so sweet and kind, so utterly in his rightful place under the dusking sky before the great brooding house, all lit with the brilliance of Simon's electric skill. He wore evening dress, which was very becoming, and the culmination of his long-held party dreams seemed to have given him an authority she had never seen in him before. He might not have done much of the work, but the brilliance of the idea was certainly all his. And now he was here to take credit.

He led Helena down to the water's edge, where the best punt was waiting, all decked out as elegantly as Helena herself. Squashy held the boat and Simon was waiting to help. They more or less lifted her in and settled her against the cushions. She knew she was on the water. Lily saw her put her hand over the side and draw it slowly along, then put the wet hand to her face to feel it. She was perfectly calm, smiling. Antony and Simon got in carefully and Squashy was given the nod to cast off, but he held still and said in a loud voice, 'I want to come.'

Antony said, 'No, Squashy. Come in another boat.'

'No, I want to come with Helena.'

He stood firm and Lily knew perfectly well that if Antony did not allow him to join them he would scream and ruin the evening.

She ran down and put her arm round him. 'Take him!' she hissed at Antony. 'He will sit like a mouse and you won't know he's there. He deserves it, just like Helena.'

Simon said, 'Yeah, Antony, he can come with us.'

'And the bloody dog, I suppose.'

Simon laughed, and then Antony laughed too and Squashy slipped into the bow under Simon's feet and Barky jumped in after him.

Lily pushed the boat off and the two boys poled it out into the deep water. The lights of the grotto trembled across the water, showing the way. The crowd on the lawn, suitably impressed, started to take to the rest of the boats, not very capably, but none closed with Helena's stately progress. No one invited Lily and all the boats were taken, so she turned back crossly, realizing she would have to walk to the party.

But she had forgotten about the rugger team which had been instructed to deal with Rose and Violet and they were now coming out of the house, laughing.

'Poor old cows! You sure you locked the door properly?'

'Yes. There was a load of food on the table and two bottles of sherry, so they should be all right. They put up a hell of a fight though.'

'All the bloody boats have gone.'

'It doesn't matter. We'll go round in the Rolls.'

Lily approached them. 'Please take me too.'

'Of course, darling. Jump in.'

Thank goodness for that: Lily had expected scorn, but the young men seemed to have improved their manners since breakfast time. They had a couple of snooty girls with them who were not obviously impressed by Lily but at least made room for her. Two of the boys sat on the bonnet and a couple on the running boards.

'Hold tight.'

At least the driver was sensible and nobody fell off. When they arrived they walked over the bridge to the grotto landing and were in time to receive Helena's stately barge as it was the first to arrive, slipping in from the open lake under the great canopy of the trees that grew crowded from the overhanging rocks on the island. They made to receive it, but Squashy jumped out and elbowed them out of the way, kneeling down to hold the punt steady.

'Leave him, leave him!' Antony commanded, as a couple of the boys made to kick Squashy out of the way.

'He's the boatman here,' Simon said crisply. 'It's his job.'

Squashy beamed and Barky growled menacingly. The boys moved back, and then saw that they were in the privileged position of helping Helena out of the punt so forgot about Squashy and moved forward to greet her. She moved with such grace, as if stepping out of a punt was something she was perfectly practised in, but it was clear she did not know where on earth she was. How could she know? Her calm expression now showed doubt and a hint of fear. Antony saw it and stepped out quickly, taking her in his arms. She knew him and relaxed, smiling. Then Lily saw that the beauty of the grotto was all for nothing where Helena was concerned. And would the now-arriving, noisy, stupid boys and their hanger-on girls appreciate it as she had earlier? Somehow she doubted it. She wanted to see it again, before she felt that it would be despoiled, and was thankful when Antony nodded to her and said, 'Put your arm round her, she knows you. We'll take her in together.'

So she went with Antony and Helena into the grotto where, since she had last been there, a beautiful chair had been installed for Helena, draped in crimson cloth like a veritable throne in the centre of the glittering room. The candles had all been lit and the flames danced in multitude reflections over the pearly walls and stalactites, along with the coloured electric bulbs. The food that she had so elaborately dreamed up was all set out in a most professional style, along with the bottles of champagne and the priceless glasses borrowed from the house. Lily had never seen a party like it, nor dreamed that anything could look so gorgeous – all for Helena, who could not see it, or even know where she was. She wanted to cry for Helena, half afraid at what Antony was doing.

But now the rest of the party-goers were crowding in and the gasps of amazement echoed all round. Antony was seating Helena on the throne-chair and not letting go of her, and Simon came forward to be beside him, so as the party-comers started to throng in with exclamations of amazement at what they were seeing, Lily decided to back out and keep out of the way. Everything was turning out so well; she could not believe

Antony's luck. The idea had been so crazy, yet he had made it happen.

It was now dusk outside and the first stars were trembling through the leaves. The birds were quiet, save for the owls hunting over the farm. She stood, pulling her brain together, as the motley collection of arriving boats struggled to find space in the narrow passage under the overhanging trees. The boys amused themselves by crashing into each other, hitting each other with their oars and pushing each other from one boat into the other as the ones in front of them took turns to land. Squashy had taken on Antony's direction as head boatman and was trying in vain to land each boat safely, but no one took any notice of him. The more agitated he got the more excited Barky became, running up and down and barking his head off.

Lily went to him and said, 'Leave them, Squashy. Let them park themselves.'

'Antony told me! It's my job!' He yanked himself away from her.

'Oh, poor diddums!' A tall young man stepped out with his friends and mimicked Squashy's garbled complaint. 'Aren't we taking any notice of you then?'

'And what a bloody noisy dog you've got! We really don't want him at the party, do we?'

'Let's get rid of him!'

'Throw him in, throw him in!' One of the boys scooped Barky up and flung him out into the clear water beyond the landing.

Squashy screamed and launched himself at the boy, and by pure chance caught him off balance so that he tipped backwards into the water. He surfaced, furious, and put out a hand to grab at the landing but Lily stamped on it and he let go with an oath.

'Make room up there!' they were shouting from the logjam.

Lily grabbed Squashy by the arm and hissed at him, 'Behave yourself. Get out of their way – they'll throw you in too if you're not careful.' She dragged him away from the landing and into the bushes.

'Barky! Barky' he shouted, hiccupping with grief. 'He'll drown! He'll drown!'

'Don't be stupid! He can swim as well as you can. Oh, they are such idiots!' Lily groaned.

Boats were landing now and just being pushed out of the way to the clear water beyond the landing. Barky was paddling his way round them as best he could. The boy who Squashy had pushed in had landed, his elegant evening dress soaked through, and was shouting, 'We don't want this bloody dog at the party. Get away from here, you cur!' With which he picked up a handful of stones, and started throwing them at Barky.

Barky yelped. Lily could see the dog's expression, enjoying the fun, turn to hurt. Nobody had ever hurt Barky before. Another boy threw a stone, then two others. They were good shots and hit the little dog fair and square so that he yelped again, this time in pain. Squashy was now screaming, fighting and clawing at Lily to let him go. Tormenting the dog was now more fun for the boys than hitting each over the head with their oars, and in a tangle of boats landing and boys shouting, more stones flew through the air and Barky's yelps turned into howls. But still he tried to get back to Squashy, paddling frantically.

Lily screamed at them, terrified that Squashy would have one of his fits. She picked up an abandoned oar and advanced on the ringleaders, but suddenly it was snatched out of her hands and she glimpsed Cedric's furious face.

'Stay back,' he hissed at her.

He swung the oar wildly just as Lily had intended, but with far more power than Lily could have managed and swiped three boys straight into the water. The other boys turned on Cedric and a free fight broke out, bodies flying in all directions, and great shouts of encouragement came echoing from the party-goers still waiting to land from their boats. Squashy stopped crying at once and ran down the grotto bank to reach Barky who was paddling determinedly on, and Lily turned into the fight to try and rescue Cedric who was being overwhelmed by force of numbers. She thought that gentlemen would not attack a lady, but was soon disabused of the idea when someone tripped her up and she went sprawling face down. Someone trod on her and she screamed.

The next moment she heard Antony's voice, loud and angry as she had never heard it before, uttering words she had never heard before, and the whole melee came to an abrupt standstill. She struggled to her feet and saw everyone as if petrified in mid-conflict, fists dropped, faces gaping.

'This is supposed to be a bloody party!'

A mortified silence, then someone said, 'Terribly sorry, old chap! We got carried away. Some idiot attacked us, this fellow here actually.'

He pointed at Cedric with his oar and Antony laughed and said, 'Cedric wouldn't hurt a fly. You must be drunk already. The food's waiting. Just get landed and come on in.'

The atmosphere had changed in a trice and someone was actually shaking Cedric's hand, and even the boys in the water were hauling themselves out laughing. Then Antony saw Lily dusting herself down, and he turned and went to her and put his arm round her and said, 'Lily, I'm so sorry. They are idiots. Are you all right?'

'Yes. They threw Barky in and flung stones at him. That's what happened. Squashy went mad.'

'They didn't mean any harm. It's all right now.'

And he put both arms round her and held her close for a moment so that she almost passed away with heavenly delight. He stroked her hair, kissed her forehead and then turned away and went back into the grotto. The boats were quickly abandoned and the party-goers all trooped in after him, leaving Lily alone, dazed, on the landing. She could hear Squashy mumbling and squeaking somewhere, comforting Barky who had apparently made shore, and a party noise emanated from the mouth of the grotto that convinced her that there was no way she could go back in. She had seen the grotto as she always wanted to remember it: she did not want to see it despoiled by these stupid louts. Her heart was thumping, whether from the

118

fight or Antony's embrace she could not tell, but she wanted peace and quiet: she felt very close to bursting into tears.

As she stood, feeling trembly and indecisive, Cedric appeared out of the grotto passage.

'Are you all right?'

'Yes.'

'Just came to see. Did you get hurt?'

'No. But I don't want to go in there – all those idiots. It was so beautiful, empty, with the lights and all. I don't want it spoilt.'

'But it was for them, for Helena, for the party. The food is lovely. It's not spoilt, Lily, not now. They will be kind to you now.'

'No.'

'Later then, when you've calmed down. It was bad for you, Squashy getting so upset.'

'Yes, I'll sit with him for a bit. He doesn't understand.'

He nodded, understanding, and went back in. Lily felt comforted and went to find Squashy, who was jabbering away to his dog, hugging him to death.

'He's all right now, Squashy. Let him free.'

'They wanted to kill him!'

'He's happy now. Look how his tail's wagging. Put him down.'

Squashy released the dog, who shook himself gratefully and set to scratching his fleas. Lily sat down beside Squashy amongst the willows on the far side of the island, where all was undisturbed. The grass was still warm, the night very calm, the full moon high over the lake and the stars so bright that they were reflected in the still water. All just as Antony had arranged. The abandoned boats were floating around in all directions, Squashy having forgotten that he was in charge, not caring any more. In a few minutes he was fast asleep, Barky settling down beside him. He often fell asleep suddenly: it was part of his affliction and Lily was used to it. Poor little sausage, she thought, thinking how wonderful it would have been to have had a strong, brainy brother around to help. With her father growing old she was never going to be free of her cares, as far as she could see. If he had been like Cedric, how proud her father would have been!

She lay down too, suddenly very tired. It was long past her bedtime and she had hardly slept the night before. She had no worries now, everything was in hand, and she too fell asleep.

She had no idea what time it was when the party ended, or if it had an end at all. When she opened her eyes it was because someone fell over her, cursing, looking for she knew not what. He was naked, which gave her a startled awakening, but when she sat up she saw that a lot of the boys were swimming, and mostly they had no clothes on. She sat up. They were all very jolly, rounding up the boats.

'Is the party over?' she asked the embarrassed boy who had fallen over her.

'Yeah, Helena's left. We're going back when we can round up the bloody boats.'

'Where's Antony?'

'I don't know.'

He must be with Helena, Lily thought. She got up quickly and started to push her way across the landing and under the tunnel of trees to the far side of the island. The tunnel was crammed with departing boats, but quite a few were already out on the open lake and were surrounding Helena's punt. There was a lot of shouting and singing and Antony and Simon were rowing very slowly and laughing. Lily stood watching. The lake with the little boats dotted over it in the moonlight had never looked more beautiful and she stood taking it in: that Antony's amazing party for Helena had been such a success and that Helena was going home having experienced what must have been the most wonderful occasion of her poor stunted life. Lily felt herself close to tears with emotion, with pity for Helena, with gratitude for everything going so right after all the hard work. She had been so frightened at times, at what they were doing.

Suddenly an eerie noise, strong and pure, interrupted the party noise. It was unearthly, piercing, and very beautiful. Lily saw that Helena had stood up in the punt and she was singing, her face held up to the moonlight. She looked ecstatic, the gorgeous sound drowning all the raucous party noise around her. Lily remembered the story of how Helena had sung so unexpectedly before at her mother's funeral; it must have had the same stunning effect as it was having now, for all the laughing and shouting had stopped. Everyone was suspended, gaping, even the swimmers. The night seemed to be filled with the amazing sound, so pure and without a melody but with the anguish of a lament. Antony and Simon were frozen in mid-stroke.

How long she sang for, Lily never knew, only that it seemed that the night was standing still for her, the swans immobile, the boats as if petrified. The light of the moon was so bright that every detail of her beauty was as if magnified: she was unearthly, her face held with an expression of rapture while the sound filled the night – not a melody, no song, but just a voice brimming – it seemed to Lily – with all the longing she felt for a life she could not have, could not see, could not hear, but a longing she could only express in this weird, heart-chilling aria. Nothing moved, not even an owl called, nor a leaf fell.

Lily could see that Antony was petrified for her standing so precariously, and was trying to creep towards her in the bottom of the boat, but even as he did so another punt, taken by one of the strange currents that flowed beneath the lake, nudged the side of her punt. Not hard, but Helena was tipped off balance. She stopped singing, held out her arms to Antony, but before he could reach her she crumpled up: the punt tipped sideways and she slid into the water.

A girl shrieked and all was total confusion. Lily saw Antony plunge in, and then Simon, and then everyone was shouting and screaming and boats were crashing in all directions. Lily found herself screaming. Squashy materialized beside her, wanting to know what had happened, and Barky added his hysterical noise to the scene.

'Helena's fallen in!'

Squashy screamed and immediately jumped into the water. Barky howled. Lily sobbed. She was not afraid for Squashy; he could swim like a fish, but where was Helena? The empty punt bobbed serenely, empty, but in the crowd of swimmers splashing and diving all around it no Helena appeared. Lily saw Antony bob up, shout something, and disappear again. Lily knew the water was very deep just where they were and guessed he was getting frantic. And yet he had been quick enough to dive in: could he not clutch her hair or her volumi-nous dress? How could she have sunk so quickly? But then she remembered her father's stories of the strange currents at the far end of the lake and previous drownings, a suicide or two, stories she had put away as ridiculous because she and the boys had all swum like fishes there with no mishap.

Had Helena wanted to die? Was the unearthly music her swansong? How could anyone guess how her mind worked, so disabled by her lack of senses?

She saw Antony surface again, leaning his arms on the punt. Simon bobbed up beside him and they spoke to each other and then dived again. Most of the others had backed away now as time was passing and a terrible silence now fell on the crowd that was as cruel as all the screaming. Only Barky's yapping echoed across the water.

Lily cuffed him. 'Be quiet!'

He gave her an offended glance and lay down. She felt a

123

terrible stillness take hold of her, freezing her tears, just as now all the boats were still on the water, the swimmers climbing back on board. They were turning away, starting to row for home, save for a few waiting. Squashy was sitting in Helena's punt, waiting to see her home. The silence was painful after the crazy party noise; only the owls called, oblivious.

Lily waited.

She lost all sense of time. The full moon seemed relentless now, when a sweet darkness needed to fall, to pull a curtain over what had happened. Antony and Simon eventually gave up, exhausted, and swam back to the punt. Squashy was waiting for them. Lily didn't want him to go back across the lake, and stood up, shouting for him.

Barky started off again, and Antony called out, 'Lily!'

'I want Squashy back!'

They rowed back to where she stood waiting, and Squashy jumped out. Lily could not say anything, appalled at Antony's despair and grief.

Simon looked up at her, grey-faced. He nodded at Antony and said to Lily, 'I'll stay with him, take him home. I won't leave him.'

'No. Good.'

'Cedric's still looking.'

'He knows the lake best.'

'Are you all right, Lily? To go home alone?'

'Yes, of course. I must take Squashy.'

'He thinks she's swum home.'

'If only.'

They rowed away and Lily walked home with Squashy, who thought he would see Helena in the morning.

'No, she's still in the lake.'

'I'll find her and tell her to go home.'

'Yes, you do that.'

'In the morning.'

He skipped along, the water flying from him. Barky trotted close.

The lights went out in the grotto.

13

In spite of what had happened Lily went home and slept dreamlessly. When she awoke it was full daylight and she dressed quickly and went down the ladder, still stupefied with what she could remember. Her father was sitting at the table. Seeing him, she started to cry.

'Eh, lass, don't take it to heart. It were nothing to do with you.'

'Have they found her?'

'No. I've been out. They've the police and everything up there, and a couple of divers. I didn't speak to anyone.'

Lily put her head down on her arms and sobbed. Her father watched her, then put his hand on her shoulder.

'There, don't go on. You could say it's a blessing, after all. God's way of sorting things.'

Lily could not say that she was crying for Antony more than Helena. It had been a stunning ending after all; she would never forget the unearthly voice echoing over the lake. It should have been a beautiful finale to an amazing party but, as her father remarked, God had sorted things. Maybe it was a blessing, but certainly not for Antony. She did not dare contemplate what it meant for Antony.

'Where's Squashy?'

'He's up there, watching. He says she's hiding.'

'Poor Squashy.'

'Aye, poor Squashy.' Gabriel's voice was heavy.

'I'll go and fetch him.'

'I'll make you a drink. You two'll be best down here while all this is going on. You don't want to get involved.'

He made her a thin brew of tea and she drank it and went out. The morning was beautiful, just as the night had been, and the lake lay innocently empty. No boats, not even the swans. Several cars were parked by the bank on the other side, and the searching seemed to be going on up by the dam at the far end of the lake, way beyond the grotto. The smart cars of the party-goers had mostly departed.

Lily felt calmer after walking as far as the grotto. It was true what her father had said, that Helena's dying was a blessing: how ever could she had lived on into old age in that weird set-up with the dreadful Rose and Violet? Helena was at peace. Perhaps her song had been a longing for death and peace, how could one tell?

She hesitated at the bridge that led into the grotto, but decided she did not want to see inside it again. Its magic would certainly be dissipated by now.

Squashy was coming towards her along the side of the lake, Barky trotting beside him. He saw her and came up.

'Helena's asleep. I can't wake her up.'

'What do you mean?'

'She won't wake up. I shook her. But she didn't.'

'Squashy! Where is she?'

'Up there, in the reeds.'

'But they're all searching, the police and everyone! You haven't told them?'

'No. I was coming to tell you.'

'Oh, Squashy!'

'I'll show you.'

Lily followed him, her heart thumping nervously. She wouldn't have chosen to see Helena's body but now she felt excited – that Squashy had found her! Dear Squashy, who thought she was asleep! There was a small inlet beyond the grotto which she knew well, as it was a place where the water was shallow and she had come here fishing with Squashy when he was in his trolley, and now Helena had taken it for her resting place.

It was very quiet, hidden from the top of the lake where all the excitement was, and Helena lay there just as Squashy thought, apparently asleep, washed into the reeds with her golden hair bobbing in the gentle wavelets, her gorgeous dress spread around her. Her face was turned up to the sun, her eyes were closed, and her expression was one of tranquillity, acceptance. She was just as beautiful in death as she had been in life, no sign of the struggle of drowning – how did one drown? Lily wondered. She had always thought it must be horrible, yet there were no signs of horror here. Only peace. Was it as her father had suggested, God's blessing, that he took her and did not let her suffer? How could they ever know?

She stood quietly, moved by the fact that she was feeling comforted by looking at Helena rather than shocked and distressed. She was so much at peace. How could one be sorry for her? It seemed a fitting end now to the wild party, the full circle through excitement and joy to peace and oblivion. Squashy was playing with Barky, undismayed. Her father was right, Lily thought, that it was a blessing.

'She's not asleep, Squashy. She's dead. You know about dead?'

Squashy considered.

'Like our mother,' Lily prompted.

But he had never known her. 'Like that cow that Cedric buried?'

'Yes. The cow died and that was the finish of her. He buried her in the ground. Helena will be buried in the ground. Because she's no longer there. She's gone, and left her body behind.'

'Where's she gone?'

'To heaven. Where all dead people go. Nobody knows what's it's like there. You only find out when you're dead, but when you're dead you can't come back and tell anyone, so nobody knows.'

Lily wasn't sure about heaven and not sure about comparing Helena to Cedric's cow, but it was something Squashy seemed to understand.

'That's why she wouldn't wake up? She's not here any more.'

'That's right.'

'Barky won't die.'

Lily did not feel up to contradicting this and coping with the eruption it would cause, so did not reply. She knew she had to go on to the end of the lake by the dam and tell the men where Helena was, but for a while she stayed. Barky licked Helena's face.

'He loves her,' Squashy said.

Lily felt bereft, thinking of Antony – what he had to cope with now, just when everything had been going so stupendously right. Was he searching up by the dam? She wanted to see him very badly.

'Come on. We'll go and tell them where she is.'

Squashy followed her along the shore, showing a lively interest in death. Do cows go to heaven? Do you meet all the other dead people? Do you have to talk to the horrid ones? What do you get to eat? Lily did not feel qualified to answer any of his questions and was glad to come across Cedric just before they got to the dam.

'Are you all right?' he asked her.

'Yes.'

'The police are here. They're asking for Antony but I don't know where he is.'

'I don't know either. But we've found Helena. Squashy found her.'

'Oh, good. Well done, Squashy. He can show them where.'

'She's down in that little reedy inlet. Where we used to fish.'

130

'Oh God, poor Helena. But what a way to go – unbelievable! The whole night . . .' He shook his head. 'I can't get it out of my mind. The police are here – not sure why, asking all sorts of questions, mainly about where is Mr Sylvester. None of us know, I don't think even Antony knows. And nobody knows where Antony's gone. He's not in the house. I guess he's with Simon, but I'm not saying anything. I don't know why they're so interested.'

'Now they know where she is they'll check her out and go away, I should think.'

'Our men are helping. They can get a cart and take her round to the house, but we need Antony. Or my parents will see to it, get her laid out properly and all that. And a funeral to arrange. Antony must sort it out with Reverend Simmonds.'

'I'll go and see if he's at Simon's.'

Lily was impressed with how Cedric seemed to be so much in charge. He went off to tell the police and the farm men, and she turned back, not wanting to see poor Helena manhandled back to the house. Cedric had been very useful the night before too, sorting out the drunken idiots. She had not noticed how much he seemed to have grown up, always having seen him in the shadow of the three superior brains. Perhaps when it came to practical things he was like herself, feet on the ground, a normal country person, untainted by public school ethics, unburdened by intellect.

She hurried back home, past Helena without looking again, and leaving Squashy to tell the tale to her father while she continued up to the village to Simon's house. She knocked on the door of the Goldbeater house. What a lovely name he had, she thought while she was waiting . . . Simon Goldbeater . . . better than Sylvester . . . but Mrs Lily Goldbeater didn't have the appeal of Mrs Lily Sylvester . . . she didn't really like Simon very much after all; he could be very superior . . .

'Oh, hullo, Simon. I'm looking for Ant. He's needed. Is he here?'

'Yes. Who wants him?'

'The police, Helena, everyone.'

'You'd better come in.'

Mrs Goldbeater came bustling down the hall. 'Oh, Lily dear, what's the news?'

'We found Helena. They're taking her back to the house. They want Antony. The police want him and he has to see to things.'

'Oh dear. I told him he should be back down there, he can't go into hiding.'

'They want to know where Mr Sylvester is.'

'Come and see him. Tell him all this. It seems like nobody knows where Mr Sylvester is.'

Antony was sitting in a chair in Mr Goldbeater's study. He looked terrible, white-faced, red-eyed, stricken. He did not get up when he saw Lily, but gave a sort of groan.

'They've found her. You've got to come. They want you.'

'I can't—'

'You've got to. There's no one else, Ant. You've got to tell them what to do.'

'There, we've been telling him that, to get in touch with his father, to think ahead what to do with the poor girl, but he's all to pieces.'

Simon said, 'Come on, Ant. You've got to face the music. It wasn't your fault, stop crucifying yourself. I'll come with you, and Lily, and we'll get John – he can start sorting out the funeral with his father. There's tons of people to help you.'

'And Cedric's in charge taking her home. Come on, Ant.'

'Yes, dear boy. Pull yourself together. You can stay here as long as you want, but they need your authority to decide what to do. Even if they find where your father is, it will be days before he can get back.'

With everyone goading him, Antony struggled to his feet. He was wearing some of Simon's old clothes and it seemed to be an effort for him to merely stand up. Certainly he had exhausted himself the day before, especially with the time he had spent swimming in the lake searching, but there was a desperation beyond the physical exhaustion. No doubt it was grief for Helena finely balanced by fear of his father. Lily wanted to hug him and say sweet things, but she could see he was hardly aware of her presence.

'They've found her, Ant, that's the best news,' Simon said. 'Come on, let's get going.'

Simon's mother saw them to the door. 'And bring him back here, Simon. He doesn't want to stay in that awful place all alone.'

With a body, Lily thought. She wondered suddenly as they walked through the village towards the gates of Lockwood Hall whether anyone had thought to free Rose and Violet.

Had they even heard the news? The thought gave her the shivers. She must remember, in case. Surely the rugger boys had let them out before they drove off home?

There were several police cars parked on the drive overlooking the lake. The farmworkers had all gone. Only Cedric was sitting on the grass, gazing out over the water. There was no breeze, still a cloudless sky, just as beautiful as the day before. But quite different.

Cedric got up. 'They've brought her into the house, Antony. Rose and Violet have taken over and made them carry her up to her room. But the police are looking for you. They're going through all your father's things, in his study, say they're trying to find out where he is, because you're still a minor. Seems a bit of a cheek to me. You'd better go and talk to them.'

They all went into the house. The kitchen was in a shambles and the house was as cold as always, in spite of the sun outside. Whoever built a great house facing north? Lily wondered. It was a horrible place, and she hated it. They walked down to Mr Sylvester's study and went in, all of them.

There were four policemen there. One of them was sitting at the desk with all the drawers open, rifling through the contents. There were piles of files and papers that he had pulled out stacked on the desk top and some tumbled on the floor. The other three were nosing into the shelves and cupboards, pulling things out, more like burglars than policemen.

'What on earth are you doing?' Simon said sharply.

The man at the desk stood up and faced them. Ignoring Simon, he said, 'Which of you is Antony Sylvester?'

'I am.'

'You others can go.'

'We're not going,' Simon said. 'What authority have you got to go through Mr Sylvester's study? You were called here because a girl drowned. You've no right in here.'

Lily was stunned by Simon's attack.

'We are searching for Mr Claude Sylvester's present where-abouts. He needs to be informed. Perhaps Mr Antony Sylvester can help us in this matter?'

'I've no idea where he is.'

'Isn't that very strange, that he didn't inform you?'

'No. He doesn't tell me anything. I don't know where he is and I don't know when he's coming back.'

'If,' said one of the policemen.

Simon shot him a daggers look. He said, 'All you are here for is to enquire into Helena's death. We can tell you exactly what happened.'

'We need the body to be identified. The young man can do that now – he is her brother, I presume?' He told one of the other policemen to take Antony upstairs.

'I'll come with you,' Lily said, and as no one demurred she followed Antony and his escort out of the study. She reached out and caught Antony's cold hand. 'We'll look after you, Antony,' she whispered. 'And don't be afraid. Helena looks lovely, just as she always did, very peaceful.'

Antony had to lead the way to Helena's room as the policeman in charge quickly got lost. As he opened the door and Rose and Violet saw who it was they sprung round from the bed where Helena lay and launched into a tirade of abuse. Two little sharks, Lily thought, snapping white teeth; she could not believe the venom.

'Ladies, ladies, please! Not in front of the dead.'

The policeman's authority silenced them. Lily dragged Antony to the bedside and he stared down at Helena's sweet face with tears running down his face and nodded speechlessly to the policeman's questions to confirm her identity. Lily cried too, and the policeman had to blow his nose, not trained to cope with the emotion. He hurried away, leaving them, but Antony had no wish to stay with a further tirade from Rose and Violet, having no strength, it appeared, to silence them. Lily supposed he accepted the dreadful things they were saying. She wanted to scream back at them but retreat was the best option.

'You must sack them, Antony, pay them off and they will never come here again. They are terrible people.'

She slammed the door behind her. Antony went on down the stairs, and never said another word.

14

They all went back to Simon's house and his parents made them welcome. Even me, Lily thought, the servant . . . what nice people they were! If only Antony had had such nice parents! Boring old John joined them and said he had fixed everything with the undertakers, and his father had made a date for the funeral and everything was underway. He would say a few words. They should ask me, Lily thought. I could say far better words than John would ever dream up. But he was a good old stick and had done all the donkey work, which was really Antony's province, Antony having fallen to pieces. But as the day drew on, plied with good food and Mrs Goldbeater's maternal hospitality, he started to come to. They sat out on the lawn over a picnic lunch and Simon's parents came out too, curious to hear what the police had been up to.

'Bloody cheek, going through his desk like that! What did that have to do with Helena?'

'Language, Simon, please! But yes, out of their brief, I would have said. They were taking advantage.'

'Very strange,' murmured Mr Goldbeater. 'Do you know when your father's coming home, Antony? He really ought to learn of his daughter's death.'

'No. He never told me.'

'Where is he? What country?'

'South America. That's all I know.'

'And that aunt of yours, she needs to know. Where is she?'

'In the South of France somewhere. But I've no address.'

The parents went indoors, and in the kitchen Mr Goldbeater said to his wife, 'I always thought there was something fishy about Sylvester. One hears a lot of rumours. Why should the police be rifling his desk?'

'There's always talk in the village,' she replied. 'What does he do for a living? No one seems to know – save, whatever it is, it makes him a lot of money. The servant bill for that place must be enormous.'

'He has to do with the Foreign Office, I believe. He goes up to Downing Street and all that, to do with armaments, they say. Just rumours. No one seems to know him at all.'

'That poor kid. He's virtually an orphan when you come to think about it. No background at all. No one loves him, save poor Lily.'

'Oh, come on, there's nothing poor about Lily! Lily's love is worth ten of anybody else's.'

'Yes, you could say, with Lily on your side, you've not much to worry about. We'll get him to stay here in the meantime. He can't stay in that dreadful house with just his poor sister's corpse.'

138

But Antony insisted on going back to Lockwood. After the lunch and support of his friends he was reviving, and said he must go home and sort out Rose and Violet and see what the police had trashed in his father's study. With Mrs Goldbeater's advice that he come back later ringing in his ears, he left the house with Lily at his side.

But Lily left him to go back to her father. 'He will be wondering where I am.'

Antony looked so white and stricken still that she hated to leave him, but he said he wanted to be on his own. He walked up the long drive to the house and was relieved to see that the police cars had gone. The afternoon was still very hot, the lake placid below the lawns, the swans drifting as usual among the reeds. He stood looking across at the grotto, reliving the glorious party, trying to put out of his mind its terrible aftermath.

He could not get out of his head the unearthly sound of Helena's voice, more a wailing lament than singing, a lament for all she could feel but not see nor express, petrifying the shenanigans of the drunken, uproarious idiots trying to escort her home – her swansong, almost as if she knew she had come to her end. Perhaps she had willed it, perhaps she had actually fallen of her own accord. He could not exactly remember how she had fallen, only the panic that sent him plunging in after her. How was it possible, he having been so swift, that he had been unable to grasp her dress or her hair, or touch any part of her, that she had vanished in seconds? In his mind he was beginning to accept that it was an act of God, perhaps a kindness that she should die in the full flower of her youth and beauty. Perhaps he had been the catalyst for her finding peace in the ever-after. It would reassure him if he could believe that.

But what his father would have to say when he heard the story, Antony did not dare think about. He did not know how he would be able to face his father.

He turned and went back into the house. It was dark, silent, like a prison. It was hard to remember it otherwise. At least Helena had lived in the sun, in her lovely room at the end of the house. He made his way towards it, along the miles of corridors and up the stairs and opened the door to her quarters.

Rose and Violet were just leaving, their outdoor clothes in place. Between them they had two enormous laundry bags, so heavy they had to drag them rather than carry them. When Antony appeared, blocking the doorway, their faces sagged.

'I see you're leaving. I was going to settle up with you but it looks as if you're helping yourselves.'

'Just a few clothes, sir, that no one will ever want. And our own things.'

'Let me see.' He made them tip out the bags over the floor. As he had guessed, wrapped up amongst sundry items of nightwear and underwear were precious boxes filled with the jewellery Helena had been given by her parents: all her little valuable knick-knacks and the smaller of the paintings from the walls, thousands of pounds worth of goods that would have paid off their wages for a few hundred years. 'Just a few mementoes to remember her by? How lucky I came by! I was here to pay you and wish you well, a reference for another job perhaps, but now – now—'

His mounting anger choked the words in his mouth. It was all he could do to stop himself from lashing out and hitting their stupid faces, knocking them to the ground and stamping on them. They cowered back from his rage, mouths open, incoherent.

'Get out! Get out!'

'But – our stuff—'

'Go! SCRAM! Before I hit you – GO!'

'But—'

'GO!'

They went, scuttling, he thought, like rats, running away along the corridor into the distance. He stood panting, startled by his own reaction. He kicked at the piles of beautiful clothes, and then stepped over to where Helena still lay. Since he had seen her last, she seemed to have departed still further towards the afterlife, her beauty fast fading, her face now waxen and stiff. She was now just a thing, no longer Helena. John had said the undertakers would call in the late afternoon and he thought the sooner she was screwed away in her coffin the better. How strange to think that only the previous afternoon none of this had happened: the world then had been so fine.

He left the room and locked the door behind him, pocketing the key. Those women would never set foot in this place again. The house was his own and he wanted peace. He wouldn't go back to the fussy Goldbeaters, kind as they had been.

He went downstairs to sort out his father's study. It was just as the police had left it, the desk drawers all pulled out and papers scattered everywhere. It was hard to know where to start. Just cram everything back, he thought, but maybe if he looked at some of the addresses he might find a way to contact his father. He sat in his father's desk chair and started pulling papers towards him.

He sat there until the evening shadows made it too dark to see. At one point he got up to give entry to the undertakers who went upstairs with the coffin; he had to show them the way and unlock the door, but they departed later without disturbing him. As he shuffled through the mountain of letters his father's presence started to fill the room, the secretive, watchful, humourless person whom Antony felt he knew morphed into a dictatorial highflyer, conversing with governments and diplomats of obscure far eastern and South American countries with extraordinary names about orders with only hieroglyphics for titles, mostly meaningless stuff or coded to make it indecipherable. What was it all about? No wonder the police could make neither head nor tail of it. If it was serious, he imagined that higher officials would come with a search warrant to take it away.

But was his father in trouble? Strangely Antony realized that, at the back of his mind, this possibility – of his father being involved in something slightly sinister – had always lurked. Why no bonhomie with friends or drinks parties, no business dinners, why the aura of secrecy that surrounded his coming and going, the phone calls in the night? Why did he never talk about his business or laugh, or confide in his son that one day he might join him, as most fathers did? He had never discussed his son's future with him, and now that Antony had finished with school, his future had arrived, and what did it hold? Antony hadn't the faintest idea.

He sat back in his father's chair and wondered if, indeed, his father had scarpered. Was he really now alone in this hideous mansion with no mentor, no money, no future? It was hard to take in. But, to be fair, his father had told him vaguely of a date for his return and it wasn't for a week or more yet; that was how he had decided on the date for his party. So it was a bit stupid to make wild surmises about his father's business.

He tidied the papers as best he could, without finding any useful information to suggest his father's whereabouts, and stuffed them back in the drawers. And then, pulling open the bottom drawer he was astonished to find a revolver lying there. He thought he was imagining things, the way his mind had been led on through the mystifying papers, but the revolver was quite real. He picked it up and looked to see if it was loaded. It was.

With it in his hand Antony walked to the window, stunned. Had the police seen this? Why would his father have a revolver? He stood staring out. The shadows lay long across the lawns and nothing moved. Only a blackbird sang from the willows, otherwise all was silence, peace. He moved the revolver from

143

hand to hand. It was a very perfect instrument, quite small and light. How strange, he thought, that he could, in a moment, end his life as perfectly as Helena had ended hers, so that his father would come back to no one. Within twenty-four hours they could both be gone. Who was there to mourn them?

What was he going to do? The talk on the lawn all afternoon had been about the future: even dreary John was talking eagerly about his place in some terrible retreat somewhere where he could contemplate his future. Perhaps he should join John and see the light? Simon had got a place at Balliol and couldn't wait to go. Antony, if he thought hard about it, imagined he would gravitate towards Brooklands and the flying, but he knew that with all the pilots and aircrew still unemployed from the war there would be no job for him there. No job for him anywhere really, without his father's help and with his school's hostility damning his leaving report. Even with all his faculties he was as useless as Helena when it came to a place in the world. Two coffins leaving Lockwood Hall would make a neat closure.

Across the lake at the far end near the village two pale specks on the bank caught his eye. It was Lily, wandering down by the water with Squashy. Seeing her, Antony felt an instinctive recoil from his morbid thoughts, shocked at the way his mind had been wandering. Dear Lily, when she had dared to give her life for him jumping out of the plane, how could he even think of doing away with himself when she loved him so much? How he took for granted her overpowering adoration! He knew he wasn't worth it, knew that she knew that; it was a joke between them, yet it was so much the part of her life that lifted her from the poor, dreary, overburdened role she had been born to that to tear it away would be cruelty indeed.

He would put the gun back where he found it.

He had a funeral to organize, unless John had done all the work.

Late that night the telephone rang in his father's study. He unhooked the receiver, trembling to hear his father's voice. But he did not recognize the caller. The voice was well-educated, peremptory.

'Claude, just a warning. Lie low for a bit. Things are looking grim.'

Before Antony could reply the caller rang off.

15

The whole village turned out for Helena's funeral, filling the church and the churchyard. Antony was the chief – and only official – mourner, and he sat at the front with Mr and Mrs Goldbeater and his friends. Before the service started he asked Cedric to go to the back where all the estate workers sat and bring Lily and her family up to the front.

Gabriel refused to move, but Lily came with Squashy, who was asking of Cedric in a loud voice, 'Is she going to be buried like your cow?'

No one remarked on the little dog that trotted into the pew at Squashy's heels.

The cortege came from the house on a farm cart pulled by Hector and Olly. The coffin was covered with flowers. Gabriel had cut the finest from his gardens for Helena, and many of the villagers had plundered their own gardens and children had made posies of wild flowers. Along with Hector and Olly decked out in their finest show harness with their manes and tails braided and decorated, the cortege was more impressive than many a rich person's departure in a large town.

There was also a tangible atmosphere of love and respect for the poor corpse, with, of course, the undertow of gossip of how the death had come about. Some newspapermen had wangled their way into the churchyard and were busy quizzing the spectators, enquiring the whereabouts of the well-known Mr Claude Sylvester, the question on everybody's lips. Miss Maud Sylvester was also wandering about in the south of France in a state of ignorance, although it was possible she might read of it in an English newspaper. Long might they both stay away was Antony's fervent prayer.

He had been asked to say some words from the pulpit, but he knew he could never lay himself bare in that fashion in public. The job was obviously John's, so the congregation was forced to listen to his heavy eulogy, which suggested that Helena's death was a blessing, a very obvious path to take, while Simon's mother shook her head and whispered: 'With all that money, why ever did that dreadful man not get her some professional help, an education for God's sake? They can help so much today.' Antony thought Simon could have made a better fist of the speech, or even Lily, and half wished he had been brave enough to do it himself after all. But bravery had never been one of his attributes.

The farmworkers, including Mr Butterworth himself, carried the coffin out into the churchyard where a grave had been prepared next to Helena's mother.

Lily held Squashy's hand tightly and when he started to cry and shout, 'I don't want to be buried in the ground!' she led him away and sat him down in a quiet corner. Barky scrambled up and licked his face.

'Don't be silly, Squashy. You're not going to die until you're an old man and it won't matter then.'

'I want to lie dead in a field or somewhere, not in the ground.'

'You can't do that. Bodies get all smelly left about.'

'I don't mind being smelly.'

'Other people don't like it. They don't want to walk past smelly bodies when they go shopping and that. Besides, the birds come and peck you, and the foxes will eat you, and the maggots grow inside you.'

It seemed that Squashy didn't mind the birds and the foxes but drew the line at the maggots and he quietened down. 'I'm not going to die,' he decided.

'No, of course not. Nor me. Nor Daddy, so there's nothing to worry about.'

When they went back to the grave the service was over. All the flowers from the wagon were being carried to cover the raw earth, and Lily found Antony being shepherded away by Mrs Goldbeater, her arm round his shoulders. She along with her friends had made a funeral feast of sorts in the field next to the graveyard and everyone was on their way there, but Lily went over to Antony's side.

'I want to go home,' Antony said.

Cedric said, 'I've got to take the horses home. I can take you back on the wagon if you like.'

'Probably that's best for now,' Mrs Goldbeater said. 'I think those newspapermen are after you, Antony. It'll be best to keep out of the way. I'll fob them off.'

'Take me too,' Lily said.

'Ride on the wagon! Ride on the wagon!' shouted Squashy.

He lifted Barky in before there could be any argument, and jumped up himself, and Lily and Antony followed. Cedric unhitched the pair of horses from the fence, sorted out the reins and climbed up.

'Thank God that's over,' Antony said.

Lily felt, for the first time, amazingly light-hearted. It was true that the funeral made one feel as if a pair of gates had been shut on the bad memories. 'It was wonderful, Antony, before that happened. A fantastic party. Just remember that part of it. It wasn't your fault. Helena—'

'Lots of people were saying it was a blessing,' Cedric said cheerfully.

'I don't see it like that. That we couldn't save her.'

'No. But it happened, so forget it.'

'Yes. Remember the good bits. And I think she died happy. She looked happy, so remember that.'

'There's some fantastic beer in the house that Ma made for the funeral do,' Cedric added. 'Come in and have a drink. That'll cheer you up.'

They saw to the horses, which took ages, undoing all their decorations. But when the horses had been turned out to graze they went back into the house and Cedric fetched the beer. Lily looked around the farmhouse kitchen and thought how lovely it was, quite unlike Mrs Goldbeater's and the vicar's and those of the posh people in the village, but so comfortable and homely, just the sort she would choose if she ever had the chance. At home they only had one room downstairs, and a scullery, so they ate in the sitting room: it was all the same. Squashy had to rescue Barky from the over-attention of the motley farm dogs that wandered in through the open door and put him on the table, but Cedric did not protest, although Lily said it was wrong.

'What does it matter?'

In the whole scheme of things very little, Lily agreed. The beer was wonderful, likewise a pork pie that Cedric brought in from the larder, and they sat growing more cheerful by the minute until even Antony laughed.

'You can stay here if you like,' Cedric said. 'Mum would be pleased to have you.'

'No. I must go home. I've got things to sort out.'

'Are the staff back now?'

'Yes. I've got to pay them – their money's overdue – see to that for a start.' And sort out the valuables in Helena's room that were lying all over the floor. He doubted Rose and Violet would be returning for their pay.

And wait for his father.

But when he went to the bank to get enough to pay the staff, the bank told him that his father's account, and his own, had been frozen. No money was available.

The bank manager was very apologetic. 'I'm afraid it's out of my hands. I can't help you.'

'Who closed it? By what authority?'

'I'm afraid I cannot disclose the details. Not to you, sir. If your father were to come in we might be able to discuss it.'

'I've got to pay the staff.'

'Perhaps when your father gets home – we might arrange something. I'm so sorry.'

Antony told the staff to stay on holiday until his father came back. He did not tell them the reason why. In fact, he was relieved to have the house to himself, but deeply worried about what was happening. He supposed it was to do with the police visit when they had gone through all his father's effects. What had they found? he wondered. And that very strange phone call . . . was his father in some sort of trouble? The indications certainly suggested it.

And the revolver.

Maybe when his father came home Helena's demise might be a minor mishap compared with what else he had to face. After all, he had scarcely set eyes on the girl in all her life, so her departure would scarcely make any difference to him. If his father had feelings Antony had never seen them revealed.

Now everything was over Antony felt a certain peace descend. He was beginning to believe that his own behaviour would be less pressing upon his father than the fact that his bank account had been frozen. All the same he was alert for the sound of a taxi pulling up in the front drive: the likely date his father had given for his return had arrived. He stayed in the house, waiting.

He waited for two days, without going out.

On the third day he began to think that his father was not

going to come back. He had tidied up Helena's effects and knew that if he sold the jewellery and paintings he would have enough to live on for a good long while, so the closing of the bank accounts was no worry. He had a house to live in – and he quite liked it now he had the whole place to himself, so silent, undemanding. The amazing summer weather bathed it in unusual warmth, the sunshine winkling its way in for all the architect's apparent desire to keep it out. Antony manoeuvred comfortable chairs into the pockets of sunshine and basked contentedly, all the while listening for the sound of his father's return. He was not afraid of his father any more. He sensed that his father was in more trouble than he was himself.

Quite early one morning, early in August, he heard at last the sound of motor tyres on the gravel drive. Antony looked out of the front windows and saw a taxi delivering his father, so went across the hall to open the front door. The taxi man was dumping his father's suitcases on the doorstep and Sylvester was taking out his wallet to pay him. He looked up as the door opened.

'Hullo, my boy.'

He was very brown and looked to Antony as if he had shrunk, the fat of good living completely stripped away. He looked more active, sharper; his eyes were furtive, glancing everywhere.

'Are you alone?' he asked.

'Yes, Father.'

'Good.'

The taxi man retired. As he went back to his vehicle another car appeared at the end of the drive, approaching the house.

Claude Sylvester looked up quickly and swore. 'I *thought* I was being followed! Shut the door, quickly.'

Antony slammed it.

'Bolt it, bolt it. Don't let him in.' And he scurried away across the wide hall like a hunted animal and straight into his office. 'Bolt *all* the doors,' he flung back over his shoulder at Antony.

Antony did as he was told, feeling completely bewildered. Then he followed his father into the office.

'What the hell's been going on here?' His father had pulled open the top drawers and seen how everything was all awry. He pulled out the top papers and flung them down in disgust. 'Who's done this?'

'The police came. They emptied everything out. I couldn't stop them.'

'Did they take anything away?'

'No. I told them they had no right.'

'Too bloody right! But they'll be back. Here already, if I'm not mistaken. Go and have a look and see what's arrived. Don't let them see you. I've got to sort a few things—' And he was sifting rapidly through the drawers, pulling out some papers, pushing others aside.

There was a heavy banging on the front door as well as the

loud pealing of the bell. Antony slipped out to take a peek through a small window in one of the towers the house boasted on either side of its entrance, but saw only one man making the racket. His car was parked on the gravel and its chauffeur was already pulling out a newspaper, as if to settle down for a long stay. The man on the doorstep was tall and commanding-looking; if a policeman, he was not in uniform, but dressed in a formal suit and a trilby hat. Antony went back to report to his father, who was busy stuffing some of his papers into a Gladstone bag that was usually lodged under his desk.

'Just one man,' Antony said. 'And a chauffeur in the car, reading a newspaper.'

'Only one, eh? That's very relaxed.'

'What's he after?'

'Me, of course, for all the crimes I've committed. Which are serious, you might as well know, Antony, I'm afraid. Life is about to change for you.'

'What crimes?' Antony felt as if the floor had shifted suddenly from under his feet. His father was smiling. Antony felt he was seeing another man entirely, not his father at all, but an intruder, sharp as a fox, quick and active, moving about his papers, smiling.

'You're a man now, Antony, and well able to live your own life. I shall have to go away, a long way away and never come back. But I think you will cope, so no grieving. We've never been close, you won't miss me.'

'But—'

'Just look after Helena, like a good chap.'

'But Helena's—'

The knocking at the front door interrupted Antony, and his father turned and said, 'Go and let him in now, for God's sake. The man's no patience.'

Antony thought his father had gone mad. He left the office and went back across the hall to the front door, his mind reeling. He could cope with minor crimes, but *major* crime had never crossed his path. Surely his father was joking? He slid back the bolts on the door and opened it to the impatient gentleman waiting on the step.

'I have reason to believe Mr Claude Sylvester is at home?'

'Yes.'

Antony was going to say 'Come in' but the man was already in. 'Take me to him.' They crossed the hall. 'And you are?' he barked at Antony.

'Antony Sylvester, his son.'

'Ah.'

When Antony opened the door to the study he saw his father sitting at his desk looking very relaxed. He looked up as if in surprise.

'Ah, Mr Higgins, I think?'

'Chief Inspector Higgins of the CID, based in Westminster. I think we have met.'

'Fleetingly, yes. Do take a seat. Antony, you can leave us.'

Antony went out. He felt faint, and went outside and sat on the lawn looking at the lake. To think he had been nervous of facing his father with the news of Helena's demise! And here was his father with not a thought in his head about his daughter, or his son either, come to that, but embroiled in what he declared without shame as major crime. Where does that leave me? Antony wondered. His father was going away and never coming back. Did he mean to prison? It didn't quite sound like it. But the policeman was already there, presumably to arrest him. None of it made any sense at all.

He felt a bit sick. The place was deserted, as it had been since all the staff had been sent home. Even old Gabriel hadn't been around, and the flowerbeds were spilling out with blooms, tangled and fallen across the paths. Lily hadn't been tidying as usual; Gabriel must have kept her away. What were they going to do for money if they had no job any more? What was he going to do, come to that? Go away? Go where?

He groaned and lay back, looking at the sky, which was still blue and cloudless as it had been for weeks. The party felt like a decade away now, lost in the mists of time. It had been a great party until Helena . . . but her accident no longer seemed of any importance. It might well be true that her death had been a blessing, as he had heard whispered at the funeral, the words sadly, kindly, on everyone's lips. If she had lived with only himself to look after her, then certainly it had been a blessing. He doubted he could even look after himself. That really hadn't come into it at Eton; the pampered lot he had grown up with were mostly as heedless as himself. He was now on a sinking ship, unless his father was playing some amazing joke.

After a while he decided to go back into the house and make himself a cup of tea. He could put his nose in and offer one to the policeman, see how things were going, get an idea of how the land lay. He mooched about while the kettle boiled: the great kitchen range had gone out since the staff left and he had to use the new gas contraption that his father had been forced to buy after harangues from the cook. While it was boiling he went out into the hall to check on the policeman's chauffeur and saw that he was now snoozing with the newspaper over his face. He went back and turned off the boiling kettle and at the same moment he heard a sharp crack from the direction of the office. He thought for a moment it was something to do with the gas cooker, but nothing was amiss there. He went out into the corridor towards the office with a terrible fear rising suddenly into his beleaguered brain. Surely it must be his imagination? But he knew the neat little revolver was still lying in the bottom drawer of the desk.

He went out into the corridor and saw the office door open. His father stood there with the revolver in his hand. It wasn't his imagination.

His father was quite cool. 'I've got to leave, Antony.'

Antony shoved past him through the doorway and saw the body of Detective Inspector Higgins lying on the floor with an expression of amazement on his obviously dead face. There was no sign of blood.

'He had come to arrest me. He thought I would go quietly, like a good civil servant. Wrong, the idiot. Come on, Antony. Is your little aeroplane fuelled up?'

'*What?*' Antony couldn't believe what was happening.

'I've got to leave here in a great hurry, can't you see? Before the chauffeur comes enquiring, before anyone finds out. I can't go out the front way obviously. Is the plane ready to go?'

'Yes, Tom refuelled it after the . . . party, and I haven't taken it up since . . .'

'Thank God for that. I'll just get a bag. You get your helmet and goggles or whatever and we'll be off. Good lad.'

It was as if some great lark were taking place. Antony waited speechlessly as his father gathered together some stuff off the desk and shoved it into his small leather bag, pulled what appeared to be wads of money from a drawer he had to unlock, stuffed it on top of the papers and laid the revolver on top. He buckled the bag up.

'Get your gear.'

'It's in the plane. The keys are in my pocket.'

'Antony, move! Wake up! Do as you're told – fast!'

Antony ran. He thought he was going to be sick. The body of the police detective was nowhere near as peaceful as Helena's had looked, the dead face seeming full of hate and pain, a rictus leer stretching the smooth, rather handsome features, blood now beginning to pool beneath his body, and Antony wanted to be rid of the sight. Soon he was across the lawn and pushing the fastest of the skiffs out into the water.

His father was nimble as a rabbit. 'You row, smoothly now. Not as if we're in a panic, in case someone's watching. Taking your old father for a trip out to the grotto, that's what we want them to think.'

'The chauffeur was asleep,' Antony said, hoping to calm him down. His father was a man he had never seen before, on the verge of laughter, alight with excitement. Antony thought he was enjoying it, his life of crime erupting on his boring home stage. What on earth had he been up to in South America? Had he killed before? 'Dad – you're going to . . . hang.'

'Only if I'm caught. I've done this sort of thing before, believe me, but it's taken them a long time to catch up with me. Now the cat's out of the bag though, it's time to leave.'

'Where are we going?'

'Le Bourget. Paris. I can get on farther from there, no trouble.'

'Across the Channel! I've never flown across the Channel!'

'A good time to start then. The weather's perfect, piece of cake.'

Piece of cake. The words went round and round in Antony's head. Nothing made sense to him any more.

16

If his father had chosen a time to kill someone and fly to France he couldn't have chosen a better day for it. It was still quite early in the morning and the sky was cloudless as usual: a perfect day to cross the Channel. Antony was now more concerned with the thought of flying across the Channel than with his father's amazing transformation into a crook. It was as frightening as anything that had already happened that morning.

He knew the way to Dover. One just followed the road. He had hovered many times over the port thinking about making the crossing, but had never actually found the courage to do it. He despised himself for his lack of pluck, and had always convinced himself that if he had had a willing passenger he would have committed himself. Cedric had been keen enough to go and study French cows, but Simon and John had never even taken a flight with him, and Antony had never thought Cedric was quite the right companion for a trip to France (although, strangely, he seemed to have changed a lot recently: he had been extremely useful at the party).

From the plane France beckoned, apparently quite close.

His father appeared to be enjoying the flight, although the engine noise made conversation virtually impossible – thank goodness, Antony thought, not in any way wanting to be a confidant of this killer in the passenger seat. He made as much height as he could, heading south, wanting to be as far away from the water as possible. Thank God there was no wind and no problem in seeing where to go . . . the sands of Calais lay white in the sunshine, and tiny fishing boats dotted the blue silk sea.

It was beautiful! Why ever had it taken a mad father to coerce him into this trip when he could have done it long before? For a few minutes Antony was euphoric. Then, as Calais loomed up amazingly fast, he realized he had no idea where to go next. Where was Paris? He had no idea. His little plane continued like a cheeky robin looking for 'abroad' and it was for him to give it directions: thank God Tom had looked after it so assiduously, for its engine never gave him a moment's doubt. Lots of pilots got killed by their craft giving up on them. Looking for an emergency landing place was always instinctive.

Now his father was poking his shoulder and passing him a note:

Follow the coast down to the Somme and then the river inland to Amiens. Then the railway line to Paris. Easy as pie.

161

Lovely beaches to land on all the way. France seemed altogether much larger than England and Antony was now actively enjoying this amazing experience, peering over the cockpit edge at the alluring little villages below. Everything was far more spread out in France, and less intensively farmed, all much more relaxed somehow. Even the river Somme, with the terrible connotations in the very name from the war that had ended only four years ago, picked a lazy route through wide expanses of sand, sparkling all the way, to find the sea, and beside it was a railway line as well as a big road, all marking the route to Paris. Further on, the ravages of war were still only too apparent but, overlaid by struggling new growth and basking in sunshine, the wounds were receding. The river led him all the way. How simple! Why ever hadn't he come before when it was so easy? (Without a killer in the passenger seat.)

Strangely he felt little compassion for his father, or even interest in what was to become of him. He had been a distant figure in his life, never displaying the slightest interest in his son; there seemed little reason now for the son to feel anything but a passing anxiety in his plight. Getting rid of him would be a relief, but there might be a welcome party at Le Bourget if word had got out. Telephones might have been ringing. But with luck the chauffeur at the front of the house was still asleep and had never seen their exit, or heard the plane take off. There was no one in the house to come across the dead body; it was probably still lying there, growing cold, undiscovered. It was hard to work out how long ago the shot had rung out. It seemed to Antony about five minutes ago, but it must be getting on for at least two hours now, even three.

A large town that must be Amiens – or what remained of it – loomed up beneath them. Road and river led them on. Antony knew that Le Bourget airport, was several miles north of Paris, so hoped his father would recognize it before they reached the capital. He began to feel nervous about making a landing in a strange airport, but trusted his father to do the talking. Did his father speak French? Antony had no idea. His was sketchy, not for lack of teaching but for lack of his own application.

His father prodded him again and pointed out to the left, and Antony saw the airport with its generous landing strip heaving into sight, with its windsock showing him that he could fly straight in. He searched the sky in all directions to make sure that no one else was coming in, and there was no action whatsoever on the ground to suggest anyone taking off, only a few craft sitting like flies outside the hangars, so to his relief his landing was very simple to complete. He touched down without a bump, the airstrip a great improvement on his rough home landing, and taxied on for what looked like the reception area. A few workers were standing around chatting and smoking and no one made a great show of greeting the incomer.

His father was already opening his door to jump out, his leather bag in his hand. 'Here, Antony, old chap, I'm sorry the way things have turned out. Take this – it'll keep you solvent for a few weeks. Go and see your Aunt Maud – she'll see you through.'

163

The packet he offered up was, presumably, money. Antony took it.

'Try not to say any more than you have to. Stave them off a bit. Don't land at home – not today at least. I'll be gone from here in no time and we shall probably not meet again, so goodbye, old chap, and thanks for your help. You're a winner.'

And he smiled widely, happily, in a way Antony had never seen before, jumped down and hurried away into the open doors of the reception.

Antony sat stunned.

Was this man truly his father or someone else pretending? Murder and mayhem seemed to have given him a new lease of life. This departing, happy man was not the father Antony in any way recognized. One presumed he had friends to go to, in another country, money to burn, and complete confidence in not getting caught. All very hard to take in.

Another small plane landed and came up past him and the men who had ignored him went to greet it. Antony decided to take off before anyone came to see who he was, the sooner the better. To be detained in France would be a disaster. The sky was clear. He taxied back down the runway, almost expecting people to be running after him, but it was clear that his visit was of no concern to the French, and so he took off and flew away, miraculously undisturbed.

Once in the sky again he felt quite faint with shock. He concentrated on picking up the road and railway to Amiens to find the way home and then, on track, felt the enormity of this sudden change in his life overcoming him. He had no idea how his father's crime might affect him; he had no idea of what he was going home to.

Not to go home, as his father had instructed: lie low if he could . . . his mind whirled. Brooklands was too close to home. He would go to the little airstrip in Wiltshire where Lily had done her parachute jump. A pal from school lived nearby and might give him a berth for the night. But no, he didn't want to have to talk to anyone . . . he would land and walk away. His plane would be safe there until he could retrieve it. He would lie low . . . he could sleep out in the fields and perhaps come to terms with what had happened whilst communing with nature . . . the thought made him laugh.

And then a seed of delight broke into his mind: he was a totally free man, his future was whatever he wanted! Answerable to no one.

He just hoped there was plenty of money in the packet his father had shoved into his hand.

17

Lily's father wasn't happy.

'Did your friend Antony tell you that he couldn't pay the staff until his father comes back?'

'He said he went to the bank and they wouldn't let him have any money.'

'So when is his father coming back?'

'Antony said he was supposed to be back two days ago. He's waiting for him now.'

'So we all live on air until then? We none of us have been paid for over a month now.'

'I've earned a bit, at the vicarage. And Mrs Carruthers wants me on Thursday, to help in the kitchen. And the pub might find something for Squashy. We'll get through till he gets back, Pa.'

Gabriel had knocked off his heavy schedule since none of the other servants had come back to work and was now fretting, unused to leisure. He had enjoyed the freedom at first, putting his own garden in order, but now his conscience was pricking him, letting the beautiful herbaceous borders up at the manor run to seed and the lawns go uncut. He found it hard to witness the neglect, but none of the lads, the so called under-gardeners, would come back to work without pay, even if he went up there to do some tidying. All the house staff who lived in the village were complaining loudly. Claude Sylvester's strange dereliction of duty was the only talking point.

Lily had heard Antony's aeroplane take off earlier in the day. Her father, being a bit deaf, hadn't heard it, but Lily had run out and seen that there was a passenger in the plane. She thought it very strange, as Antony would have told her if he had been planning anything. She had wandered up to the big house only the day before and had a chat with him, and he had seemed perfectly relaxed and not up to any tricks, saying he expected his father home any minute. He was worried about telling him of Helena's death, but had said nothing about flying anywhere.

Squashy, catching on to his father's complaints about how they would all be starving if Sylvester didn't come back soon, went out to go fishing and stock the larder. He never caught anything save tiddlers, but lived in hope. Lily was doing the washing in the scullery when Squashy came back, very excited.

'There's soldiers up at the big house. All over the place. I saw them!'

'Soldiers! Don't be daft.'

'Lots of people.'

Lily stopped squeezing sheets and went outside. Across the lake it was true that there were several people wandering across the lawns, but they weren't soldiers. 'They're policemen!' They seemed to be beating about the flowerbeds, looking for something. Lily was shocked. 'Whatever's happened?'

She called her father out of the cabbages in the back garden and he came grumbling.

'Look, Pa. Policemen! What's up, do you think?'

He had no answer, save his brain connected the police intrusion with Sylvester not having paid him for over a month.

'The old man's in trouble perhaps? He's acting queer, not paying us. Unless it's young Antony.'

'No, he's not in trouble.'

He wasn't there, she knew. He had flown away in his aeroplane, with someone in the passenger seat. Lily felt strongly that she wouldn't tell anyone of seeing that flight. Not a word. Probably a few other people had seen the plane depart, but it hadn't flown over the village, so it wouldn't be common knowledge. Maybe some workers up at Butterworth's might have seen it, even Cedric, but it was possible that no one knew of it but herself.

Antony had scarpered, and who had been in the back seat? His father? Had he just been giving his father a lift to somewhere, or were they fleeing together for some unknown reason? She felt very frightened. The police never came to their little village, and certainly not in numbers, only a pair at the most.

She said she would go up to the village and get a loaf of bread. Her father wouldn't approve of her going to gawp, as he would put it, but curiosity drove her. The police being there was surely connected with Antony's flight. But I don't know anything about that, she convinced herself. Not a word.

168

Everyone was out gossiping, stunned by their village being a hotbed of crime. They were saying that there had been something on the radio about Claude Sylvester being wanted for questioning concerning his latest trip to South America, but as only two people in the village had this new-fangled radio and they were not given to street gossip no one knew any details. Everyone was saying that of course they knew something fishy was up when all the staff had been sent away without pay.

'But that was young Antony's doing, not his father's,' someone else remarked. 'So's he could have that terrible party.'

'So where's young Antony then?'

'The police'll have him. He's up at the house.'

'Yeah, waiting for 'is father.'

'Someone said there's been a murder.'

'That can't be true!'

'Perhaps young Antony's been murdered!'

Lily kept her head down, listening. She realized that no one knew about Antony's departure in the aeroplane; they all thought he was up at the house, either dead or alive. If she hadn't seen the plane, she would be in a real panic listening to the wild conjectures being offered up. As everyone knew she was a familiar in the big house she was asked if she knew anything about it or whether she had seen Antony lately, but she just kept saying no, lying through her teeth.

When she wandered up to the gates of Lockwood Hall she found a chain across the entrance and two policemen standing guard. There was a group of people there, amongst them Simon.

'Do you know what's happened?' she asked him.

169

Simon's face was pale. 'They say there's been a murder. But they won't say any more.'

'Oh, Simon!'

He was thinking it was Antony, she could tell. But her secret was so crucial she could not reveal it even to Simon. He was bound to tell his parents, and then everyone would know. She just whispered to him, 'It's not Antony. I know. I've seen him. But I'm not saying a word.'

'Oh, thank God!'

'Don't tell anyone I've seen him, whatever you do.'

'No. Let's keep out of it. God knows what's happening.'

But as they spoke a police car came down the drive and the guard policemen went to meet it, removing the chain. They spoke for some time and Lily heard shreds of the conversation: 'Everyone must be questioned. The whole village . . . the suspect is Sylvester. We've got to find him . . .'

'I'm going back,' Lily whispered to Simon. 'I don't want to be questioned.'

'What do you know, for God's sake?'

'Nothing!'

'Me neither, if poor old Ant is involved.'

By the time Lily had gone back through the village and bought her loaf the word was out that it was a policeman who had been murdered and the suspect was Claude Sylvester, of whom there was no trace. Not a word about an aeroplane. Everyone was to be questioned as to what they might have seen early in the morning. Lily went home and reported all this to her father.

'Well, dang me! And him a gent and all, a proper gent. And what about young Antony then? Is he involved? He was up there, wasn't he?'

'I don't know, Pa.'

The news had traumatized the village. In the morning the newspapers all led with the story: the well-known financier Claude Sylvester being wanted by the police in connection with the shooting at his home in Surrey, Lockwood Hall. He was known to have arrived home early on the morning of the fifteenth of August and been interviewed there by Detective Inspector Higgins of the Metropolitan police. Later in the morning the body of the detective was found in Sylvester's study, shot through the head, and since then the whereabouts of Mr Sylvester was unknown. He had lately been travelling in South America.

Later in the day when the evening papers came through Claude Sylvester was headline news. And what headlines!

CLAUDE SYLVESTER
TRAITOR AND MURDERER!

Sources today reveal that Claude Sylvester, lately suspected of the murder of D.I. Alexander Higgins at Lockwood Hall in Surrey, is also suspected of selling copies of secret files, concerning the government's involvement in arms deals, to South American companies.

The small print continued with details in a vein that Lily found difficult to understand, the words being too long and incomprehensible for her limited education. She did her best to read it to her father who was still finding it hard to believe that this story concerned his erstwhile boss with whom he had had many pleasant conversations about the herbaceous borders.

Lily noticed that although the newspaper knew that Sylvester had vanished they seemed so far not to have any news of how, nothing about an aeroplane nor a word about Antony. No policemen so far had come to question her, although they were obviously combing the village and nearly everyone had been grilled. When she next saw Simon he said they had been a long time with his parents who had told them all they knew, but not much bothered with him. He said that they did not seem to know that Antony had been living up in the house.

'Surely he was there when his father came home? He was expecting him, wasn't he?'

'Yes, he was there.'

'He must have seen the murder, or heard it, surely?'

It was evening and going dusk and Lily was talking to Simon out in the garden of his house. It seemed she was the only person in the world who knew how Mr Sylvester had managed to disappear. The knowledge of it was weighing on her; if Simon had already been interviewed she thought he might as well share her secret.

'I saw Antony fly away in his plane, with a passenger, who must have been his father.'

'Crikey!' Simon was stunned.

'I haven't told a soul I saw it. And if they ask I shan't say. It flew the other way, not over the village, so no one else did see it. But I did.'

'Blimey, you're a hot witness! And nobody's been near you?'

'No.'

'Where did they go? I wonder. It must have been abroad, surely? Over the Channel. God, poor old Ant! His father must have had his pistol in Ant's back, giving orders! So where are they now?'

'Ant will come back, don't you think? He wouldn't want to go off with his father.'

'No, but there's nowhere for him to come back to. The house is all sealed off,' Simon said grimly.

'What do you mean?'

'All boarded up. Keep out and all that.'

'But he lives there, all his stuff is in it.'

'Well, let's go and have a look. Maybe there's some way of getting inside.'

It was easy enough to enter the property without going up the front drive where the gates were locked and a policeman still stood on guard. They walked through a thicket off the lane and came to the little stream that wound down to the lake, a way they were perfectly familiar with. Following the stream brought them out onto the lake proper and the lawns below the great sprawl of the house. It was true what Simon said: all the windows and doors had great boards nailed over them, making the place uglier than ever, more like an abandoned prison than a home.

Lily remarked on the poor trampled flowerbeds. 'Pa's out of work now. I don't know what on earth we'll do.'

'He'll get work in the village, won't he? He's got a very good reputation.'

'Our cottage belongs to Mr Sylvester. Perhaps we'll be boarded up shortly. Crikey, Simon, I hadn't thought of all this!'

It was true, she hadn't. So wrapped up in Antony's plight she hadn't thought of her own. She realized now that her father had got the message some time ago.

The sun was going down and the house was casting its heavy shadow across the lake. It was just like the evening before the party, with the same swans drifting on the lake, the water turning gold, the willows still hung with the lights that would never twinkle again. The lawn where they sat was growing shaggy and the lovely smell of mown grass no longer hung in the soft damp of the evening.

Lily suddenly felt close to tears. 'What is going to happen?'

'What, to you? Or Ant? It'll be all right, Lily, you've lots of friends, and the police have nothing on Ant. None of it was his fault.'

Simon put his arm round her as she sniffed miserably and she knew that he was a good friend too, not as good as Antony, but the companionship went back so far. It was as little children they had first romped down by the lake, making mud pies and swimming like fish, chasing each other, making dens in the woods and cooking sausages on sticks, mocking Squashy, fighting, climbing trees, quarrelling, laughing . . . it had been a way of life, the gang together, she the only girl. And now they seemed to have been catapulted onto a world stage. The dull, benign figure of Antony's father, who had given them the freedom of his domain, was now in line to be hanged. It didn't seem possible.

'Antony will come back here, I'm sure. He's nowhere else to go,' Simon said. 'Only to his Aunt Maud and he hates her like poison.'

'Gosh, she might come, mightn't she? How awful. I hadn't thought of that.'

Lily went home comforted by Simon, but not sure of anything any more. The next day the papers proclaimed that the police had now traced Claude Sylvester to Le Bourget airport, from where the trail went cold. If he was trying to return to South America, which seemed likely, all possible shipping ports were on the lookout for him, but it was assumed that he had contacts in Paris or elsewhere in Europe where he could lie hidden for the time being. He was known to have travelled widely in his job.

'Knew lots of sticky politicians,' they said in the village.

No mention of his son. Where on earth could Antony be? Lily worried. But at least, although her father had lost his job, there didn't seem to be any move on the part of the authorities to take over the workers' cottages. Along with Gabriel's there were five others in the row and no one had heard anything amiss. They now assumed they were safe. They didn't have anyone to pay rent to, but Gabriel put it on one side every week in case. He was going up to see Butterworth to ask if

175

there was any work suitable for him on the farm, but without much hope. Mrs Carruthers in the village told him she could do with another man if he was hard-pressed, but working for Mrs Carruthers was notoriously awful. Even Lily could tell him that. Do this. Do that. Gabriel was used to working on his own, trusted. Old habits were hard to break. Also, she wouldn't have Squashy anywhere near.

'Old bitch,' was Gabriel's verdict. 'I'd rather starve.'

Missing Antony, Lily began to think, was the least of her problems.

18

Three days later, when Simon came home after a day out fishing, he found Antony sitting in the kitchen devouring what remained of the supper the family had already eaten. Mrs Goldbeater was hovering over him like a mother hen, beaming her welcome.

Simon stopped in surprise. 'Holy cow! The wandering boy! Where's the aeroplane? We never saw it.'

'I've left it in Wiltshire. I brought it back. Stayed clear for a bit and now find I've no home any more. It's all boarded up.'

'We've just been telling him, Simon, he's got to go to the police. He can't stay hidden. After all, there's nothing he can be found guilty of.'

'Aiding and abetting?'

'Well, hardly, when it's your own father you're aiding, especially when he's got a pistol in his hand,' Mrs Goldbeater said firmly. 'But there's no hurry. The boy's worn out, he needs a good night's sleep and then we'll sort it all out.'

She bustled away to make tea and Simon sat down

opposite Antony who was mopping up the last of the stew with a lump of bread.

'God, I feel better for that. I was bloody starving. Keeping clear, when I saw it was all in the newspapers . . . I just wanted to get home. Now I find out I haven't got one.'

'No. It's now government property.'

'So where does that leave me? God, what a mess! The old man shooting that geezer – I couldn't believe it! And making me fly him to France! Crikey, Simon, but that was magnificent – we must do it together some time. But the whole thing – it's like a dream, or a nightmare, I can't work out which.'

He certainly looked as if he wasn't quite of this world, his face drawn, his eyes wary, his clothes covered in bits of the countryside, seeds and thistle burrs – unlike the usual quite dapper appearance he usually displayed. Simon realized that Antony wasn't used to not being cosseted by servants, loaded with money by his father, wanting for nothing.

'You've been living rough?'

'Yes, all the way from Wiltshire. I kept out of sight mostly and slept out. I thought the police were looking for me.'

'They don't seem much bothered. They don't even seem to know how your old man got to Le Bourget. The only person who knows you flew away is Lily. She saw you. And she's not said a word to anyone. Only to me, because she was so upset.'

'She saw me? Crikey, I tried to keep away from everyone, especially the village, and even the farm – I made a big loop away. But of course I had to go right down to her house to turn round and take off. Why was she upset?'

'She loves you, mate. And keeping mum when the police were all over the place asking questions was quite hard. She was frightened of giving you away. She's only told me a few days ago.'

'Oh, poor Lily! I must go and see her. She's a brick.'

'There's some ginger sponge here, Antony. The custard's a bit cold but there's plenty of it.' Mrs Goldbeater came back to the table with reinforcements.

'That's ripping, Mrs G. Thanks. I'm feeling a new man.'

'You can have a bath when you're finished, and I'll make up a bed for you. You must be really tired.'

'I ought to see Lily. Simon's told me she—'

'She's upset, Ma. You know how she is about Ant. She was crying just now, down by the lake – I saw her when I was fishing, but I left her alone. I was trying to cheer her up only a few days ago. They've got no money coming in and now their cottage belongs to the government so what's going to happen? And Ant gone missing. All that.'

'Yes. There are a lot in the village with suddenly no money coming in, it's very distressing. To be leading such a double life – it's very hard to believe, such a quiet gentleman. Did you have any idea, Antony?'

'No. I didn't know my father very well, to tell the truth.'

'Well, no one did, it seems. What a shock, in the village. We've not recovered yet. And there's no word of his being caught yet.'

'I don't think they'll find him. I got the impression he was really enjoying himself. He wasn't a bit frightened, not like me.'

Antony finished the ginger sponge and when Simon's mother had retreated back to the kitchen he said to Simon, 'If you say Lily has been upset, I ought to pop down and show my face, cheer her up. I didn't know she had to tell lies to the police. No wonder she was worried.'

'Yeah, that would be nice. She's not very good at dissembling.'

'No. She's not a natural liar like us. I'll slip out before your ma tells me not to go.'

'Fine. I'll tell her you're coming back.' He saw Antony out to the door and said, 'By the way, good to have you back. She wasn't the only one worried about you.'

'Thanks, mate.'

Antony took the path down to the lake. It was dusk now. Strange to think that this wasn't his any more, but government property, already going to seed. Nobody in the government was going to look after it, that was obvious. Poor old hideous old house . . . And what about me? Antony wondered. Where to go after a couple of days with the Goldbeaters and an interlude with the police? No answer.

He squished through the reeds at the bottom of the lake and came out onto the path that ran in front of the row of workers' cottages. Luckily there was no one about; most of them were in bed when the light went. But a lamp was lit in Gabriel's cottage, thank goodness; he had never intended them to get out of bed.

He knocked at the door.

It opened cautiously and Lily stood there.

'Antony!' She flung herself at him with such ardour that he nearly fell over backwards. She wrapped her arms round him, sobbing, burying her face in his sweaty old shirt.

'Hey, steady on! Put me down, you lunatic—'

'I thought— Oh, Ant, I thought you were dead! Where's your aeroplane? You never came back . . .'

'Well, I'm back now. Put me down, Lily. I'll explain. I just came over because Simon said you'd been upset. I went there, only place I could think of really when I found the house all boarded up. Mrs G fed me and I slipped out just to see you.'

'Come in, come in. Pa and Squashy have gone to bed. If we're quiet they won't hear us.'

She took his hand and dragged him over the threshold. In the lamplight he could see that her face was shining with relief and joy and that tears still ran down her cheeks. A tangle of wool and half-darned socks lay under the lamp where she had been working.

'Oh, Ant, I've been so worried about you! Here, sit down.' She gestured to Gabriel's chair and almost pushed him into it. 'Tell me what happened.'

It was strange to Antony to be ensconced in this threadbare little cottage straight from the elegant modernity of the Goldbeater home. He had never been in it before – how poor it was! It obviously did not get any of the devotion from Lily that some of the village women spent on their similarly impoverished homes: no flowers, rag rugs, embroidered cushions or treasured china dogs. Lily was an outdoor girl, Antony knew that, and her home was spare, clean(ish) and masculine, Lily herself the only pretty thing in it. Gabriel's chair was hard, but Antony felt himself relaxing for the first time in what felt like weeks and realized he had no desire to return to the cosseting of Mrs Goldbeater. Just seeing Lily's joy made him acknowledge that he had made the right move.

He explained to her everything that had happened while she sat listening on the hard bench that serviced the table. When he had finished he felt so tired that he knew he hadn't the strength to get back to the village. He had scarcely slept at all since leaving the aeroplane: sleeping out had not come naturally to him.

'Can I stay here tonight?'

'Yes, of course! I'll show you a bed.'

The only empty bed in the house was hers, but she did not say this, nor did he question her. He followed her up the ladder to where two small rooms sat side by side. In one slept Gabriel with Squashy beside him, where once his wife had lain, and in the other was Lily's bed pushed hard against the eaves to make room for a dressing table made out of boxes and a chair with a few clothes thrown over it. The bed looked to Antony so appealing that he unlaced his shoes, kicked them off and fell into it.

'Oh bliss, Lily! I am so tired.' And he fell asleep before she could make an answer.

She crept down the ladder, her heart surging with joy. To see him again, know he was safe: her whole life took on a different complexion. She wanted to sing and dance. She went to the door and went out. It was dark now and the lake lay

182

glittering in the light of a small, bright moon lying on its back over the willows. So quiet and beautiful, what she always took for granted. Seeing Antony again banished from her mind all the depressed thoughts she had been having recently about their future; they paled into insignificance now.

She walked along for a bit, calming herself down, ashamed at how she had thrown herself at him – how could she help it? It made her laugh now. He must think she was a real idiot. Well, she was where Antony was concerned. What was in it for her, in the future? Nothing at all. It wasn't as if she hadn't always known.

After a little while, calm now and still happy, she went back indoors and shut up for the night. There was nowhere for her to sleep, no sofa, only the floor, or Gabriel's hard chair. She went silently up the ladder to see if Antony was comfortable and stood for some time looking at him heavily asleep, sprawled on his face, one arm dangling down. His face was brown and scratched, the dark hair dusty and tumbled, his clothes dirty. He looked like a gypsy, not a public schoolboy.

God, how she loved him!

Without another thought she slithered silently down beside him. There was just room and he did not stir. She would be gone in the morning, he would never know. But she would remember sleeping with him all her life.

A few days later she had a dream. It was so vivid she never forgot it; it stayed in her brain as clearly as if it was something that really happened. So clear, in fact, that in later life she sometimes wondered if it was no dream at all, but the truth . . .

She dreamed she was making porridge over the stove for her father's breakfast when a strange spasm of sickness took hold of her, and she ran outside and vomited into the potato patch. She couldn't understand it – she was never ill and she certainly hadn't eaten anything that could upset her. But after she was sick nothing more seemed to ail her and she forgot all about it until the next day when it happened again. Lily was not ignorant when it came to the basic facts of life and she knew what this condition usually presaged, but she knew it could not have happened to her. Nevertheless, as the weeks went by she could not dispute the fact that she was pregnant. She was not showing much in her stomach, but by the fifth month she definitely felt movement and her breasts were telling her that she was pregnant. She told no one. She did not dare. She took to wearing her mother's old loose pinafores that covered her front, and old Gabriel never noticed any change. What he would do when the baby was born she had no idea. The thought of another mouth to feed would destroy him, let alone coming to terms with her sin.

The baby was due to be born in May, and Lily felt her pains come on one evening after a day of hot sunshine. She went out into the woods behind the house, and as the sun went down she found herself a sheltered spot beneath an oak tree. In her dream, the pains of birth were blurred but the baby was sharply realized: a tiny blonde-haired girl, perfect and pretty in every way. Her cheeks were pale rose petals, her little fingers perfect, softly coiled, her hair like golden thistle-down, but no breath fluttered her nostrils. And even as Lily held her close, the warmth of the tiny body faded.

'She's dead, like Cedric's cow,' said Squashy, who was there. 'We must bury her in the garden somewhere. I'll dig the hole.'

'No, she must go in the churchyard. She's a baby, not a dog.'

'I'll fetch a spade.'

They took the baby to the churchyard and looked for a good place, but hidden so that nobody would notice. They passed the beautiful Sylvester grave and the grave of their mother, and behind some old elm trees with low branches they found a patch of long grass where nobody went.

Squashy dug a big hole and they laid the baby in it.

'Her name is Rose,' Lily said. 'She's my baby Rose. She will be happy here. I will plant a rose on her grave.'

'And flowers,' said Squashy. 'She needs flowers.' He filled in the hole, and on the disturbed earth sprinkled a packet of seeds that he took from his pocket.

A few days later she decided to walk over to the churchyard and see the place where they had buried her baby. It was another hot day: summer was just starting and the wild swags of hawthorn blossom were just fading, and throwing down petals like confetti. The smell filled the air. She went to the churchyard and walked down the main path past the beautiful Sylvester grave, past her mother, and out towards the elm trees where the grass was unmown and no footsteps showed. The deep shadows of the elms fell across her, blocking out the sun but, beyond, the long grass shone brightly, and a wild pink rose, all alone in the grass, was just putting out its first buds exactly where they had buried the baby.

She went on and stood looking down at it and saw that in the surrounding grass were the spent and faded flowers of cowslips and violets and white wood anemones. If she had come earlier the patch would have danced with wild flowers, just the patch around the rose, the patch where her baby was buried.

Was Rose real?

Was it just a dream . . . ?

19

In the morning Antony went back to Simon's house and Lily went with him. She knew she shouldn't but she did. The dream still danced in her head, so strong, so real – what was called wishful thinking, she supposed (though not for the fate of the baby), but her love for Antony, although so real, had never had a carnal element in it, not for either of them. She was too young, only just fifteen, it was a childish thing, and he didn't love her in that way; he never had.

In the dream the baby had come as if by magic, and magic was the word that best described her happy hallucinations where Antony was concerned. The dream was disturbing, but it must be put away. It mustn't spoil her fragile world of make-believe. It had been magic enough to lie beside his heavily unconscious body for a few hours, feeling his warmth and listening to the soft, regular music of his breathing. No more.

Gabriel was too depressed to give her orders. He spent his time now in his own garden, extending it into some rough ground beyond his boundaries to grow more food. He had always brought all he needed from the vegetable gardens at the Hall, now fast going to seed. He could not bear to go up there any more, it hurt too much. Lily told him he was stupid – the vegetables were still growing amongst the weeds and other people from the village were stealing them – but he would not go.

'I don't know what we're going to do,' she said to Antony.

'Same here. My father's a— Well, I won't say it . . . but leaving all those people in the lurch, apart from being a murderer. I want to get in the house and see if there's any money around. I know there's valuables.'

'The police turned it over, searching.'

'Yes, but I know places they could well have missed.'

'But it's all boarded up.'

'It only needs a crowbar to a window – Cedric could do it standing on his head. We'll have a go – but don't tell Simon's parents. They're depressingly law-abiding.'

'No.'

Of course the Goldbeaters were put out by Antony's disappearance the night before, but when Lily told them he fell asleep in mid-conversation (a slight exaggeration) they understood how it had come about, forgave him, and supplied him with another large meal. Lily, who only ever had a slice of bread for breakfast, was also offered toast and marmalade.

Simon's parents made it clear that Antony must go to the police and tell them what had happened.

'And then you must go to your Aunt Maud. You're not of

age yet and she will be responsible for you. At least you'll have a roof over your head in London.'

Antony was silent. Lily knew that the last thing he intended to do was go to his Aunt Maud.

'Simon's father has to go into Guildford tomorrow. You can go with him, Antony, and he'll take you to the police and get things sorted out. We can't see they'll have any grounds to hold you as you had no hand in the shooting. It should be quite straightforward.'

'And I've got to go back and get my plane.'

'Yes, but first things first. Guildford tomorrow, then the plane, then off to London.'

What a bossy old boot she was, Lily thought. As soon as the meal was finished they went out. Antony wanted to avoid the village, with so many people wanting to know his story, and suggested they went to Lockwood Hall straightaway, to see if they could get in. Simon came with them to help. Although the driveway had a chain across it and there were notices saying KEEP OUT all around the boundaries, there seemed to be no watch on it. It was obvious that most of the village had been snooping around, judging from the pilfered flowerbeds and now almost bare vegetable garden, and when they got to the house it was clear that there had also been quite serious, but unsuccessful, attempts to break in.

Antony seemed upset. 'Bloody jackals! What a nerve, thinking it's up for grabs.'

'What do you expect, with the place abandoned? There's nobody guarding it.'

'Quite easy to break in really. Not the doors, but a window round the back. With the right tools – Cedric will have them.'

They inspected the boarding of the windows that overlooked the lake and decided that one underneath Helena's apartments looked the most likely.

'A couple of big crowbars should do it easily. Lily, go up to the farm and find Cedric and get a couple of crowbars. We'll wait here.' Antony dropped down to the grass and lay on his back, hands behind his head. 'Off you go.'

'Why me?'

'Because you love me and want to please me. If you come back with two crowbars I will love you more.'

'No you won't. You're a pig.'

'Yes, I'm a pig. A loving pig.' He snorted happily. 'Get a move on.'

'I hate you.'

But she went, Simon not offering. She was used to the treatment they meted out; nothing was any different. But Cedric would be on her side; she depended on him more these days because he was kind and took her side, although the two of them would never win. They were bottom of the pecking order, only Squashy even lower.

Cedric was fiddling about with the reaping machine but fetched a couple of crowbars and came back with her to where Antony and Simon were still lying on the lawn. They talked for quite a while, Cedric having to learn all the news, and then got up to attack the house. Cedric had already surveyed it and agreed that the window at the back, underneath Helena's apartment, was the least secure. Someone had already loosened the boarding but obviously hadn't had a man-enough tool with them to finish the job. Cedric got to work with one of the crowbars and Simon helped with the other and Antony sat on the grass and watched. Lily noticed how strong Cedric was compared with Simon; he made quite short work of it, levering off the boards and then smashing the window so that they could get in.

Antony got up and went first. Cedric helped bunk Lily up and the two boys followed.

The house was dark with all its windows blanked, and smelled of dust and mould. It was horrible, Lily thought, knowing that a man had been murdered there. Cracks of light came in here and there and Antony led them for what seemed miles of corridors to his father's office, wanting to know first of all if it had been stripped by the police.

It had. The desk drawers were pulled out, all empty; every shelf and cupboard had been cleared, even some floorboards pulled up. The detective inspector's blood still lay in a great stain across the carpet, with a cloud of flies buzzing over it. They all stood and looked at it, trying to come to terms with Antony's fusty, silent father being a murderer. Lily felt sick.

'It's weird,' Antony said. 'But when we left he was like another person, sort of excited, pleased. Not frightened. I got the impression that he was actually enjoying himself, as if he had suddenly come to life after all those dreary years of whatever it was he did. As if he knew how to outwit everybody, like a sort of hunted fox. That was the impression he gave me. He was happy!'

'Well, they haven't caught him yet. Perhaps he'll get away with it.'

'I bet he's lying low with friends in France, and when the hue and cry has died down he'll go and live somewhere out of the way, perhaps back to South America. Amazing. I wish I knew him better. I don't suppose I shall ever see him again.'

His words, although spoken without regret, made Lily feel incredibly sad.

'It's horrible in here. I want to go,' she said.

'We'll go and fetch the things out of Helena's room. That's all I want. Then we'll go.'

The pillowcases stuffed with valuables still lay inside the door where Rose and Violet had dropped them. Sorting through them, they abandoned all the female things, the dresses and furs and embroidered underwear, and made piles of the valuables hidden within – the jewellery, the silverware, the Fabergé eggs, the inlaid boxes, the Venetian glassware, the knick-knacks of gold and silver set with rubies and emeralds, the most beautiful of the silk scarves . . .

'Cor blimey, mate, you'll be able to live on this lot for years.'

Best of all the pictures, of which the two servants had only tried to take the smallest. Simon took the Van Gogh sunflowers off the wall, and a Botticelli nativity, a Dutch flower piece, a bright Matisse, a Turner seascape and a small Rubens portrait.

'You're rich as Croesus, Ant, no problems.'

'But where can I keep it? I can't live here any more.'

They had already discovered that the electricity, the water and the gas had all been turned off.

Simon said, 'We can take it to my place for now.'

'Your parents will go potty, seeing this lot. I don't really want anyone to know. They'll insist on putting it in the bank, obviously. And then everyone'll know I've got it.'

'Where then?'

'The grotto,' Lily suggested.

'People have been in there since the party. I've seen 'em,' Cedric said. 'My father blasted some of 'em out only last week. Threatened them with a shotgun.'

'Somewhere no one will look.'

'In my place,' Lily said. 'My bedroom. My father never looks in there. Not ever.'

'In *your* house?' Simon's voice was derogatory.

But Antony said, 'Yes, that's a good idea. But not let him see us put it there.'

'He said he was going to do the gardens in the pub today. If we go now he won't see us.'

'What about Squashy? If he knows the whole world will know.'

'I'll sort Squashy.'

'OK. Let's go.'

They packed all the stuff carefully in the pillowcases and left the building, making sure no one was about to see them. It did not take long to walk to Lily's house. She went ahead on

193

a reconnaissance to see that no one was there, but all was quiet, the door left open as it always was, with no sign of Gabriel or Squashy.

The boys came after her and the loot was carried upstairs and stuffed away under her bed, (deep in dust, she was ashamed to notice). Lily noticed Simon and Cedric looking all about them, never having been invited into Lily's house before, and she could tell from their expressions that they were amazed at its poverty. If it had not been for the memory of Antony lying so happily in her bed and her own joy in his company, she would have been hurt and embarrassed, but as it was she was able to smile to herself. She thought Antony enjoyed her house more than Simon's (apart from the food, of course).

As if to prove it he sat down in Gabriel's chair when they came downstairs and said, 'Well, that's very handy, Lily. No one will find it, you're sure?'

'No.'

'If they do they'll think you've stolen it,' Simon said coldly. Lily could tell he didn't like being in her house and was anxious to return home. 'Are you coming, Ant?'

'No. I'll come later. I've got to see about getting my plane back.'

'Shall I tell Ma to expect you later?'

'Er, yes, I suppose so.'

'You'd be welcome at ours too, if you want. My ma wouldn't mind,' Cedric said.

The two boys went off and Antony grinned and said to

Lily, 'I'd rather stay here actually. I'm not used to being mothered.'

'Being told what to do. She's so bossy. I could make up a bed for you in the barn if you like. People have stayed in there sometimes. It's dry and clean.'

'Oh, Lily, if only—'

He looked at her sadly. Lily wanted to hug and kiss him but knew she couldn't. He had no home, no family, no ambition, no nothing, and looked about ten years older since his father's escapade. She could not think what on earth he was going to do.

'I would like to get a job at Brooklands but so do so many people, much better qualified than me. But I have got an aeroplane. First things first. I shall go and fetch it and take it to Brooklands.' Ambition flickered.

'Yes, that's a good idea. Maybe you can stay at Brooklands, or somewhere near, and get to know people and get a job. And come back here sometimes, to take your loot.'

'Yes. I might go now and keep clear of Mrs G. Didn't they say they would take me to Guildford tomorrow to see the police? That's not a good idea, for God's sake. If I go now to get the plane, you can tell them that, can't you? Not where I intend to take it, although they might guess. But I doubt they'll come looking for me.'

'You're going now?'

'Yes, I think so.'

'You can always come back here if you've nowhere else.'

'Take your bed off you? That's not fair, Lily, and I don't

think your father approves of me. But I'll keep in touch – I can always fly in to see you, and collect some of my loot to sell.'

Lily could not bear to think of Antony going. She tried to delay him, made him a cup of tea, chattering. It proved a big mistake, for as they sat outside, drinking, a familiar figure appeared, coming towards them from the road.

'Oh my God!' Antony breathed.

It was Aunt Maud.

SEPTEMBER, 1922

20

She said, 'This whole thing is a most terrible stain on the family name. I cannot believe it of Claude. I always suspected he was into some shady deals – I'm not stupid – but the fact that he is a traitor to his country is beyond belief. A traitor and a murderer, my own brother, it has been the most terrible shock, and for you too, dear boy, it must be very hard to bear.'

(But it was quite fun, Antony was thinking – not the murder, but the bit afterwards was great, and his father coming to life in a way that revealed another character completely, one that Antony thought he would have got on with much better . . . if only he had known . . . he might have gone with his father into a new life, a hunted fugitive . . . what larks . . . God, how she did go on!)

'As long as you are not sullied by his ghastly behaviour, I think we can expunge his memory from our minds by keeping you away from that dreadful place and finding you a good position here in London. I have many professional friends and am sure I can place you in a law firm or a bank in the city. With your education, even though I know you are wilful and idle, you are mannerly and literate and you might be able to start at the bottom in a worthy profession and make yourself into a passable human being. It's called work, Antony, and in this age of massive unemployment you should feel yourself very lucky that you have a stronghold here in London with me . . .'

Et cetera, et cetera, blah blah blah, on and on.

Antony tried to sit looking mannerly and literate rather than wilful and idle, and realized slowly the full horror of what the old bat was planning. His life, no less! Compulsorily marched to London, to her house in Hampstead, he had had no say in anything, hardly able to get a word in edgeways . . . 'I've got to get my plane . . .' 'We'll send a message to the aerodrome and get a man to fly it back to Lockwood.' 'But we don't own Lockwood any more.' 'Rubbish!'

My plane, my plane! he kept thinking. And my treasure under Lily's bed . . . It had only been a temporary solution.

He slumped back in his armchair while her voice ran over him. Her sitting room was even worse than the one in Lockwood, charmless, cluttered with the accumulation of generations of bad taste, of useless little tables covered in bric-a-brac, fusty velvet curtains draped against a view of brick walls, unread books in stacks behind grimy glass doors, firmly locked. It smelled of Ludo, the dog of indeterminate breeding who occupied most of the floor space, his four paws splayed out for visitors to trip over. The bedroom she had shown him was worse than his room at school. Having none of his stuff to clutter it with, it was a stark monk's abode with a brown lino floor, an empty cupboard or two and a washstand with bowl and ewer.

'You will be comfortable here,' she said wrongly.

He had brought nothing of his own with him. He had none of his stuff, no clothes, no gear: she had not allowed him time to sort anything – not that he could have salvaged anything from his bedroom without Cedric's crowbars again, and no doubt the old girl would never have stood for that. She had countenanced no argument. Lockwood was boarded up.

'We shall have to get permission to access your belongings later.'

'But I'm staying with Simon's parents. They've invited me.'

'I've spoken to them. They agreed that you should come to live with me. When I called they told me I would probably find you down at that girl's cottage. Such an unsuitable friendship, Antony, to be on such intimate terms with your servants – I always saw that you were slipping into careless ways. I discussed it with Claude, but he seemed to take no interest. And that tragedy with Helena – well, I said to myself, it was only to be expected, the way you were allowed to run riot all over the place, to do what you liked. The poor girl . . . but in retrospect one can only be thankful . . .'

Antony wanted to scream. He wasn't thankful that Helena had died! She had deserved more; she had deserved to be educated and helped and given a life; he would have done it for her if he had ever had a chance. (Wouldn't he? He stifled the small doubt that his conscience raised.)

So now he was a prisoner of this terrible termagant.

'I'll take you to see a friend of mine in the City, whom I am sure will start you in his office. A firm of solicitors, very respectable. I am sure you will make your way there. You realize that a young man like yourself is in competition with all these thousands of men displaced by the war: it is very hard to find a job today. You need the help such as I can give you. You are very lucky in that respect. I have many influential friends . . .' And on and on.

The small over-full sitting room was stifling him. He was used to the acres of Lockwood Hall's interiors. He wanted to scream.

'Can I go for a walk before supper? See the heath?'

'Yes, you can take the dog with you. He needs a run. Just turn right outside and the heath is at the end of the road. Don't go far, you'll get lost. Make sure you notice where our road is when you cross over to the heath.'

She was much higher on the bossy scale than Mrs Goldbeater, and Antony wasn't used to it. Had she suspected he would scarper off to the nearest railway station to make for home? He was inclined to do just that, but knew she would come after him, and certainly he didn't want to be lumbered with the dog. Is that why she had demanded he take the dog with him? He suspected so. Large and clumsy as Ludo was, he leaped up with agility when the lead was rattled, and bounded to the front door.

'Supper will be at seven. Mrs Walker is cooking it now so don't be late.' Mrs Walker was the live-in factotum, a woman much in the same mould as her employer.

Getting out of the house was like coming up for air after a long underwater swim – oh for the lake outside Lily's house on this sweet autumn evening! He could not believe how he had been so neatly captured. Lolling about with Lily one minute, then into a taxi and away the next. At least he still had most of the packet of money his father had passed him safely in his back trouser pocket.

As he walked towards the heath with Ludo trotting beside him, he realized slowly that he had little option other than to stay with the old bat for the time being. He couldn't safely go back to living in the old house: the Goldbeaters would stop him, and he couldn't stay with them either for more than a few days. Besides which they were intending to take him to the police station, and at least Aunt Maud hadn't suggested that. His treasure was safe (or fairly safe) with Lily – the only worry was his aeroplane.

He needed to get that to Brooklands. He decided to write to Tom and get him to arrange it somehow. He would send him a wodge of money to pay for its collection and housing at Brooklands until he could get back to it. Which he would, he vowed. Brooklands was his idea of paradise, and as he crossed the road onto the heath he decided that Brooklands was where he wanted to be, even if it was only bumming around and sleeping rough in the back of a shed. When he had sorted himself out and the hue and cry over his father had died down he determined to go back there.

Now on the heath and with Ludo running away off the lead he felt his optimism return. Staying with Aunt Maud was just a blip in his ambition, useful for a week or so of being well-fed at least. The heath was extraordinary, like being back in the country: he couldn't believe it, the grass and trees stretching away ahead of him as if London, right on its heels, didn't exist. For ever, it seemed. Lakes as well, with ducks and swans, just like home. He walked for a long way, kicking the first autumn leaves, throwing sticks for Ludo, feeling his over-stretched emotions beginning to subside. What had happened was amazing, but now he was his own man. He would do what he wanted, humour Aunt Maud for a few days and then do what he wanted.

When he noticed that dusk was falling he turned back for home but discovered he was completely lost. He could tell his direction by the setting sun, which had been on his right when he set out, so now, what was left of it needed to be on his left. Fortunately he soon realized that Ludo knew the way, so he attached him to the lead again and let him trot ahead. Ludo was by miles the best thing about being with Aunt Maud. The dog came to life when let out and turned from a great slob on the carpet into a prancing bearlike animal. Antony thought he was Alsatian crossed with what could only be bear, what else? But unlikely. He would be better off with Squashy, Antony thought, and decided to take him with him when he went.

He got into deep trouble for being late for supper, upbraided for his lack of consideration, his selfishness, his stupidity, etc.

but Ludo was thumping his tail and obviously showing that he thought Antony was good news – Antony didn't think he got much of a walk most days with his over-stuffed owner. But his supper, though having languished for an hour in the oven, was very good, and fuelled his optimism in spite of everything.

'Tomorrow we'll go to Savile Row and get you measured up for some decent clothes,' Aunt Maud decided. 'And you can get a haircut and some new shoes. And then we'll see about a job.'

'Yes, Aunt,' said Antony politely.

Mannerly and literate. The best of him. He dredged it up.

'Yes, I think he will suit. The vacancy is coming up in October, with poor Mr Derbyshire coming to the end of his working days, I'm afraid. The boy will have to start at the bottom, of course, but if he shows aptitude and the right attitude he will be able to make his way with us.'

The thought of working with this man in this office made Antony feel faint. *Never!* his whole being cried out, even as he was smiling in his best sycophantic manner. It was a solicitor's office in Clerkenwell, housed in a hideous brick building pretending to be a Gothic vicarage, hemmed around by equally hideous offices, their walls very close. Out of all the windows the view was only of high brick walls with a mere sliver of sky at the top, not a leaf in sight. The windows were grey with grime. The office was divided into several glassed-around cubicles where clerks worked at desks on typewriters surrounded by piles of papers. Antony forbore to admit he could not type. It had never been on Eton's timetable. He had played about on his father's machine, the limit of his expertise.

No way would he ever set foot in this place.

'Yes, sir,' he agreed, smiling. 'Yes, of course.'

The old boy was the male equivalent of Aunt Maud, overbearing and ugly. Maybe he was a very good solicitor. The office seemed busy. All the workers were male, some fairly ancient, others not much older than himself, all intent on their papers, not a smile to be seen. No joking, no joshing, not a coffee cup to be seen. He would wither and die on day one. He would not come.

'Well, I'll be in touch, Miss Sylvester, when the date comes up for the young man's initiation. I'm sure it will be a very fruitful collaboration.'

'Thank you so much, Mr Hargreaves. I am very grateful to you, as I know the circumstances are a little difficult. I am sure the boy will prove a credit to your judgement.'

Antony presumed that this was a reference to the fact that his father was a wanted traitor and murderer. The name Sylvester was still in the news – not a pretty connection – and Aunt Maud had already told him that not many employers would take him on, not without her outstanding influence amongst her hand-picked circle of upper-class friends.

A couple of weeks had passed in which he had been reshaped in her image: smart, immaculately dressed, severely coiffed, sycophantic in address, obedient and polite. But every day saw him closer to escape. Tom had written to say that the aeroplane was safely at Brooklands; no police or officials seemed to be interested any longer in Lockwood Hall and it was rumoured that it was to be put up for sale. Antony intended to avail himself of some of the fortune held at Lily's house and then go and try and make a bit of a living by giving aeroplane rides or offering a taxi service with his aeroplane – according as to what he might be allowed to do, or forbidden to do, from Brooklands. He knew the place was cluttered with flying-crazy young men like himself, all looking for a job, all getting in the way of the professionals who were already working there. One more like himself would make no difference.

He needed to go fairly soon now to rescue his valuables. Tom said Squashy had discovered the pictures and hung them downstairs in their kitchen: the Botticelli over the range, the Rubens over the sink and Van Gogh's sunflowers in a space beside the dresser. Gabriel had not remarked on the decorations, but Tom thought it was only a matter of time before someone stole them. None of them ever locked the front door, rarely even shut it.

Seeing his fate in the solicitor's office and reading Tom's letter, Antony decided then that it was time to leave. He would take Ludo with him, a present for Squashy in exchange for his pictures back. Ludo deserved better than Aunt Maud. She scarcely took him a yard on the heath, only far enough to do his business, as she described it. Antony took him miles every day, the only pleasant hours of his life with Aunt Maud. Taking the bus home with Aunt Maud after his interview with the solicitor, Antony decided to depart the following morning.

In the evening, after Aunt Maud had gone to bed, he stuffed his few possessions, including a selection of his new clothes, into a bag and hid it under some laurel bushes in the garden of a house a little way down the road. He confirmed that there was still a considerable amount of money in the wodge his father had given him, secured it safely in the pocket of his outdoor jacket and hung it on the bedpost. He was all ready to go. He would first eat a large breakfast, then, as usual, take Ludo for a walk – all the way to the station and then on a train for his old home.

It was so easy. Ludo loved the train, suspecting that he might be going back to that place by the lake where another dog lived, and spent the journey looking eagerly out of the window, Antony allowing him to sit on a corner seat, oblivious to the disapproving looks of his fellow passengers.

At the nearest station to his old home he alighted and set off to walk the last five miles or so, taking footpaths and byways that he had roamed from childhood. Ludo went mad with all the new wild smells of the countryside, and lumbered eagerly in all directions until his tongue was hanging out and his eyes popping. Antony found him a stream for a drink and rested a bit. It was now well into autumn and the day sharp and, sitting there on a log, it came home for the first time to Antony what a step he had suddenly taken. The visit to the solicitor had accelerated what had been a rather vague intention to leave his aunt, but, now that he was hungry, he realized his plans were not exactly well-considered; in fact he hadn't thought out anything at all beyond a wish to hang out at Brooklands where he suspected he would get scant welcome.

Going back to the Goldbeaters' would undoubtedly land him back where he didn't want to be; going to Cedric's was impossible because he wasn't into farming and his presence would embarrass them, he being the gaffer, the way they were used to seeing it, so who else was going to feed him and find him a bed?

It would have to be Lily for now. This worried him somewhat. He always felt anxious about exploiting Lily's love, giving so little in return. But he had to go back there to see to his treasures, so he had no choice. Just a night, he thought – not in her bed this time, but in the barn she mentioned. Then he would try and see Tom. Perhaps Tom had a spare bed? Antony was a bit vague about Tom's domestic background.

Not feeling quite so optimistic now that the full force of finding himself homeless had entered his consciousness, he called Ludo to heel and set off again. He made a detour to a pub to get some food – not in his own village as he didn't want to be recognized – and in the mid-afternoon came down through the woods behind Lily's cottage and saw the familiar lake and his old home flaunting its ridiculous battlements against a grey, wintry sky, looking as abandoned as he felt himself. Bereft, suddenly. He felt a surge of self-pity, and found it difficult to stifle what was almost a sob in his throat.

Then Ludo was barking and another dog came skedaddling round the corner of the cottage, yapping a welcome, and Squashy was shouting, 'It's Ludo! It's Ludo come back!' and there was Lily, speechless amongst the garden flowers, looking so lovely that Antony's mouth fell open.

'Lily!'

'Antony, oh, Antony!' and she flung herself at him, sobbing violently, burying her face in his chest so that his face was full of her mass of golden hair. He gasped, trying to fend her off and then, at her passion, putting his arms kindly round her and hugging her and saying sweet words to calm her down. Somebody loved him at least.

'Oh, Antony, I thought you were gone for ever! I have been so miserable! Everything is so awful now without you. I hate it! It was so lovely before, and now everybody has gone and we've no money and I have to work for Mrs Carruthers and she is so beastly, and Dad is so gloomy and there's only Squashy laughing – hark at him! Have you brought Ludo for him?'

'Yes, I've stolen him. I've run away, Lily, and I've nowhere to go. I want you to help me.'

'Yes, oh yes, Antony, I will do anything for you! Come in, come in, I'll make you a drink. Dad's not here, he's ditching up at Carter's.'

Gabriel was too old to do ditching, Antony thought with a pang. He surely must help this family, left in the lurch by his father . . . he would give them the Van Gogh. It did look very splendid on the only bit of wall where there was a space, lighting up the whole room. Lily moved the Botticelli from over the range where she started to stoke up the kettle.

'I always move it when something's boiling, so the steam doesn't hurt it. We do love the pictures, Ant, they make the place so pretty.'

Crikey, Antony thought, that's saying something! A Matisse of dancing ladies bounded over the wall beside the scullery and a Dutch flower painting was squashed between the chimney breast and the cupboard where pots and pans were kept.

'Of course we know you will take them away soon, but they like to be looked at, don't they? Not kept under the bed.'

Antony had a nasty feeling suddenly that perhaps the pictures, like all his father's stuff, now belonged to the authorities (whoever they were) – the same people in black cars who had commandeered and boarded up the house and confiscated the whole contents of his father's office. If he tried to sell them, he would have some explaining to do. Didn't dealers always ask for what they called provenance, where the picture had come from? Did they not belong to him after all? He put down this nasty thought, which had never occurred to him before, as Lily prattled on.

'Tom will be very pleased to see you – I think Brooklands don't want your plane, not without getting some rent or something for storing it. But you can see to that now. Don't let Mrs Goldbeater see you though – she was ever so pleased that Aunt Maud took you away. She said she was just what you needed, a firm hand.'

'A firm hand? Hand of death more like. She got me a job with a solicitor. So I left.'

'What do you want to do then?'

'What do I *want*? What I want, and what I will get, are probably very different. What I *want* is a nice job in flying, preferably out of Brooklands, a pilot for someone, or taking somebody somewhere, like a taxi, or teaching someone the first things about flying. I don't know enough really, I've got to get the paperwork, I suppose. I'm not much good as a mechanic, unfortunately, so that's off. I'm not much good at anything really, when I come to think about it. But if it's just *want* – I want to jump out with a parachute, like you did.'

'Oh, Ant, that was so wonderful. When I'm sad I think about it. I shall always think about it, till the day I die.'

'Well, perhaps if things go right we will do it together. Me for the first time, and you again. Hire a plane, and jump together. That would be terrific.'

He was talking rubbish, he knew. Where was the money coming from if he didn't get a job, if he couldn't sell his treasure . . . But the knick-knacks in silver and the jewellery – surely he could dispose of them without questions being asked? Say his grandmother left the pieces to him. His mind rambled on as Lily made him a cup of tea, her confidences having set up so many questions which stupidly he hadn't given a thought to, setting off so blithely with Ludo on the lead. And Ludo too . . . he could hardly take him to Brooklands with him, and a big dog was difficult to keep if he left him with Squashy.

'Do you get by, for food, I mean? Are you earning enough? And the rent for the cottage?'

'No one's asked us for any rent since your father went, which is handy, but we're all afraid they're going to sell off the cottages along with Lockwood when they get round to it. Then only God knows what we shall do. We get rabbits to eat, and Mrs Butterworth is very kind and sends Cedric over with a pie sometimes and a bag of potatoes, and of course now there's plenty of fruit and blackberries and Dad's got cabbages and stuff, so it's not bad. It'll be worse after Christmas, of course, but then it always was.'

She spoke so prosaically, like a hardened housewife, which Antony sadly supposed she was, at only the age of . . . what? Fourteen?

'How old are you, Lily?'

'Fifteen.'

'Blimey.'

She was still a child really, yet so hardened by responsibility. He supposed he was the opposite, still a child through being unburdened by responsibility. Until now. No one had taught him to take care of himself, and he realized it had been really childish not to have thought ahead about the realities of leaving Aunt Maud.

'Well, I shall be around hopefully, not far away,' he said. 'I swear I shall never go back to Aunt Maud. I've got to make my own way. Even if it can't be at Brooklands.'

'How, Antony?'

There was no answer to that. 'Don't ask.'

He drank his tea. Squashy was romping about outside with the dogs, Ludo skittering about like a puppy, barking with joy. Antony had never seen him so happy.

'I've got to go and see Tom, about the aeroplane, Lily. And now I must collect Helena's things too, to sell. I need the money. You can keep the pictures for a bit. I'll be near here if I go to Brooklands, so I shall come back and see you quite often.'

'Yes, you must come back. I love you so. I've missed you terribly.'

'Yes, but you always knew I had to go away some time.'

'Yes, of course, but I can't help myself. Will you leave Ludo? It makes Squashy so happy, look at him!'

'Yes, of course.'

That was one problem solved. He had never thought ahead about arriving at Brooklands with Ludo. He had never thought ahead about anything really.

He collected the pillowcase full of Helena's treasures, which was still fortunately under Lily's bed, and departed before Gabriel came home. He didn't want to face Gabriel, although the old man usually said nothing. But Antony could always sense the disapproval. He felt bad about old Gabriel. He had to give them some of the money when he sold some of the stuff, he decided.

But the wodge his father had given him was shrinking fast.

He crossed the lake and went up the erstwhile lawns to the house. Everything now was forlorn and broken, overgrown, abandoned. He could not believe how quickly the place had fallen into disrepair. What a grim place it was, glowering over the dusking lake. The air was cold now, the nights drawing in, and Antony started wondering where on earth he was going to sleep. And he was fast getting hungry again and could not help thinking of the large, tasty suppers he had got used to at his aunt's. He prayed Tom might help him: they had always been quite good friends in the past.

But when he knocked on the door of Tom's cottage behind the garage he did not get a friendly welcome.

'God, mate, where've you been all this time? Come to pay your debts, I hope. I'm getting dunned for money from Brooklands – rent for the storage, bill from the pilot, threats of bailiffs coming in, you name it. You really landed me in it. What do you think I do for money? I'm the same as all the other bastards your bloody father dropped in the bin. Your name's not good around here, I can tell you.'

Antony saw his hope for rest and food and consolation evaporate sadly in the dusk. He had not truly given a thought to paying back Tom what he must have spent.

'I'm going to Brooklands tomorrow. I'll square it with them.'

'Thank God for that. Make sure you do so.'

And with that he shut the door in Antony's face.

Antony was shattered. Tom had been a larky friend the last time he had been with him. If it had not been for Lily's devotion his homecoming was not proving a very good idea. Going back to Simon's house would land him in the Aunt Maud situation, not to be contemplated, going back to Lily's and

213

facing Gabriel just as bad. He could not face going into the village for food, where no doubt he would meet a lot of the people in the same frame of mind as Tom. The Butterworths at the farm had no love for him; he had always treated them like servants, and even Cedric as a hanger-on, not in the same bracket as Simon and John.

He spent the night, hungry, asleep on the back seat of the Rolls-Royce which still resided, unused, in the garage of Lockwood Hall.

21

Antony awoke in the morning freezing cold, starving hungry and deeply fed up. Outside it was drizzling with rain. There was no one about. He sat for a bit, listening to his empty stomach rumbling sadly and had to fight off the inclination to return to Hampstead Heath. It was impossible. So was asking Tom for help, or anyone else for that matter. Things could only be better at Brooklands, for they could not be any worse than where he was now. At least his plane would be there and he could fly away somewhere if the worst came to the worst.

There was a bicycle in the garage and he decided to use that to get to Brooklands. He could not remember whose it was. Tom's probably. Too bad. He loaded his gear on the carrier and tied it on firmly with some old string lying on the floor and pushed it out into the rain. At least the pedalling might warm him up, and somewhere along the way he would find somewhere to buy breakfast.

This proved correct, so when he arrived at Brooklands he was, if wet, in a slightly more optimistic frame of mind. He found nothing had changed much, save the place was getting smarter with its growing popularity as a car racing venue. The motor racing now overshadowed the aviation, the aeroplanes and their motley conglomeration of sheds being shoved together at the end of the vast concrete ellipse that comprised the race track. Watching these races, with their ever-present shadow of imminent and ghastly death overhanging them, was now a huge spectator sport and apparently the place was crowded with spectators on race days. Luckily today was not one of those.

Antony presumed he ought to get the money thing sorted first, but he wanted to assure himself that his plane was actually there and safe and that it was worth paying for before he parted with any cash. He asked the nearest men he met about where the office was and where his plane might be, and when they found out that he was the son of the famous traitor and murderer Claude Sylvester he found himself getting as much attention, or more than, he really wanted.

Amazingly, it was his way in to being offered cups of tea, cheese sandwiches, a seat in a work shed and a fair share of admiration. Not many air trips had been made with a gun in the pilot's back: he was a one-off, a local hero. They wanted to know all about the murder, how much blood, how the escape was contrived, where was his father now? When he had satisfied them with the answers to most of the questions, he plied them with questions of his own and discovered that there were very few jobs going – just a possibility if he could fly and owned a plane. There was nowhere to sleep, nowhere to get a

216

meal unless you were a rich member of the racing club, and no jobs at all for someone who couldn't use tools and knew nothing about engines. Nothing, really, that he hadn't guessed already, but there was goodwill, which was something he was beginning to cherish. He decided he would turn some of Helena's knick-knacks into money, pay his debts, check in for a bed and breakfast close by and hope for the best.

Nothing in his life so far had been as hard as what he faced now. If he hadn't had a goal: to get a job in flying, he supposed he would never have found the strength to go through all the drudgery of a hanger-on's life at Brooklands.

He found himself a cheap boarding house nearby; he paid Tom's debts with the remains of the money his father had given him, and sold some of Helena's jewellery in London to make enough to live on for a few months. With his public school confidence he found it quite easy to mingle with the moneyed people who came to Brooklands for the racing and flying, and at weekends he worked in the restaurant as a waiter, a job which he found far more to his liking than anything Aunt Maud's solicitor friend was offering. The conversations he overheard kept his ambitions afloat, and with young men of his own kind he even found himself drinking at the bar and discussing, as well as the amazing speeds reached on the motor circuits, the current achievements in flying: the opening up of commercial airlines to fly passengers all over Europe, long-distance flights across the world, the racing for the Pulitzer Trophy and the Schneider Trophy in America, and even the start of an affordable fun aeroplane designed by Geoffrey de Havilland to sell cheaply to people like himself. The burgeoning of flying was all the news, and Antony found himself far from alone in his hopes to be a part of this exciting world.

But the frustration of not being a part of it crucified him. The young men he talked with mostly had jobs in the industry, some as pilots, others working in the offices of the flying firms. Antony had no desire to work in an office; to be a pilot even for a pittance for some rich young idiot was the height of his ambition. But he soon realized that many of the craving jobless like himself had far more to offer than he did. They did not have Eton accents, but they did have oily hands and could take an engine down, or discuss the intricacies of rudder design, and still they could not get a job. Unemployment was rife everywhere: even his weekend waiter's job was envied, although it did little to pay for his living expenses. He became a familiar figure hanging around like many others. Actually owning a plane, even if he could not afford to fly it, gave him the right to hang around, at least.

Helena's store was evaporating, and some of it seemed to have been lost, or more likely stolen, in his careless swapping of lodgings. He could not understand how quickly money vanished. He had meant to take some back to help Lily and her family over the winter, but he never did, thinking of her only at times with a sense of guilt. He told himself that if he

218

got a job he would honour his promise to her to take her on a parachute trip: to jump out himself was still his own crazy desire, but he could not bear to face Lily with nothing to say for himself. Her crazy love for him must surely have died by now: he rarely gave her a thought. He just longed for the winter to be over and his miserable existence to take a turn for the better with the blessed coming of spring.

Lily had always known that Antony would go away sooner or later, leave home, get a job, do something. Leave *her*. She had always known it. Since he had escaped Aunt Maud and set off for Brooklands her spirits had lifted, knowing that he was his own man again and not very far away, but as the winter progressed and she heard no word she began to think he must have found the job he had always hankered after and, literally, flown away. Nobody had had word from him, not even Simon or the Goldbeaters. If he was close, she thought, she would have known.

Cedric said, 'He doesn't think of anyone but himself, Lily, you know that. He doesn't know other people have feelings.'

'He knows the feelings I have for him.'

'Yes, everyone knows that.' Cedric laughed, but kindly.

Lily said, 'He had feelings for Helena – what he did for her.'

Cedric forbore to say, 'Yes, he drowned her' and nodded in agreement. 'I'm sure, sooner or later, he will fly back here to see you.' He wanted to cheer her up, depressed to see Lily so forlorn.

He did not believe, if Antony made his way successfully, that he would ever come back to see them. Why should he? They meant nothing to him. Simon, possibly, but Cedric knew that to Antony Lily was just a funny little girl who adored him and danced to his tune. She amused him. He used her. He took her for granted. Her devotion meant nothing to him. Cedric had little admiration for Antony, although, like everyone else, he enjoyed his company. Antony had certainly enlivened his childhood, just as he had Lily's.

Yes, they missed him.

But Antony was no help to Lily now that times were hard. The winter was stretching the small family since there was no real income coming in. The cottage could well be taken away from them, then where could they go? Gabriel and Lily scratched for the meagre jobs the village provided and lived with the cloud of eviction hanging over their heads. Lily worked the hardest and had the two men to cook for and feed, and no Antony to weave her dreams around.

Simon was away at university. Cedric was the only one of the old gang she saw when he came down from the farm with food his mother sent: the leavings of a joint of lamb or a new-baked fruit cake. When he had the cart he would bring a bag of potatoes. He would have brought some of his sisters' discarded clothes for Lily, but that would have been a charity too far, insulting.

Lily knitted every evening by candlelight from unravelled

wool some village ladies gave her, and made amazing jerseys. Squashy had one with a portrait of Barky on his chest, his dearest possession. She longed for the spring.

She gave up longing for Antony. Antony was for fun. Life wasn't fun any more.

JANUARY, 1923

22

In the middle of winter, when Antony was close to despair, Clarence Frobisher flew into Brooklands – very badly, his landing causing considerable excitement and laughter, and much curiosity as to the character who professed to be an aviator. Fortunately Clarence was not a sensitive soul and took the derision with charm and good humour, and asked only, 'Is there anywhere I can get a drink round here? I need one after that.'

'Come with me. I'll stand you one,' Antony said quickly.

Clarence was a rich young American whose father had indulged him, as had Antony's, in his fleeting ambition to be a pilot. In the bar, especially after discovering that Antony was the son of the famous crook Sylvester, Clarence warmed to the socially adept young man who was so welcoming. Like everyone else he wanted a blow-by-blow account of the murder and Antony's flight at gunpoint, and after that he asked what Antony was doing at Brooklands now; did he fly?

'Because I've got the plane,' he added. 'But I don't seem to have much talent when it comes to flying the damned thing. I was hoping to find a pilot here, so I can do my travelling and sightseeing and partying in Paris and suchlike without the worry of being my own pilot.'

'I'm looking for a job as a pilot,' Antony said, trying to sound casual. 'I've got my certificate, and plane of my own, and I need a job.'

'Yeah, it seems there's no shortage of out-of-work pilots. I've already discovered that. Why is it so easy for all you young kids, but I can't seem to get the hang of it at all? Good enough to amuse myself, but I haven't the confidence to take my friends up. We none of us want to die, after all. If I stay here a bit perhaps I'll find the right man. Maybe you, who knows? I'm not going to jump into it. But you can show me the ropes around here, eh? Who runs the joint, where I can stay? We can be friends, eh?'

You bet, thought Antony, his heart leaping at the possibilities. It was the first time anything like this had come his way, just when he had been thinking of giving up on the whole thing. Day after day, mooching about, sweeping up, handing spanners to mechanics, valeting machines, kicking his heels, forever with an eye out for an opportunity . . . it had been getting hard to bear and more dispiriting by the hour. But Clarence, literally descending from the blue, was opportunity writ large.

He was about twenty-one, Antony supposed, a large, well-nourished young man with blond hair and fat laughing cheeks, extremely affable but with, one suspected, a sharp intelligence. He was pleased to find Antony, a youth on his same educated wavelength, and invited him straightaway to join him in finding a decent hotel to stay in, hire a car, have lunch and generally be a friend. He was lavish with his money, which seemed to come from a hugely generous allowance.

'My pa said to find myself a pilot – he wants me to stay alive. But there's no hurry – I don't want to fly much until the summer. It's damned cold up there at this time of year.'

And down here, Antony thought, nearly always frozen and too mean to spend money feeding the gas meter in his dank abode. He did not dare reveal to Clarence his lowly residence and did not point it out when they passed it in the hired car that Clarence drove with the same bravado and lack of skill with which he had landed his plane. They found a very elegant hotel set in its own parkland and woods, and Clarence arranged for his luggage to be delivered there and treated Antony to a sumptuous lunch. Later he delivered Antony back to Brooklands and promised to see him again in the morning.

Antony could not believe in his luck. Word had got around, of course, that this maniac of a Yank was looking for a pilot, and out-of-work pilots were already dropping in looking for him. They were mostly older, adrift from the war, mostly disillusioned and hardened by their experiences, and Antony could only hope that his already established friendship would put him ahead of these men who undoubtedly had more ability than he had.

But Clarence was friendly to all and he was no fool; Antony

could only wait on tenterhooks, doing his best to foster the friendship without seeming sycophantic. He started to fly again, to retain his skill, and took Clarence up once or twice to impress him, and Clarence was encouraged enough to start taking flying lessons in his own plane. This machine was a converted de Havilland bomber, a DH 9C, which carried three passengers. If Antony wanted the pilot's job, this was presumably the plane that he would have to fly and, taking his life in his hands, he persuaded Clarence to take him up with him and let him try it.

Amazingly, he did not find it at all difficult. He even landed it smoothly, without the alert emergency fire engines and ambulances having to start their engines. It occurred to him while he was flying that this was an ideal machine to use for his parachute-jumping ambition, should he ever get that far.

Luckily the flying lessons did not discourage Clarence from his intention to employ a pilot. 'I don't want to bother parking the plane and refuelling it and all that rot when I'm out with my mates,' he said simply.

'Thank God for that,' Antony breathed.

But he could not disregard the men that came to Clarence with far better credentials than he had himself. Hours of flying experience and seasoned mechanics as well – Clarence was kind to all and encouraged a few of them, Antony could not help noticing, by writing down their names and addresses in his little notebook. He said he had friends coming over in June, and by then wanted to have a pilot employed, but until then he was not in a hurry.

'My good friend Mart is arriving next week, and I'm arranging to have him put up at Birch Hall with me.' Birch Hall was the plush hotel that he had made his home, a far cry from number six Victory Place where Antony had a fine view of a gasometer and a railway shunting yard.

Mart wanted to buy a plane and was another rich young American, full of enthusiasm. To Antony's astonishment it transpired that he was crazy about parachute jumping, now apparently all the rage in America, coupled with wing-walking (which Antony had no wish at all to experience).

'You heard of Slim Lindbergh over here? Charles Lindbergh? He did pitches all over, wing-walking and parachute jumping – couldn't actually fly. Couldn't afford to learn. He just hung out being dogsbody for a rich owner and getting a pittance for the circus act – until his father got a bank loan to buy an old army plane. That gave him the idea of enrolling in the army as a flying cadet, so he got to be a pilot, and then he was in a collision with another plane and he had to jump for real . . .'

Antony lapped up this thrilling conversation, hanging on Mart's every word. Mart was older than Clarence, but every bit as friendly. He had been happy to include Antony for a drink in the bar, but now Antony had to bite back his enthusiasm when the talk came to parachuting, not to butt in, for it was not his place. Clarence was obviously not very interested in Slim Lindbergh's exploits and the conversation veered elsewhere, but all Antony's old enthusiasms surfaced again, and he wondered if here was his chance to experience it for himself, if Mart was going to buy a plane and learn to fly . . .

Fortunately Mart was in no hurry to leave Brooklands and as the winter turned into spring and summer beckoned, Antony got the opportunity to discuss parachuting with him.

'You've actually jumped?' he finally asked the American one evening.

'No, I haven't, only watched. It takes more guts than I think I've got.'

'I took a girl up, and she jumped. But I haven't.'

'*What?*' Mart was obviously stupefied.

Antony was surprised at his reaction. It had only been a bit of fun, after all. Had Lily been terrified? He had not got that impression; she did it because he asked her to. She always did what he wanted.

'What girl was this? Is she famous – does she do it for exhibitions?'

'No. She's just a maid-of-all-work at home. I wanted to try it but there was no one to fly the plane if I did it, so I asked her, and she did it.'

'What, just like that?'

'Well, we went off very early so that no one would see. We didn't want to get into trouble. I asked my friends but none of them would, but Lily – she said yes.'

'Some gal!'

'She said it was lovely and she'd like to do it again. It didn't bother her.'

'Gee, I'd like to meet this gal! Where does she hang out?'

Antony found the conversation now getting out of his control. He could not conceive of Lily coming here and meeting

Mart. He had not really given Lily a thought since he had left Lockwood on Tom's bicycle.

'Not far away, near my old home. But she's only a maid. Very young, just a kid really.'

'Well, I could buy her a teacake surely? You don't get many maids with those sort of guts.'

Antony tried to envisage Mart driving to Lily's old cottage and inviting her out for a teacake, and failed. 'I could bring her over some time, perhaps.'

'Yeah, kiddo, you do that! If she wants another go, I bet we could go up in Clarence's crate. I might even get up the courage to try it myself.'

'I want to do it!' Antony couldn't help himself. 'I've always wanted to do it, but there was no one to take me. I only took Lily because I wanted to try it out myself, a sort of practice. I bought myself a parachute and obviously it worked a treat. It's still at home, doing nothing. It could do with an airing!'

'Are you serious?'

'Yes, very. I want to do it so badly.' Antony couldn't hide his enthusiasm.

But he had found a fellow enthusiast in Mart.

'We'll get Clarence to fly us in his crate then! We'll all have a go – not all at once, of course. But you get your chute ready, and I really want to meet this girl – hey, it'll be a real whizz!'

Antony saw enormous complications but Mart brushed them aside. Getting Mart to meet Lily without anyone in the village seeing him, avoiding Gabriel, Mrs Goldbeater . . .

'We'll motor over to your old home and collect your chute

228

and you can take me to meet this girl. I really want to know her. You say when—'

'I could fly home and bring her back.'

'No, we'll drive over in Clarence's motor! We've got nothing to do all day until I find myself a plane and sign on for a few lessons. I'm still waiting for the weather to warm up a bit, I'm not in a hurry.'

It was out of Antony's control. Thrilled as he was to see his opportunity of doing a jump, the social difficulties of introducing Mart and Clarence to Lily and taking her for a teacake rather took precedence. For all he knew she might have left the cottage by now if the authorities had kicked them out . . . and what of his pictures?

She had no idea where he was now, he realized. He hadn't ordered things very well, as usual. Events overcame him, it seemed, before he had thought out how to deal with them. But the chance of someone taking him up to do a jump . . . it was really unexpected and a chance that he couldn't let slip through his fingers.

It was true that the weather was not yet warm enough to make flying a pleasure, but with the arrival of spring the trees around Brooklands had begun bursting with leaf and blossom, the cuckoo was calling and the first housemartins were building nests under the eaves of the work sheds. For once Antony felt a stir of optimism. Without the friendship of the two Americans he guessed he would have given up by now.

But where to go if he could not get a toehold in the flying industry? He was still loading all his hopes onto getting the job with Clarence, which seemed very likely as the friendship developed. He knew he was counting on it now, in fact, and knew already that his flying expertise had impressed Clarence.

So going off on a glorious spring day with his two eccentric friends to seek out Lily was not altogether a looming disaster: it was up to them what they made of her. For himself, realizing how he had neglected her since their last meeting and how much she professed to love him, he began to feel slight qualms as they approached his home village. Sitting in the cramped dickie seat behind the two Americans, he bent down to retie his shoelaces as the car came to the village, not wanting anyone to see him.

'Left here!' he shouted, and Clarence turned onto the farm track that led down to the lake. Straightening up, Antony felt a most unexpected blast of homesickness overcome him as the old familiar scene met his eyes: he nearly cried out, and felt his eyes fill with tears. This is where he had been, if unloved, utterly carefree and content, larking with his friends, swimming in the lake, whizzing down the mowed grass in his little plane, wanting for nothing. 'Dad, I want . . .' And the money came, no questions asked. What a life!

Hurriedly he snuffled himself together, wiped his face with a grubby handkerchief, and said, 'The last cottage, mind the dog—'

For Ludo lay outside, basking in the sun, and Squashy was plodging on the edge of the lake with the eternal fishing net. He came running up when he saw the car, and as Clarence braked to a standstill Squashy screamed, 'Antony! Antony!'

and threw himself at the car, beating on the side with his fists.

'Hey, pack it in!' Clarence shouted, and caught him a cuff round the ear.

Squashy screamed blue murder and Lily came running out of the house. She saw Antony and screamed as loudly as Squashy, and Antony, climbing hurriedly out of the car, nearly fell over backwards as she flung herself at him.

'Antony! Antony! Oh, at last! Where have you been? So long – where—?' She was completely overcome by sobs, burying her face in Antony's chest. From behind he could feel Squashy kicking him and shouting, 'Pig! Pig! Pig!'

'Oh, for heaven's sake!' He put his arms round Lily and hugged her and mumbled some sort of comfort, and then Ludo was jumping up and licking his face. He wanted to die.

Clarence and Mart stood watching with some embarrassment, and then amusement as the dog joined in.

'You're very popular round here, mate,' Mart said.

'It's my home.'

He managed to disengage himself from Lily who, after her first shock, started to pull herself together. Through the tears her amazing blue eyes were still on fire with adoration, but she backed off, taking in his companions and the impressive car. Antony could not believe she had kept on loving him unseen for so long all through the winter months, when he himself had pretty much forgotten all about her. It threw him, and he found it difficult to make the required introductions.

'This is Lily—' Christ, he didn't even know her surname!

Was Gabriel the Christian name of her father or his surname? He had no idea. 'The one who parachuted with me.'

'Jesus!'

Clarence and Mart stared with unfeigned admiration. It was a fact that Lily was still a skinny thing, but she had a presence out of all proportion to her size. Straightening up, wiping away her tears and tossing back the great mane of her golden hair, she did in fact look as if she could well jump out into the sky with complete lack of concern, and probably wing-walk as well if asked.

'These are my friends, Lily – Clarence and Mart. They come from America. I met them at Brooklands. They are very interested in your parachute jump. They can't believe a girl could do such a thing.'

'Well, I did,' she mumbled. 'You can tell them.'

'Yes, I did, and they were very impressed. They want to talk to you. Is your father in, or can we come in for a cup of tea and have a chat?'

'Yes, if you like. It's not very tidy.'

She was recovering, slowly. She shook hands with Clarence and Mart, and led the way into the cottage. Antony realized that she had grown quite a lot since he had seen her last, and was now on her way to being tall. And skinny was now the wrong word for her – she was slender, willowy perhaps, having lost her gawky childishness and gained the beginnings of a bosom. She moved with an easy, athletic grace. She was no longer a child.

Antony was unprepared for the impact of Helena's

gorgeous pictures which still crowded the walls of the cramped living room, so totally out of place and yet so glorious. He had forgotten how crazy they appeared in such a setting, and he heard the two Americans' shocked intake of breath as they shook their heads to make sure their eyes were not deceiving them.

'Jesus, Ant, are these for real?'

'Yes, they're mine – at least, my father's. We hid them here for the time being.'

'They can't be safe here, surely? The door open, anyone could see—'

'No one comes down here much, only the neighbours, and no one comes in the house. Gabriel keeps himself very much to himself – that's the kids' father. Where is he, Lily? Is he likely to come in soon?'

'No, not till dusk.'

'God in heaven, what treasures! A Van Gogh, surely? And this portrait – is it a Rubens?'

'Yes. They're real. But I can't sell them, not with their belonging to the government now – now that all my father's things have been taken. I suppose I've stolen them actually, although I don't think of it like that. What can I do?'

'We'll have to think of a way to help you. There are plenty of people back home who would give them a home, no questions asked, believe me.'

'Well, they're safe here for the time being.' Antony did not want the business of the day to be side-tracked by the paintings. He turned to Lily. 'Do you know where my chute is now? I got it repacked after you jumped. And left it somewhere.'

'It's in the garage with the Rolls-Royce. In the Rolls, I think. To keep the mice off.'

Antony was not keen to go anywhere near the garage since he had stolen Tom's bicycle, Tom's cottage being so close, and he wondered how he could manoeuvre Lily into fetching it for him. But Clarence and Mart were already questioning her about her jump and she was starting to relive that amazing day in her dull life, all her animation returning, the tears dried, the old laughter ringing out. Antony had forgotten how gorgeous she was, and all the fun days with her and the boys flooded back as he watched her. He had taken it all for granted in those days – how things had changed!

It was obvious that Clarence and Mart were now set on taking Lily up and getting into parachuting. Antony watched Lily blossom with excitement.

'And Antony too – he could come up and we could jump together! He wanted to do it so badly, didn't you, Antony? You took me up as a sort of practice, to see if I might get killed, didn't you? It was so wonderful – you must come too this time!'

'To see if he might get killed?' The two Americans were laughing.

'Well,' said Mart, 'if we get this chute of yours, Ant, there's no reason why the two of you shouldn't make a jump together. There's room in Clarence's crate – if he flies it and I come to push you out. It takes four. And then if you two survive I reckon I could have a go myself – I really love the idea. If you heard how Lindbergh described it, and now Lily too . . . to overcome the fear, and then such an experience – it's mind-blowing. I want to do this thing.'

'Us first, me and Antony!' shouted Lily.

'What a gal!' shouted Clarence.

The unlikely meeting was proving hilarious, but Antony was anxious to be away before Gabriel came back, for he was uncomfortably aware that what he was getting Lily into was not really in Lily's best interests. He told himself that she needed some fun in her life, that he would be doing her a good turn, but at heart he was worried. Come to that, for all his talk, he was worried about his own part in it: was he going to be brave enough when it came to the point of no return? Even reclaiming his chute . . . a great uneasiness was beginning to spoil his day.

'We must go, before your father gets back, Lily. We don't want to get you into trouble.'

'We'll take the motor and collect the chute, eh?'

'Can I come too?' Lily was loath to let Antony out of her sight.

'And me! And me!' Squashy shouted.

'There's not enough room!'

'There is! There is!'

They made room, even for Barky, tumbled over each other in the cramped dickie seat, and Antony found himself with Lily in his lap, her cheek against his. He could not believe he had forgotten her all this time.

'I've never stopped thinking about you, Antony, every day. I could not believe you would not come back, even if only for the pictures.'

'Oh, I'm so sorry, Lily. I'm a rat. Nothing has gone right for me. I can't get a job. I had to escape Aunt Maud—'

'She came back here, looking for you. She was terribly angry and wouldn't believe we hadn't seen you. But in the end she went off to see Mrs Goldbeater, and she wanted to take Ludo home with her, but Squashy started to scream, you know how he is—'

'I screamed,' Squashy put in. 'I really screamed and she went all purple. I kicked her.'

Antony groaned. He seemed to bring out the worst in people.

Lily directed Clarence into the front drive of Lockwood Hall, avoiding the chain across the entrance and using the track the farm took to get onto the road. They came up to the garage and Antony shrank down in his seat, whispering to Lily, 'I mustn't meet Tom, whatever happens. I've stolen his bicycle.'

Lily relapsed into peals of laughter. 'I'll go and get it. You are a coward, Antony! Tom's a darling.'

'Not to me he isn't.'

They all piled out except Antony, and the two Americans took some time admiring the Rolls-Royce. Fortunately Tom did not seem to be around and the chute was retrieved and stuffed back into the car.

'We can walk back from here, me and Squashy and Barky,' Lily said. 'But promise—'

236

'We promise! We'll be back for you in two shakes, darling, to take you skyjumping, and your boyfriend here too.'

Lily giggled. As Antony arranged himself more comfortably in the back seat she turned to him and whispered, 'Goodbye, boyfriend.' The old childish love for him shone shamelessly out of her eyes.

'Idiot!'

But she only laughed.

They drove back to Brooklands, the two Americans exclaiming all the way about the marvels of Lily, and Antony silent and deeply disturbed about what he had set in motion. Did nothing ever run smoothly for him? He was excited (and terrified) about making the jump, but even more disturbed by what the repercussions might be for Lily. He had never asked her whether they were thriving, or starving, or what poor Gabriel was doing working until dusk, or whether Lily herself had a job. He had seen for himself how Squashy was growing from a rather cute brainless little boy into a far from cute lout, probably unable to hold down a job, poor Lily's responsibility. The cottage (apart from the pictures) was as threadbare as it had ever been.

But it wasn't his business, he supposed.

Back at Brooklands he felt that with summer approaching he must soon find himself a job here. Surely his friendship with Clarence would count for something when it came to the pilot's job. But, as always, when they parked the car, there were the usual hangers-on waiting to talk to the two rich Americans. Envious glances came Antony's way as he disentangled himself from the dickie seat with the parachute in his arms.

One man, Antony noticed, was becoming familiar, a hardened ex-serviceman called Rob. He nodded to Antony and, eyebrows raised, asked, 'You used that thing?'

'Not yet.'

'Hi, Rob.' Clarence greeted him pleasantly. 'Shall we have a drink?'

They wandered off together and Mart said to Antony, 'Let's go and see where we can hire another of these things.'

Much as he wanted to enquire about parachutes, Antony would far rather have been invited for a drink with Clarence.

APRIL, 1923

23

Lily could scarcely believe Antony had come back to her. She had had no idea where he was and had answered the dread Aunt Maud quite truthfully when she said she did not know. Knowing that he wasn't at Tom's, she had always assumed that he had gone back to London with the dread Aunt Maud and felt sorry for him. And now it seemed he had been enjoying himself quite near at hand – he had managed to get something at Brooklands, after all – but had never bothered to come and see her.

So nothing was any different. She wished now that he had stayed away. Seeing him again reawakened all the crazy passions she thought she had put behind her. He had always been a dream, of course, the unattainable, but there was nothing else in her life to dream about. All the fun had gone with the boys departing. The village boys who made advances got very short shrift and only Cedric was received with any grace. Lily did not have a good reputation in the village, her lack of respect, quick temper and unladylike ways causing her to lose jobs in spite of her acknowledged capability. She was strong, able and intelligent but hard to get on with. Wild, they called her.

But in spite of her shortcomings there was sympathy for the small beleaguered family now that the threat of eviction hung over them. The row of workers' cottages were part of the estate commandeered by the government, due at some point to be put up for sale. Lily herself did not dare consider what might lie ahead if they lost the only home they had ever known.

Antony had never thought to enquire, she realized, how things were with them. He seemed to have some smart rich friends, but he did not boast of any achievements in the flying world, or even of having a job. The parachute jumping was what had brought him to see her, but only to get his parachute back. She could not deny that the prospect of doing another jump, and with Antony too from what she gathered, was wonderful, but hedged around with difficulties: to keep the intention from her father, to escape for a day without Squashy, even to come back safely. How to get there for a start.

She tried to push it out of her mind.

But the following morning there was a visit from Mrs Goldbeater. It was a beautiful morning and the door of the cottage was open, and the woman was standing there before Lily had any warning.

'Hullo, my dear, can I have a word?'

Lily could see that she had already seen the pictures, for her jaw was dropping immediately after her words were uttered. With a strong sense of foreboding, she invited the woman in.

No use apologizing for the untidiness, the dust, the sewing scattered around, the empty porridge plates on the table . . . what was the point?

'My word, these are Sylvester's pictures, surely?'

'Antony left them here.'

'How extraordinary! But of course, they are not his any longer – how can the boy think . . . Oh dear . . .' Her voice trailed away. Then, rallying: 'It's Antony I've come to see you about actually. I believe he was here in the village yesterday?'

How did this gossip come her way? Who saw him?

'He came to see me.'

'You must know that Miss Sylvester, his aunt, is very anxious to trace him. I know you said you had no idea where he was, but now you must know. It is really important that she is able to find him. There is so much unfinished business to tie up. The authorities are very keen to interview him and it is no good his running away from that. He is still a minor and in Miss Sylvester's charge. She is his only next of kin. Antony is such a silly boy to think he can just wash his hands of all that has happened. And these pictures stored in your cottage – it is truly ridiculous! The boy has no sense of responsibility whatsoever . . .'

The poor woman had such a lot of indignation to express that Lily stopped listening. She knew that Mrs Goldbeater had a good heart, and if Antony had stayed with her a bit longer no doubt she and her husband would have helped him get himself sorted out. But the shadow of the evil Aunt Maud would not have gone away.

'Now tell me, Lily, where is he? Did he leave you an address?'

Lily thought hard, and remembered how Antony had abandoned her and only come back to her because he wanted his parachute. The more she thought about his neglect of her, without sending a word, the more hurtful it was. And even now he had only come back because those two American loonies had wanted to see her.

'He's working at Brooklands.'

The words slipped out, and as soon as she had uttered them she guessed she had made a mistake. But even then she felt justified. After all, he had his American friends to support him now. Aunt Maud was surely no longer a threat and she did not know his address after all.

'Well, that's something. I can pass that information on to Miss Sylvester. She can look into it. Thank goodness for that. We can't help being a bit worried about Antony, you see – what happened here was so dreadful. The boy has never known a real family life – he is quite rudderless and has no concept of responsibility. He is really not fit to be out in the world on his own, poor lad. We would help him if he would allow us.'

Being looked after by the Goldbeaters would be far nicer than by Aunt Maud, Lily thought, so perhaps there were possibilities there. Antony could live with them and still work at Brooklands and then she would still see him.

But how Mrs Goldbeater did go on! Not really unlike Aunt Maud. Then, as she turned to go, she hesitated and said, 'And you, Lily, are things all right for you? Your father, oh dear, he shouldn't be working on the roads at his age, and he such a competent gardener. He was too proud to come asking for work – you know, I am sure he could have got gardening work if he had asked around. Would you like me to try and find something for him in the village, if I can?'

Yes, she jolly well would like, but she did not want to be beholden to Mrs Goldbeater, and her father would think she had been asking favours on his behalf.

'I don't know. He will think I asked.'

'Oh, I'm sure we can get round that. I will see what I can do. You've so much on your plate with Squashy and your old dad as well, such a burden for a young girl.'

She meant well and Lily tried to look grateful, but was glad to see the back of her as she went off home. Guilt nagged her now about having told her that Antony was working at Brooklands, but at least the information was vague and perhaps not all that useful. Or so she told herself. Aunt Maud would make a bizarre figure amongst the hard-bitten hangers-on at Brooklands and she might not want to risk making a fool of herself poking around the workshops. Or so Lily hoped.

The only good thing to dwell on was the thought of making another parachute jump. The idea of going up in an aeroplane again and making a jump with Antony was so blissful that even to think of it brought a great smile to her face.

She started to sing as she got out the broom and set to work on the chaotic mess that was her home.

MAY, 1923

Antony woke up with a hangover and lay in bed for some time, not inspired to leap out of bed and face a new day. The night before Clarence had invited him to a meal at his elegant hotel and there had been a long discussion about making the parachute jump. Antony's parachute was repacked, and Mart had bought another one for Lily to use. Mart was there, full of enthusiasm, and also the out-of-work pilot Rob, with whom Clarence now seemed to be very friendly.

Antony could see – it was quite plain – that Rob was sucking up to Clarence in the hope of getting the job that Antony so badly hankered after. Antony thought him an oik, not in the same league as himself, but he certainly could talk with great expertise about maintaining the plane as well as flying it, which Antony knew he could not. Several other hopefuls were always trying to muscle in on the hope of getting this plum job and Clarence had mostly dismissed them, but he seemed to like Rob. Rob was a good bit older than Clarence, having been in the RFC during the war, and seemed something of a father figure to the ebullient American. He was a man of few words, but a certain authority seemed to emanate from his lanky frame which Antony could see impressed Clarence. The more Antony saw of them together the more he saw his bright prospects slipping away.

He was also getting very short of money and already owed his landlady a month's rent. Having taken Helena's jewellery up to London he discovered that the experts required more than his assurance that 'his grandmother had left them to him in her will'. They wanted provenance, surety, and were not impressed by his now rather shabby clothes and air of desperation. He guessed they thought he had stolen them.

'Perhaps a letter from your lawyer?' Or a request to see the will in question, or a meeting with his parents, perhaps? Nothing that he could comply with. He sold a few pieces to rather shadier persons on downbeat premises and still hadn't enough to see him through to the end of the month. Perhaps Clarence and Mart would buy the Van Gogh, no questions asked? But he did not dare venture the idea.

Jumping out with the parachute – once his dearest wish – now that it was near to being realized was turning out to be merely a most terrifying obstacle in the path of his disintegrating life. He was no longer in the mood to enjoy it. Once, with the wild Lily, it had all been terrific fun: he would never forget her overflowing delight, her euphoria, her amazing blue eyes flashing with pride and love – yes, love for him which had always engulfed him in her presence. What had happened, what had he done to her, to discard such innocent delight? Lying in bed with the rain pattering on the window, he felt so wretched that he wanted to die. If the parachute failed to open, he would be happy at last. Perhaps a good idea. That is, if he even found the courage to jump. He wasn't even sure about that.

But the idea was going ahead with his gung-ho friends. He had set it in motion, and he could not stop the wheels turning now even if he wanted to. Mart was desperate to see his dreams put into practice, eager to have a go himself once he had tested it out with his friends – at least, that's how Antony perceived it. Also thrilled to have discovered a *girl*, for heaven's sake, who had the guts to do such a thing.

'This Brooklands is just a fantastic place, my old bean,' he exclaimed to Clarence over dinner, having downed most of a bottle of Clarence's champagne. 'How great that I caught up with you! And I shall soon get my ticket – my instructor is very encouraging – and then I can get my own crate and we can try this chute jumping lark ourselves.

Alcohol sparked the conversation and even the reserved Rob had been induced to relate some of his flying adventures, which Antony saw raised him even higher in Clarence's esteem. No wonder Antony today had no inclination to get out of bed. Rather snuggle deep down and forget.

By the end of the month the weather was set fair and the parachute escapade was set in motion with no hope of back-tracking. Antony had no hand in the arrangements: the two Americans were in charge, choosing the date, weather permitting, the arrangements to collect Lily, the most convenient whereabouts to make the jump and how best to make the aeroplane easy to jump out of. (Wrenching the door off seemed to be the easiest solution.)

Antony had a say in where to do the deed: over the same small airfield in Wiltshire where he had taken Lily, where no questions were asked and there was no one to see what went on save a few distant farmers. There was no inclination to do it over Brooklands, even should they get permission, for they knew they were considered idiot amateurs by most of the fraternity they mingled with and a crowd would gather more to laugh than to applaud.

Clarence was worried about actually flying the plane, and even considered asking Rob to fly it, but as there was only room in the plane for four of them that meant he would have to stay behind. Mart was determined to go. It was 'his baby', he said, and the two jumpers would need all his help to time the jump properly 'and push 'em out if need be'. He grinned widely. 'We want them to land in the right place, not out in the bushes somewhere. Then we can go down and join 'em. I'll supply the champagne!'

Antony wanted to join in the happy anticipation of the two Americans – after all, it had always been his dearest dream to do a jump. But that had been in his carefree days and now the jump seemed more threatening than alluring. His mind-set had changed, and his once happy-go-lucky future had turned into a bleak and depressing prospect.

The weather was set fair. Clarence arranged to collect Lily very early in the morning, when she could steal out of the house unseen, and Antony was commanded to report to the airfield to coincide with her arrival.

'We'll be off before anyone comes nosing around,' said Mart. 'No questions asked. Gee, I can't wait for this! Then we'll do it too, Clarence, eh? Are you game?'

Clarence obviously wasn't but smiled politely.

'Yeah. All systems go.'

JUNE, 1923

24

On the morning of the jump Antony was awoken at dawn by his alarm clock and saw that there was to be no reprieve: the dawn was perfect, the faintest mist proclaiming heat later softening the grey fame of the gasometer beyond the factory walls. He got dressed and left the house without bothering to eat or drink, and pedalled off for Brooklands trying to work out in his confused mind whether he was excited or scared, happy or depressed.

Perhaps today would sort things out a bit, lead to some decision-making on his part: he could not carry on without any promise of his life improving. But he still had no idea of what he could do. Forget it, he decided, and try to concentrate on the jump.

Now the moment was approaching he realized he was terrified. He remembered how he had bullied Lily into doing it, and she had never complained. What a girl! Thinking of Lily he was then bedevilled by guilt at how he had treated her. How she had thrown herself at him . . . that she still loved him . . . ! His thoughts were disintegrating so fast that he forced himself to think only of the jump. Bowling along through the summertime woods full of birdsong there were only good things to think of, surely? Soon he would be swinging through the sky, the whole world at his feet, fulfilling his most ardent wish ever since he had discovered flying.

There were very few people about on the airfield, it was so early. He had even beaten the two Americans to it, and had to wait, biting his nails nervously, until their impressive Bentley hove into view. It pulled up beside him and Mart jumped out.

'Clarence is going off to collect your girlfriend. Rob's coming over to see us off. He knows quite a bit about parachutes, wants to see you're fitted up properly. He doesn't trust us, you know – thinks we're a load of tyros. Which we are, of course. Wishes he was doing the flying himself.'

Clarence waved cheerfully and drove off. Knowing Clarence's skills, or lack of, Antony rather wished Rob's wishes could be fulfilled, but put the thought out of his head. The less he saw of Rob the better. It wouldn't take Clarence long to pick up Lily, as she had promised to be waiting on the road.

Antony and Mart wandered over to Clarence's plane, Mart exclaiming about the pleasures of life, the amazing breakfast they had been served at the crack of dawn at this swell hotel Clarence was living in.

'Funny thing, last night an old bag checked in, same name as yours, a Miss Sylvester. You know her? Terrible old boot.'

Antony remembered his father shooting the detective inspector and felt exactly as the detective inspector must have felt the moment the bullet hit him between the eyes.

'Oh Christ! Not her!' He almost staggered in his stride, made a choking gargle of horror.

Mart looked at him in surprise. 'Hey, are you OK? Something I said?'

'Miss Sylvester – my aunt.'

'Oh, bad luck. I see. Jeez, poor you.'

'Did you say . . . you know me? That I'm here?'

'No, old bean. She tried to engage us in conversation but I'm afraid we were rather rude. We certainly didn't tell her you were our best friend and we saw you every day.'

'Thank God for that! She mustn't find me.'

'Well, you'll be up and flying soon, away with the fairies. And we're landing in Wiltshire somewhere, aren't we? So she's not going to find you today, at least.'

'No, nor ever. I can't come back while she's around.'

'We'll fend her off – she's not going to interfere with our fun today.'

But the day's fun for Antony was no longer in his mind. He could not believe in his bad luck at being discovered by Aunt Maud. Never, never was he going back to her. He found it impossible to respond to Mart's chatter and then presumed that Mart thought the nerves were getting to him, but the nerves concerning the jump had been entirely banished by the hell of Aunt Maud's reappearance. Fortunately they did not have long to wait before Clarence came back with Lily at his side.

She jumped out and flung herself on Antony just as she

had the last time. 'Oh, Antony, isn't it marvellous! We can do it together – you can do it at last, just as you always dreamed!'

She was positively dancing with joy, glowing with excitement. Antony recalled unexpectedly the look on his sister's face before she drowned, the same unearthly beauty sparked by unimaginable inner emotions, and felt he saw it in Lily as she pranced before him. He had never seen her so lovely, his dear little flower exploded into full bloom. He thought he was going mad.

But he could see that the two Americans, laughing, were captivated by this eager spirit.

While they were all standing round exclaiming and laughing they were interrupted by the familiar roar of Rob's cranky motorbike. The professional had arrived to add the necessary air of seriousness to the expedition. He obviously found them wanting in all departments.

'This isn't just a laugh, you know. Lives depend on getting it right. First, you know where you're going, Clarence? You've got to be spot on target for the jump, so they land in a safe place, not on top of a town hall or in a sewage works.'

'Yeah, Ant knows the way. He told me. Follow the Portsmouth Road, and veer off after the Hog's Back and make for Basingstoke. Then – he can tell me as we go along.'

'You know it, Antony?'

'Yes. I can tell him.'

They then started to discuss height, tactics, procedure. Antony had to forget Aunt Maud, concentrate on getting the parachute right, the safe way to jump, many things he had never thought to explore the day he had so blithely taken Lily up and told her to go. Rob was a severe teacher and Antony knew that he wished he were taking Clarence's place as their pilot – he gave him the impression that he hadn't a great deal of faith in Clarence's skills, but without saying anything clearly to dent their confidence.

Antony began to wish again that Rob was indeed going to be the pilot, then realized with another ghastly blow to his hopes that it was obvious that Rob was going to get the job he himself so dearly desired. Good friend as he was to Clarence, he could never compete with this man's sheer competence. By the time he was safely embraced by his parachute, bundled on board, snuggled in the cramped space almost into the giggling Lily's lap, he knew that his future was in complete ruins, and when he landed in Wiltshire he would have nowhere to go, no hope of a job, no money, not even a roof over his head.

So much for his day of delight: the longed-for day of his first parachute jump.

Rob shouted his last instructions, the engine roared into life and Clarence started taxiing down the airfield. The noise of the engine now made talking very difficult, but as they took off and made height Antony had to look out of the doorway and concentrate on the roads below, to direct Clarence. Looking out of the doorway made him feel ill, and the thought of shortly launching himself out of it made him feel iller still. What should have been a glorious red-letter day in his life had turned to dust and ashes before it had even started. Thank God the little aeroplane was putting the miles between him and Aunt Maud: he would certainly not be making the return journey. With luck, his parachute wouldn't open, and he would have no more to worry about.

Beside him he could feel Lily almost vibrating with excitement. 'It is so lovely, Antony! You will be so thrilled!' she shouted in his ear. 'I can't believe I am doing this with you!'

The day below was still not awake, the roads empty, the fields gauzy in the early morning mist. The lush green of spring leaves and new grass spread like a great carpet beneath them, and in the sky above them a half moon still faintly hung, fading before thin wisps of harmless cloud. To be up there, like God, seemed an amazing privilege: he could not help thinking that, in spite of everything. Their little plane was an aberration with its stink of fuel, rattling through the silent dawn, and yet gave them this magical gift of seeing the world through completely new eyes. He could not be unaware of it, however confused his mind.

'Is that Basingstoke?' Clarence yelled over his shoulder.

'Yes! The course is something like two hundred and twenty from Basingstoke. You can see the Newbury road, then keep south of Newbury. Due west and you'll see the place.'

'Once we've picked it up we have to make height.'

'Lots!' shouted Lily. 'So it lasts longer, floating down. High, high as you can!'

Antony could feel himself beginning to sweat, in spite of the cold wind that came blasting in through the door. He was terrified now the moment was approaching. Clarence yelled that he could see what he thought was the airstrip. Antony verified it, and felt the plane start to make its first circle to gain height, Clarence not wanting to lose the place as it grew smaller below. Rob had decided on the best height for them and Clarence was watching his altimeter, sweating as badly as Antony with his anxiety to get it right. The morning was windless and they needed to jump directly above the small strip of grey asphalt. Mart stood poised to make the decision for the exact moment. Lily was to go first, and Antony the moment after, when Mart said he would give him a shove.

Not to hit Lily, to see her get clear and pull the ripcord, then he was to go. They had discussed it in detail and now there would be no excuse for making a mistake. Antony had heard unpleasant descriptions of what might go wrong. They still lingered uneasily in his brain. Why was he doing this thing? And when it was over, what then? Did he really want to come back to the hopeless mess that was his life? His brain churned wildly, as panic took over. He looked back, white-faced, at Mart.

Mart's eyes were narrowed, concentrating on the ground. 'Lily, ready to go?'

'Yes! Yes!' she screamed, and leaped in one movement into the doorway and away.

Antony could not believe this was happening.

He clung with both hands to either side of the doorway, the wind blasting him.

'Go! Go!' screamed Mart and gave him a great thump on the back.

He went.

Hurtling down, his brain went into manic overdrive. He did not want to land: to meet Aunt Maud, to become a beggar, a down-and-out like so many that haunted Brooklands, sleeping rough in the broken-down sheds, to face being the failure that he truly was. He was falling, frozen, sweating, hallucinating, perhaps screaming, he never knew.

He passed Lily, swinging blissfully beneath her great white canopy, so slowly he could not believe it. He could not believe what he was doing, or rather not doing: pulling the ripcord. He had it in his hand, but something in his scrambled mind held him back, seeking peace, seeking oblivion. The fading moon went round and round above him; the ground was quite clear now: he could see two little ants running, looking up, their faces like white daisies in the grass.

They were getting terrifyingly bigger.

He pulled the ripcord, but knew it was already too late.

So blessed peace it would be.

25

Lily landed what seemed to her a century after Antony, far away from the terrible scene she had witnessed. Scared witless, she made a bad landing and could not get to her feet, entangled in the billowing folds of the canopy. Her left ankle would not bear her weight and, once up, she fell. She could not free herself from her harness, her fingers not obeying her petrified brain. She could hear herself sobbing, swearing at the beastly, clutching parachute.

'Leave me! Leave me!' she screamed, and at last kicked herself free.

Pain seared up her leg, but she ran regardless. Long before she reached Antony the plane had come down and made a terrible, panicky landing, passing her on its way down the strip. She got a glimpse of Mart still standing in the doorway. He screamed something at her, but what it was she had no idea. Antony was still a mile away, it seemed, and she saw two other people running towards the spot. Clarence taxied the plane back to where the now-opened parachute lay sprawled uselessly on the grass and Lily was still running. Mart jumped out.

The pain in her ankle was so bad and the stitch in her side so crippling, that she had to come to a halt. She stood there sobbing, and after a few minutes saw Mart coming towards her. He held out his arms to her and she fell thankfully into his embrace, burying her face into his cold leather jacket, into the darkness. She never wanted to come out.

'There, there, Lily, hold up. Hold up, sweetheart, it's all right.'

'It isn't! It isn't!'

'He's still breathing.' He nearly added 'for now', but held it back. Then, 'What was he thinking of?' He picked Lily up bodily and, holding her like a baby, started to walk slowly back. Lily saw that he was walking towards the clubhouse, not towards Antony, and struggled violently to get down.

'I have to see him! I have to be with him. He needs me!'

'Lily, you don't want—'

'I do! I do! You must—'

He let her down, but held her as she staggered.

'There's nothing you can do. They've gone for a doctor, an ambulance.'

'I have to be with him!'

'All right. All right.'

He put his arm round her and held her up as she limped desperately towards the inert figure sprawled on the ground. Clarence was crouched beside it, and two or three gawpers, perhaps from the aero club or from the fields, working in the dawn.

'Cor blimey, 'e's a goner for sure,' Lily heard one of them say.

'Antony!' She dropped down beside him. She had braced herself for something terrible, but in fact, whatever his injuries might be, they were not obvious.

Blood was trickling from his mouth, his eyes were closed and his skin was blueish-white. He lay at a strange angle from the hips, but was so muffled up in flying clothes that it was hard to make out any details. It was plain that he was deeply unconscious, so anything she might say for comfort was not going to penetrate, but she said it all the same, muttering and sobbing, aware all the time that she was making a fool of herself.

The two Americans were now murmuring together: 'Whatever possessed him? Did he do it on purpose?'

'Perhaps he froze with fear.'

'Well, he was frightened, that was for sure. But surely—' Mart shrugged. 'I just don't get it.'

'It can't have been accidental. He must have meant it.'

'Then changed his mind at the last moment.'

'That's what it looks like. The chute was working OK. It was checked and double-checked.'

They stood looking helpless, and Lily started to pull herself together. She was the one who knew Antony best, after all, but could see the awful possibilities. Perhaps it might be best if he died.

'He's got no family,' she said to them. 'No one, save a terrible aunt.'

'Jesus, we met her! She booked in at our hotel last night. Miss Sylvester.'

'Did he know?'

'Yeah, we told him this morning.'

Lily was silent, stricken by the thought that she had told Mrs Goldbeater that Antony was at Brooklands. So of course Mrs Goldbeater had told Maud Sylvester. So it was her fault that Aunt Maud had discovered Antony. Is that why he didn't pull the ripcord? She found it hard to credit. Life was so beautiful.

But then she thought: he has no home. He has nobody. He has no job. He has no money. He has me. He will always have me. But what good am I? She lay beside him and cried. She watched for his breath, so faint. They all left her alone.

Eventually an ambulance came bouncing across the field and two men got out with a stretcher. With help from Clarence and Mart they bundled the broken body onto the stretcher and loaded it in the ambulance. Mart said he would go with him. They would not let Lily go. The ambulance men forbid her, saying there was no room. Only for one, which was Mart.

She was left with Clarence, to gather the chutes and fly home. They did not speak. Clarence, his thoughts in complete disarray, was trying to concentrate on his flying, trying to recall the way back to Brooklands, terrified of not finding it and having to make a forced landing somewhere. (Thank God, he thought, he had now enrolled Rob to do all his future flying for him: he was not a natural.) His concentration on the present luckily kept his mind off the truly terrible thing that had happened. It would overwhelm him later, hovering now in his consciousness, but seeing poor Lily safe, not to mention himself, was crucial. All the light had gone out of Lily, her vital shining life. She was like a crushed shell.

He found Brooklands, more by good luck than good navigation, but could not bear to land where he would face Rob and the other enthusiasts, not yet. He needed space. He taxied to a far corner of the airstrip, closer to where the car enthusiasts hung out, turned off the engine and handed Lily carefully out onto the ground. He put his arm round her, steered her to the motorists' clubhouse where there was no one around that he knew and ordered a taxi. While they were waiting he bought two brandies and more or less poured one down her unwilling throat.

'It will blank it out, make it better,' he said. 'Just a bit.'

'I want to be with him.'

'I will take you, whenever it suits. But not now. Now you have to go home.'

The taxi came and they drove back to Lily's home. The still, soft morning had blossomed into a perfect early summer's day, cloudless, without a breath of wind and when Lily came down the track to the lake she saw it spread before her in the sunshine just as in the days when she had larked there with the boys and Antony had mocked her declarations of love, when they none of them had a care for the future or a thought for anything but the laughing present.

A century ago. Even the brandy could not take the edge off this overwhelming feeling of loss, and she started to cry again.

She heard Clarence groan. He was not practised in consolation and was obviously wishing he had taken Mart's probably less exacting role.

'I'll be all right,' she sniffed. 'You can leave me now.'

'I'll just see you into your house. Will there be anyone there?'

'No. I don't want anyone.'

'We'll keep in touch, let you know—'

When he dies, Lily added to herself. They went into the empty cottage.

'Shall I make you a cup of tea? I will – it's what you take for shock. Sit here, rest that ankle. You really need to go to bed.'

At that Lily laughed. 'In the middle of the day?'

Laughing and crying: she supposed that was what life was all about. It hadn't been all roses, after all. But nothing as bad as this. Clarence sat on the table, waiting for the kettle to boil. It was going to take a long time; the fire was low. Lily put some wood on to hurry it up while Clarence's eyes rested on the amazing pictures scattered over the walls. A glorious thought came suddenly into his head.

'Will you sell me the Van Gogh?'

'It's Antony's.'

'You said he wants to sell them.'

'Yes, he does.'

'If I give you the money you can give it to him later.'

'If he dies—?'

'Then you can keep it.'

Lily thought her mind was too frazzled to make a sensible

262

decision. What did the picture matter to her any more? She had never particularly liked it. If he wanted it, it would go to a good home. It was true that Antony had shown little interest in the pictures, stashing them in their cottage just to suit himself.

'You can have it if you like.'

'I can give you all the money I have on me, for now. Then if – when – Antony gets better and wants a bit more we can talk about it. Would that suit you?'

'Yes, I think so.'

She wanted him to go, kind as he was. But he made her the tea, very strong, with about a week's worth of sugar in it, and she forced it down to please him, while he unhooked the picture from the wall. The taxi was waiting for him on the road.

'We'll let you know the news of Antony, don't worry. I'll find out what hospital they've taken him to, then if we go to visit we'll take you with us. We won't let you down. It was all our fault, going into this, after all. Here, take this for the picture. If you change your mind you've only to say. Otherwise I shall take it back to the States with me.' He groped in an inside pocket and brought out a roll of notes secured by a rubber band. 'I'll just keep one for the taxi. Here you are. Take it.' He pulled one note out for himself, and thrust the rest into Lily's hand. 'Go and rest now. He'll be all right. I'll come back to see you shortly.'

He picked up the painting again, tucked it under his arm and left the cottage.

Lily looked down at the roll of notes in her hand. There

were too many to count. They seemed to be in notes she had never seen before, with the figure fifty written on them. Later, when her father counted them, he said there was a thousand pounds there.

Enough to live on for ever!

APRIL, 1926

26

The Lockwood estate, including the house and the workers'
cottages was finally put up for sale nearly three years later. By
then the whole place had run wild, and the beautiful lawns
round the house had been cut by Mr Butterworth for hay
every summer. But there were no eager buyers, only a handful
of developers who soon realized that the cost of demolishing
the fortress-like house would far outweigh the profit from
building new. There was anxious talk of it being used for a
lunatic asylum or even a prison, but the affluent house-owners
in the surrounding area made a strong and successful stand
against that idea, and even a man who wanted to start a private boarding school soon saw that the architecture was not
given to inspiring youngsters, so dark and forbidding. But one
day a gang of demolition workers moved in with their impressive machinery and word came that the site was to be cleared,
and the workers in the cottages were given a year's notice to
quit. Nobody knew who had bought it.

With Clarence's roll of banknotes still sitting in a vase on top of the kitchen cupboard, Lily was not worried by the notice. She had been looking for a convenient cottage to buy ever since she had received the money, but there had been no hurry and she was loath to leave the only home she had ever known. Amazingly, Squashy got himself a job with the demolition firm, trundling stone and bricks in a wheelbarrow to the waiting lorries, the first time in his life that he had found anything so satisfying to his simple brain which he actually got paid for doing. Barky and Ludo followed and became the mascots of the workforce, getting fat on titbits from the men's bait at lunch time.

As for Antony . . .

'Far better that he had killed himself properly,' Simon said. 'Instead of only half killing himself.'

'No!'

'Well, I wouldn't want you to see him, that's for sure. I shan't take you, Lily, however much you scream and shout.'

Lily had begged and pleaded, to no avail. Antony had been in a London hospital for nearly three years now. Lily, who had never been to London in her life, had set off one day the previous year to visit him with one of Clarence's notes in her purse, got hopelessly lost as soon as she got off the train at Waterloo, asked for help, was manhandled, robbed of her money and only saved from being seriously assaulted by the fortuitous arrival of a bowler-hatted gentleman with a ferocious boxing talent. He had rescued her, comforted her, taken her back to Waterloo and put her on a train for home with a cheese sandwich and a couple of half-crowns. Gabriel, hearing the story, thrashed her, locked her up until he was tired of cooking his own meals and, when he let her out, forbade her ever to give another thought to the good-for-nothing Antony Sylvester, or else he would send her to live with his old aunt Enid in farthest Wales.

Lily, sobbing, had never heard of Aunt Enid – was he making her up? She knew he wouldn't do it. But her brief experience of London and its ways did not encourage her to try again, although she never gave up thinking of Antony: the habit was too deeply engrained.

Keeping friendly with the Goldbeaters was her only way of keeping in touch. Simon had followed a good honours degree from Oxford with further study at a university in London and could visit Antony without too much inconvenience. He only went when hounded by his mother, for hospital visiting was not on his list of pleasurable pursuits, in no way to be compared with driving fast cars, playing golf, drinking, gambling and visiting nightclubs. But he was able to report back.

Mrs Goldbeater relayed the news to Lily. 'Poor lad! I would go myself, Lily, sometimes, but that dreadful aunt of his is nearly always there, and I really cannot stand her. Of course, without her he would be doomed, wouldn't he? She pays for all his treatment, the very best of care. He'd be dead without her, abandoned with the paupers, Eton boy or no Eton boy. Mr Goldbeater has been in a few times, but it depresses him so, and he says the poor boy never really knows who is there or not.'

He would know me! Lily always thought fiercely. His face

would light up! When she said this to Simon, Simon said simply, 'Yes, Lily, I think it would.'

The two Americans, in spite of promises, had never taken her to see Antony, and only been to visit him themselves once or twice before packing up and going back to America. The escapade had shaken them badly and they felt, perhaps correctly, that they were under a cloud in Brooklands and that it would be much simpler to forget the whole thing back at home.

But the next time Lily saw Mrs Goldbeater she was told that Antony was being moved in May to a hospital in the country, a convalescent home near Richmond.

'He has made some progress at last. They think that in a year or two he might be able to go home.'

'He has no home.'

'He has his Aunt Maud. She is his home now.'

'I think he would rather die.'

'The instinct to live is very strong, Lily, even when faced with the likes of Aunt Maud. The point is, there is no alternative for him.'

'I would look after him!'

'Talk sense, Lily! He will need nursing all his life. And that is very expensive. But perhaps you could visit, now that he is closer. Simon can take you the next time he goes. I will arrange it. But bear in mind, Lily, he's probably not the Antony you used to know, not after all this long time.'

She spoke kindly, gently. She had visited Antony herself once, unfortunately at the same time as Aunt Maud, and the visit had been so painful she had no wish to repeat it. But Aunt Maud was paying the unending hospital bills without demur and would take her nephew home with her when the time came, so how could any of them criticize her?

'Do you ever hear from those American boys these days? They did visit Antony at first, didn't they?'

'Yes, they promised to collect me when they went again, but they never did. They said it would upset me.'

'They were probably right. They must have felt responsible too, although of course it wasn't their fault.'

'They gave me some money. They were very rich.'

Lily knew that now she was going to buy a cottage, the whole village would wonder where she had got the money from, so best to set the gossips at rest in good time. Mrs Goldbeater would spread the news. No need to say they had taken a picture.

'That was kind. We worry about how you are managing, Lily, now that your father is failing. If there's anything—'

'No, we're all right. Squashy's earning and I get plenty of jobs. We grow a lot of our own stuff and Mrs Butterworth sends things.'

'Ah, poor Mrs Butterworth, she's failing too these days, you know. Her husband is very worried about her. Of course, it's not been the same at the farm since Sylvester went. It's been very hard for them, Mrs Butterworth getting ill . . .'

She chuntered on and Lily excused herself, having extracted all she wanted and not bothered with village gossip. Simon might take her to visit Antony when he next came home: that was the news she wanted. She would make quite sure that this time he wouldn't be given a chance to opt out.

Of course he didn't want to take her. He didn't want to go at all, but was not without a sense of decency, given his public school upbringing.

'I'll take Melanie with me,' he said to his mother. 'Females don't mind hospital visiting.'

'You've got to take Lily. I promised her you would.'

'Oh, Ma, honestly! You know what she's like – she's so wild! She'll probably throw herself on him and cry and carry on—'

'Just this once, Simon. She's eighteen now, not a child any more. She'll behave herself, I'm sure. It's not asking too much. Then your duty is done.'

Simon knew when he was beaten. He hated seeing old Ant in the state he had come to, and had to try hard on his visits not to reveal the fantastic life he was living and arouse envy in poor Ant, which was almost impossible. What else was there to talk about now? He had considered, but never succumbed to the idea of taking Lily, but now his mother was adamant. If she was coming though, he doubted whether Melanie, his girlfriend now, would come too. Antony had always said he was going to marry Melanie – fat chance of that now. What an idiot he had been to half kill himself: the way he was now he would be better off dead. But he had rarely put his mind to doing anything properly, even committing suicide. Even the magical party in the grotto, he had only ordered things to be done, not done them himself. What a night that had been! Simon had to admit that without Antony the days of his youth at home would have been incredibly dull. Oh yes, and he had learned to fly . . . give him that much.

When he saw Lily again he was thrown by her appearance. Melanie Marsden was milk and water beside this tough, gorgeous eighteen-year-old with her wild, unbobbed golden hair and confident, fierce blue gaze. She was no longer the gangly kid, but a tall, slender and striking young woman and – to Simon's now adult, discerning eye – very sexually attractive. But he wasn't going down that road.

'I can come with you?' Not a plea, but a command.

He laughed. 'Yes. My ma insists I take you.'

Simon had been right; Melanie had decided not to come when she heard Lily was coming. So he drove Lily to the hospital, just the two of them, in his little sports car, enjoying showing it off to someone as admiring as Lily. Lily had scarcely slept since she knew that the date of the visit was planned and, now the time was so near, tried hard to keep herself calm and grown-up in Simon's presence. But the excitement was a fire bubbling inside her, very hard to contain.

'He's starting to walk again, Ma says,' Simon told her, 'so that's something.'

'It's been so long!'

'Lucky he survived. At least, I suppose so, although sometimes I wonder – when I first saw him I assumed he would die. Broken spine, pelvis, legs – just about everything – what a mess, you can't imagine! What an idiot!'

Lily made no reply. She found she was beginning to sweat with the anticipation of seeing Antony again after all this time, unable to imagine what he might look like, broken and ridden with pain for such a long period of time. Their childhood now seemed a century ago. Simon sensed from her pale silence what she was going through and took her arm kindly as they drew up outside the hospital door. Trees and lawns surrounded the place and there was a happy riot of birdsong ringing in their ears as they went up the steps and through the swing doors.

Lily had never been in a hospital before. She huddled against Simon as he enquired for Antony from a nurse, and he felt her shaking against him. He was terrified she was going to pass out.

'Steady on, Lily. It's not so awful. Pull yourself together! He doesn't want to see you all wobbly and daft. Show him the old Lily, for goodness sake – you're here to cheer him up!'

She tried. She followed the nurse down the long white corridor, up some stairs, along another corridor, and into a side ward with half a dozen beds in it, filled with afternoon sunlight from a large window across the end. She looked at the men in the beds and saw nobody she knew.

'Simon—!'

'Look, dafty, the end bed.' Simon's voice was soft and kind.

'No!'

She could not believe it was Antony, half sitting, half lying against high white pillows. The tumbled black hair was grey now at the sides, the bright face haggard, seamed with lines. He looked forty at least.

'Antony!' She could not help herself: she flung herself on

the bed and buried her face in the blankets over his chest.

He put his arms round her and hugged her. 'Lily, my darling Lily! After all this time! Where've you been? I've wanted you so!'

She was weeping again, although she had vowed not to. Simon was laughing, and then Antony started to laugh, and so she choked, and turned her tears into laughter. She lifted her head and looked into his eyes. He had never properly held her in his arms before – not that this time he had had any choice.

'Oh, Antony, I still love you so!'

'You're mad, Lily! After all this time? I'm just old rubbish now.'

'You were so stupid! So stupid!'

'Yes. Truly stupid, I agree.'

She pushed herself up, embarrassed now, aware that there was an audience from the other beds and a few jokes being thrown.

'I'm sorry! I'm sorry!'

'Gosh, Lily, you've really grown up since I saw you last! I wouldn't have known you if you hadn't flung yourself at me. Grown up, but not changed. Don't ever change, Lily! You're the best bit of what happened before. I lie here and think about it, nothing else to do.'

'It's all change now though,' Simon put in. 'They're knocking the old place down.'

'Yeah, I hear it's been sold.'

Lily was glad that the conversation had changed to

normality. Simon brought up two chairs and the two men started to talk while Lily just sat and stared at Antony, drinking him in. How changed he was! What had she expected? – she supposed the old laughing, teasing boy she remembered. She had no imagination, she knew. He laughed now at times, but winced with the pain of it. Was he ever going to get better? she asked him.

'I am better,' he said.

Three years . . . so slow!

'I walk a bit. Learning to run, to escape Aunt Maud.'

'Does she come?'

'Oh, she comes all right – passes the time for her, planning my life for me. Holding a job open for me with her solicitor friend, looking out for a nice gel who can look after me, with prospects of marriage. She'll buy a nice little house for me, just round the corner from her place so she can look in every day, make sure my wifey is looking after me properly – oh, the excitement! Making plans for the future, she says, gives me something to live for. You had nothing before, she tells me, idling around without ambition. Oh, what bliss it was, idling around – eh, Simon? We really enjoyed that. But of course, knowing what lies ahead for me now encourages me to get better, doesn't it? I can't wait. No more idling around. No more idling in bed. She said that to the sister and got her comeuppance there. It was really beautiful. Sister hates Aunt Maud as much as I do, which is quite saying something.'

'Crikey, Ant, you can't go along that road! My parents could help you better than Aunt Maud, you know that!'

'I've thought about it – nothing else to do but think about it. But it's the money, isn't it? Think about it, Simon. I'm going to be crock for ever. It takes money and that means Aunt Maud. I can't sell the pictures because technically I've stolen them from the government, which purloined all my father's estate, and I've nothing else. I need the old bag just to keep me – it's as simple as that. When I'm turned out of here, on crutches, not a penny to my name, not even the glimmer of a recommendation from the old school, where do you think I'm going to go? I don't stand a chance of getting a job without her twisting her poor friend's arm. Your parents wouldn't stand for it, of course they wouldn't – a week or two at most, out of kindness, but I'm someone's burden for ever. It's hard to believe, but I'm *lucky* to have Aunt Maud.'

There was no humour any longer in Antony's diatribe. Lily's heart turned over for him.

'I've got some money for you, Antony! I sold one of the pictures to Clarence. He gave me a thousand pounds and I've never spent it! It's still in a jam jar in the kitchen. You can have it. You can have it all.'

She quite dismissed the idea of the money being her life-line, to buy a new cottage, the comfort she had nursed ever since the accident. It quite flew out of the window, seeing Antony's anguish.

But he laughed and said, 'Please, it's yours, Lily. I wouldn't dream of taking it from you. Good old Clarence! Now you are going to be homeless you will need it, surely? You and your family.'

'Yes, but we can manage. We can rent a cheap place.'

'It's lovely for you, a fortune. But it wouldn't go far for me, honestly, can't you see? I wouldn't dream of taking it.'

'I'll buy a cottage and you can come and live with us! I will look after you.'

'You've already got Squashy and your old dad to support. Come off it, Lily, talk sense. Just imagine trying to talk Aunt Maud into the idea! Her whole life is now devoted to what she calls making a man of me. I can't deny her the pleasure.'

'She is so horrible!'

'Horrible and very rich.'

'Pity your old man didn't leave you well provided for before he made off. I bet he's still got plenty stashed away somewhere.'

'Said to be in Mexico. Who knows?'

'Who says?'

'The powers that be. I've had them in here, you know, asking questions. He'll never come back. They're still after him.'

'Yeah, they always will be. He's not only a murderer but a traitor and they don't like that. A hanging, for sure.'

'I think traitors are shot.'

'Oh, good. That's nicer than hanging.'

The two men continued their usual bantering conversation just as if no years lay between the present and the days of their schoolboy larks. Lily did not join in, merely feasting her eyes on the gaunt husk that had once been the love of her life. He had been so lovely, useless but lovely. She could not stop loving him in spite of the disappointment he had turned out to be. The stupid, stupid idiot to have done that to himself! But at least there was no whining, no self-pity. The sister whom they saw as they departed said he had been incredibly brave and never a word of complaint.

'Our star,' she said.

My star, Lily thought. The light was fading.

THE 1930s

AUGUST, 1931

27

Mrs Butterworth, said to be 'failing', lived on for another five years, and saw the new Lockwood Hall completed before she died. Like everyone else in the village she thought it an aberration – a white stucco boxlike structure, ultra-modern, with big windows and a flat roof.

The new owner, a wealthy young architect, was, unlike his building, much appreciated. He had no desire to evict the tenants of his inherited estate cottages, nor sell off the farm. Gabriel had been offered his job back, but was too infirm to accept it, crippled with arthritis. He now only pottered around his own garden, and Lily was unable to leave him for long. In his angry old age he was a hard task-master. Driven by the need to make money without leaving home, Lily had turned back to her old dressmaking skills and used some of the money out of the jam jar to buy a sewing machine. This burgeoning career was so far proving more successful than she could have hoped, the only light in her disappointing life. The great excitement of the Sylvester saga was now forgotten and the anxiety about the future of the estate was set at rest, so Mrs Butterworth's funeral was the only gossip-worthy event in the summer of Lily's twenty-fourth birthday.

Simon came home for it, prompted by his mother: 'You owe it to your old friends.'

He did not demur, attracted by the knowledge that Melanie Marsden would be at the funeral, not to mention the wild Lily. He now had a well-paid job with a firm of insurance brokers in the City. He lived in Chelsea and did not come home often.

Lily longed to see him. It was a hard to believe it was five years since he had taken her to see Antony in hospital and she had never seen Antony since. Mrs Goldbeater had told her that he was soon to leave the convalescent home in Richmond and go back to London, to Hampstead, to live with Aunt Maud, so then she knew she would never see him again. She had gone to the convalescent home once under her own steam, finding the journey very difficult, and when she had arrived had come face to face with Aunt Maud. Antony's bed was empty and Aunt Maud was sitting beside it, knitting.

She had glared at Lily and said bluntly, 'What are you doing here?'

Instead of saying, 'What do you think, you stupid old bag?' Lily had stammered that she had come to see Antony.

'You're not a relation. They only allow relations to visit. Didn't you know that?'

'Where is he?'

'He's undergoing some therapy or other. He won't be

back until tea time so there's no point your waiting, is there?'

'I've come a long way.'

'Nonsense. It's quite near.'

Aunt Maud had come by taxi – Lily had seen it waiting outside. The journey to Lily, however, completely unused to finding her way around the suburbs, had been difficult. Scarcely ever having left home, she realized that she was a complete country bumpkin, with no prospect of bettering herself until, if ever, her father died. Even then there would still be Squashy, a perennial worry now that he was discovering the blandishments of sex.

So she had left without seeing Antony, weeping all the way home.

The day of Mrs Butterworth's funeral was beautiful, the coffin taken to the church in the farm cart with the decorated horses just as Helena's had been, with family and friends walking behind. Lily walked with Cedric and his siblings, having helped at the farm during Mrs Butterworth's long illness, mostly with the cooking. The girls were married now and lived away. They had been grateful for Lily's input, glad that the burden hadn't fallen only on them.

'Gawd knows what the boys'll do now without their mum,' they said cheerfully.

Lily reckoned she already had two helpless men to care for without taking on any more burdens; she did not offer. Thank

God she had the dressmaking. She knew she had a flair for it and decided to exhibit her prowess at the funeral by wearing her own model in delphinium blue chiffon, outdoing even the ladies from the big houses who were all in black. She knew Mrs Butterworth would have laughed at the sight of her in black: 'You wear your brightest on the day, dear, I'll be lookin' down cheering you on.'

'Crikey, I didn't recognize you,' Simon said rudely. His eyes were roving for Melanie, who looked stunning in grey silk with a lilac hat and gloves.

But Lily knew she outdid her.

'I must admit you do look rather splendid,' he acknowledged. 'Have you got a boyfriend these days?'

'Antony.'

'But you never see him.'

'It doesn't make any difference. I love him just the same.'

'I never see him either, not now that he lives with Aunt Maud. It's asking too much of a friendship. But she's working on getting him a house of his own. So we might get a chance then.'

'He never writes to me.'

'Do you write to him?'

'You know I can't write – not a proper letter. I don't have to show him how ignorant I am!'

'He can't write either. His writing arm was smashed. Anyway, when did he ever write a letter? Only to his dad for more cash, as I remember. If he gets a house of his own we'll visit him.'

'Who will look after him?'

'Aunt Maud is going to get him a live-in nurse.'

'I could do that!'

'Except you're not a nurse, Lily.'

'I would look after him better than any nurse!'

'Oh, Lily, if only!'

Simon was truly sorry for Lily with her amazing, misguided devotion to Antony who wasn't worth it, never had been. But he was glad to see her with her spirit apparently undented, her jam jar full of money scarcely touched and her budding career as a dressmaker looking hopeful.

But not long after Mrs Butterworth's funeral Lily was shopping in the village when Cedric came by in a wagon, pulled by the beautiful shire horse Olly.

'Want a lift home?' He pulled to a halt beside her. 'I've been delivering corn to old Ambrose, on my way back now.'

'It's out of your way, my place.'

'No, I can go round the lake. I'm not in a hurry. Jump up.'

She handed up her basket and clambered on board with a foot up on the shaft. She was as agile as a child.

Cedric laughed. 'You're no lady, Lily, showing your knickers.'

'Don't be rude!'

She hadn't seen him since the funeral, but had become close to him during his mother's long illness. She was always comfortable with him, good old Cedric, the village boy his smart friends had always looked down on, using him as a useful entry to the farm and the fun that could be had up there, shooting rabbits, sliding down the haystacks and riding on the carthorses.

'I've been thinking, Lily, would you marry me?'

Lily wasn't sure if she had heard right. 'What do you mean, marry you? Why should I? I don't love you.'

'No, but we get on, don't we?'

'I love Antony.'

'You can still go on loving Antony. I wouldn't mind. I just thought it would make sense, if we got married. Ma said it would be a good idea, before she died. She said you were a gem.'

'A gem?' Lily was finding the conversation difficult.

'Yeah, well think about it. We like each other after all, and you'd have a nice home. We'd take care of Gabriel and Squashy if you want.'

Lily could find nothing to say. The shock had silenced her. She had taken Cedric for granted ever since she could remember and now, looking sideways, she saw a strong, brown, handsome, self-confident young man, ideal husband material. But marriage? She had never thought of getting married, save to Antony. She had never seen anyone she fancied, save Antony, even though plenty of the lads in the village had made advances. And got short shrift.

After Olly had continued his way down the track to the lake and Cedric had offered nothing more, she said, 'What about your brothers, and your father?'

'Oh, they wouldn't mind.'

'It'd be all cooking.' She had seen how it had been with

Mrs Butterworth. She saw now that they were all tired of going without a cook in the house. 'It's just to keep you comfortable, isn't it?'

'Yes, a bit. But you'd have security, a much nicer house than that awful little cottage, men to help you, not you always helping two men. And my brothers – they'd move out when they marry. They're courting, and there are two cottages empty that they'd take. And we like each other, after all.'

Lily remembered all Cedric's kindnesses, his unspoken support, his spirit on the night of the party, how he had stood up to the drunken posh boys, how he had swum and swum looking for Helena, how caring he was of Squashy and how he had never taken offence at the rough way the others treated him. She had never found fault with him.

He said, 'And our lovely horses would be yours too, Lily, think of that.'

'I am thinking,' she said. She jumped down outside her house and he handed down her basket.

'No hurry,' he said, and clicked to Olly and the cart rolled away down what had once been Antony's airstrip, still mown out of habit.

Lily stood watching, feeling as if she had been hit over the head with a shovel.

Later, she talked it over with her father. He was quiet, thoughtful, but did not say much. It was her life, he said. She thought he would like her to be married to Cedric, but was nervous of doing without her, although he would not say as much.

'He said he would take care of you and Squashy if I marry him.'

He snorted at that and said he could take care of himself. Lily knew he couldn't, not adequately. But Cedric had said no hurry.

The next day Barky died of old age, and the ensuing uproar with Squashy took her mind off the impasse. He hugged and shook Barky, willing him back to life, and then would not put him down, hugging the body in his arms and crying.

'We have to give him a nice funeral, Squashy, like for Helena and Mrs Butterworth. We have to lay him in the ground and cover him with flowers.'

'I don't want him buried in the earth! He won't like it. He'll hate it.'

'But he's not here any more, Squashy. He's gone to heaven, like Mrs Butterworth. That's just his body left behind, his shell. His heart and his soul have gone to heaven. And we just have to cover up his body, which is no good any more, else it'll start getting smelly.'

'Not in the ground! Not in the ground!'

He went to bed that night hugging the dead dog down under the blankets. In the morning the dog was stiff and cold and looked horrible.

'See, Squashy, he's gone away. That's not really Barky any more, just his old body which we must put away. You can see it's not Barky any more.'

But Squashy went round all day carrying the body in his arms. Soon it began to stink out the cottage.

'Enough is enough,' said Gabriel. 'Get that bloody dog buried.'

Lily went outside and dug a large hole on the edge of the potato bed. In the afternoon, having lost the argument with Squashy about letting the dog out of his grasp, she walked up to the farm and sought out Cedric.

'Please, if you can help me with Squashy, I'll marry you. Barky's died and he's gone potty.'

Cedric smiled. 'Is it as simple as that for you?'

Lily didn't know what he meant. She ignored his words and explained how Squashy was refusing to bury the dog. He said he would come up later. Lily went home, wondering if she had promised to marry him. She wasn't sure.

Later in the evening he came along the lake with the farm dogs trailing at his heels. They weren't used to being taken for walks and looked slightly bewildered. They were a motley crew, used for rounding up the cattle, for ratting and guarding the barns at night. Only a collie bitch lived in the house and she trailed two overgrown puppies. Ludo barked his head off at them, wagging his shaggy tail.

'Hey, Squashy, my dogs have come for Barky's funeral. You don't mind, do you? I told them Barky had died and gone to heaven and they wanted to come and see his remains laid away.'

Squashy looked bewildered. One of the puppies came up and jumped up at the dead dog in his arms.

'Lily has already made a place for him. My dogs will wait for him there, and you come with Lily.' He walked towards the potato patch where Lily had dug the grave. His dogs followed him and he lined them up beside the grave and told them all to sit. His dogs were very obedient and sat in a long row, looking expectant.

Lily could not believe her eyes. 'Oh, Squashy, how lovely! They're waiting for Barky. Take him over there and lie him down.' She had filled the bottom of the grave with hay and thrown in a few wild flowers and thought it looked very nice. 'Come on, Squashy. His friends are waiting.'

She led the way and Squashy laid poor dead Barky down in his grave, kneeling amongst the dogs. His tears splashed down.

'We'll cover him with hay and he will be nice and warm, and then when the earth goes back we'll make him a cross with his name on it, and plant some lovely flowers on top, just like Helena had, do you remember?'

Squashy nodded. All was well. He said, 'They like a nice funeral,' nodding towards Cedric's dogs and using a phrase much used in the village.

Lily heaved a sigh of relief. Cedric filled in the earth while the dogs still sat obediently, and then he waved them off and they all went leaping about with Ludo, and Squashy ran after them laughing.

'Oh, Cedric, you are magic!'

Lily's relief made her feel quite weak. Cedric came and took her in his arms and said, 'So now you'll agree to marry me?'

'Yes. Yes, I will. I promise.'

And so the engagement was announced.

SEPTEMBER, 1939

28

After she was married, Lily never tried to see Antony again. Simon told her that he was now living in a home of his own, just round the corner from Aunt Maud. He had married his nurse, which was why Lily would not go to see him again.

'I could not bear it.'

'You might feel better about it,' Simon said. 'It's clear that he doesn't love her.'

'Why did he marry her then?'

'Aunt Maud's orders, of course. Aunt Maud pays very well so the nurse was quite agreeable. She doesn't love Ant either, it's quite plain. It's just a business arrangement.'

Simon had married Melanie Marsden. Soon after Lily's wedding to Cedric, he had made his proposal and been accepted. He had fancied her then, but now he was married he told Lily that he found her rather boring. 'You made the best deal, Lily, marrying old Cedric. He's worth ten of Antony.'

'I still love Antony best. I told Cedric. He doesn't mind.'

'Yes, he's incredibly good-natured. You're very lucky.'

Over the years, Lily had three boys and Simon had three girls. They both wished for a child of the sex they hadn't got.

The third birth for Lily was a difficult one, and the old village doctor told her she ought to call it a day. 'Three lovely boys. What more could a woman want?'

Stupid old duffer, Lily thought. *This* woman wanted Antony, a daughter, a better sewing machine . . . Easy to answer . . . not another boy, for heaven's sake! – sweet though they were. William, John and this one, Freddie. Good boys, strong and funny. She had been terrified she might have one like Squashy. And the last one, so hard to produce – the labour terrified her, remembering her poor mother, but the child turned out unblemished, a beautiful golden, red-haired boy, the image of Cedric who, for this last birth, unable to bear the tension, came to help, encouraging her with exactly the same words he always used for the cows: 'Eh, come up, me old beauty! Don't be a lazy old cow now, you lazy old sod . . . put some beef into it . . .' Lily, amongst the groans, found a moment to laugh: a glimpse of the old doctor's shocked face and the sweat on Cedric's brow, delivering a calf.

'We so wanted a heifer!' Lily sighed, when they told her it was a boy.

But Cedric was overjoyed, kissing and hugging her. How easy he was to please, she thought. Not a hint of regret, what a sweet husband, even if not Antony.

The war had just started. What a time to raise boys, when young men, remembering the last war, were still called cannon fodder! But hers, thank God, were too young for her to worry.

And Cedric, to Lily's guilty pleasure – for surely everyone ought to want their men to 'do their bit'? – was declared exempt for being in a reserved occupation. Squashy, too, was excused, for obvious reasons. It was only Simon, the idiot, who volunteered early and became a commissioned officer in the British Airborne Division.

Home on leave, he said to Lily, 'We jump out with parachutes, Lily. That's why I chose it, because when we were kids I was always ashamed of not doing it with Ant, and leaving it to you – a girl, for God's sake – to play at his game. I know my parents forbade me and I was a good boy then and did as I was told, but I was still terribly jealous of you. I've despised myself for it ever since, not going up with Antony, not joining in. So I thought now I could get even – all because of you Lily. It's really great.'

'Even after what happened to Antony?'

'But that was his own choosing, wasn't it? He changed his mind too, but a bit late in the day unfortunately.'

'I'm not sure I want to be responsible for you joining a parachute regiment. Isn't it very dangerous?'

'Hark who's talking! It's great, I love it.'

'Have you jumped yet?'

'Yes, several times, but only in training. It's fabulous, just like you said.'

'But when you do it for real—'

'Oh, the whole war is dangerous, whatever you do. You could just as easily get a bomb dropped on you here. I can tell you, Lily, it's fantastic after the insurance office in the City.

Melanie made such a fuss about my being called up, but it's the best thing that's ever happened to me.'

He had told Lily earlier that with Melanie and their three girls life had become 'rather frilly'. 'Not my scene really.' She had laughed at the time. But now she saw how his parents had aged, and how they lived so in fear of his death, Mrs Goldbeater with tears in her eyes. 'We don't know where he is, what he's doing. It's all so secretive.' The village whispered that while her husband was away Melanie had a boyfriend in Guildford, a rich young man rumoured to trade in the black market. When Mr Goldbeater became very ill, Simon at last came home on compassionate leave, and called again on Lily.

'I can't stay long, just wanted to see how you're doing. My old ma needs me.'

He looked so spare, all the effects of rich living pared away, lines of anxiety etched round his eyes, a whole new burden of responsibility ageing him. Lily was shocked at the change – her laughing, cynical friend now almost a stranger. Is this what parachute jumping did for a man?

'I'm glad to see you so well and happy, Lily. Your lovely boys – I wish I'd had boys. I've scarcely seen Melanie – not much point really, now that she's got a new lover. I don't blame her – why should she hang around in limbo waiting for me? She tried to stop me going – how she tried! So I can't complain. But no regrets. I wouldn't change anything.'

'You're glad you joined up?'

'Yes. The only useful thing I've ever done. Worthwhile, I

294

mean. And you – still working your butt off, as ever? Forgotten Antony at last?'

'Never! I shall never forget him.'

'You are slightly mad, Lily. You know that? If you saw him now, how could you love him? He works in that dreadful solicitor's office which is run by Aunt Maud's friend, goes there every day in his wheelchair, comes home to dreary old Maureen, reads the newspaper, goes to sleep by the fire . . . church on Sunday with Aunt Maud, the dreariest life you could ever dream up, all the sparks extinguished. Better that he had died, that a bomb had dropped on him.'

Lily felt a wild compassion shake her, a fierce memory of old Ant scoffing at what Aunt Maud had offered him, his face alight with scorn. She could not answer. She had never seen or heard of him since his marriage . . . Impossible to go to London in the war, Cedric would never allow it. Nobody did unless they worked there. But she still remembered Antony. She still loved him, in spite of being told she was mad. She used to sit by the lake sometimes, coming back from seeing to Gabriel and Squashy – just a few minutes by the grotto, or by the little inlet where Helena's body had washed up, and her childhood would flood back: the first flight, seeing the world below as if one were God himself up in the clouds, proud of his work, looking down, admiring his gorgeous land like an ethereal entrepreneur. Then seeing it again in the embrace of the parachute, so softly falling, like an autumn leaf, having survived the first, mind-splitting terror, overcoming instinct, lapping up its reward in the sweet fall – never forgotten, to be mulled over in her rare moments of peace. And the memory of the beauty and magic of the grotto on the night of the party, evoking feelings that she did not recognize, had never known before Ant.

Antony had shown her these things: how would she ever have known what life could be without Antony? A glimpse: the euphoria recalled . . . was it was what Simon was seeking when he volunteered?

They would never have known without Antony.

THE 1940s

JULY, 1946

29

When Antony's wife became pregnant, less than six months after VE Day, Simon did not tell Lily. He wasn't sure why: he somehow thought it might upset her Antonian dream world. Antony told him that as he had done absolutely nothing with his life, he thought a last throw at making a mark of some sort on the universe would perhaps see him to the grave with a slightly lesser sense of self-disgust than might otherwise be the case. His wife Maureen agreed with him, although she did not particularly want a child.

'Yes, it will be good for you.'

The perfect nurse. Poor little devil, the baby, being brought up by this paragon and her mentor, Aunt Maud – Antony then thought he might have made a terrible mistake, but the deed was done. There was no going back. The little girl arrived, bawling, on a hot June night.

Another mistake, like his trouble with the ripcord.

With missing the chance to go with his father . . .

With ignoring Lily's sweet passion.

'I shall be glad to be out of it,' he told Simon.

'Don't say that, old chap.' But Simon, if he had been Antony, knew he would have felt the same. He couldn't see Antony lasting much longer.

'Do you still see John, the vicar?'

'Yeah, he comes back to see his old pa sometimes.'

'He's never been to see me. You'd have thought that, as visiting the sick is one of their things, he might have made the effort. If you see him, tell him I shall ask him to do the christening. For old times' sake. And we'll ask Lily and Cedric to come, and Squashy.'

'And the dogs.'

'And you can be the godfather. And Lily the godmother.'

'Oh Jesus, Antony, she doesn't know about the baby yet. I haven't told her.'

'Why not?'

'I thought it might upset her.'

'Why?'

'Because she's still in love with you.'

'How can she be?'

'I ask myself that. But she swears she is. And Cedric doesn't mind.'

'Well, good old Cedric. He always was a good egg. But he's not got a lot to be jealous about, has he? I reckon he got the prize there. You must tell her then, that I'm depending on her.'

'OK, I'll tell her.'

Simon had survived the terrible battle of Arnhem but had been wounded in the retreat, repatriated, and demobbed when the war ended a year later. He had come home to look after his ailing parents, and managed to slip up to London occasionally to visit his old haunts and friends, and just the once to visit Antony. He had not told Lily anything about the baby. He thought it was high time she forgot about Antony completely. Let sleeping dogs lie had been Simon's wish. But now it seemed he had to open old wounds. He could not deny Antony what he thought might be his dying wish, even for Lily.

She was a tough one. But he knew it would be a bitter blow.

He told her, tactfully, sitting by the lake on their own, and Lily wept, as he had guessed she would, and said she wished it was hers.

'Oh, if only!'

Simon put his arms round her and hugged her. He hoped Cedric wouldn't see, but he knew that he loved Lily more than he had ever loved Melanie, and he too had missed his chance and they were all idiots, but nothing could be done about it.

'It's a girl. He wants you to be a godmother, and me a godfather, and old John to do the christening. He's got it all worked out. Then he says he can die happy.'

'Is he going to die?'

'Quite soon, I think. You will see. But he's depending on seeing you at the christening. It's been so long. You won't let him down, will you? I expect he will include Cedric and Melanie in the invitations. So we will all be on our best behaviour, no tears, Lily. Just old friends, remember.'

301

'Yes.'

Simon departed, back to his chores at home, but Lily sat on, digesting Simon's astonishing news. Why hadn't he told her before? She supposed he thought it kinder that she didn't know, and was probably afraid of coping with her histrionics. She wept easily. She couldn't stop now, sitting hugging her knees on the side of the lake, remembering the gorgeous boy with his tumbled black curls and teasing eyes whom she had put out of her life but never truly forgotten.

She did not want to think of Antony old and crippled and near death. His life had turned out to be everything he most abhorred, stuck in the solicitor's office, wholly dependent on his dreadful aunt, adventure a dream. Whilst hers, lacking ambition, had turned out to be happier than she had ever imagined, the cares of looking after her two men lifted from her shoulders by Cedric's generosity, her daily life, mother-hood, all she needed for satisfaction. She was used to and enjoyed hard work, and her success with her dressmaking sideline, the admiration it engendered, gave her a heart-warming sense of pride. It was impossible to want more.

The contrast between herself and Antony, and how it had turned out for them, struck her with a terrible anguish – that they neither of them had been able see the consequences of their decisions, or lack of decisions, and life had just rolled over them, inconsequential, giving to one and taking away from the other.

And now, with Simon's news about the baby, it made her see that it was all to happen again, cruelly, the poor child the

302

fruit of another of Antony's wrong decisions, born to a hired mother, to be shortly fatherless, and no doubt fall into the arms of the dreaded Aunt Maud. For surely there would never now be news of Antony's father – no grandfather for this little baby.

What good could she and Simon do as godparents, when it meant broaching Aunt Maud? There was no way she could leave the farm to travel so far just to see her little god-daughter, take her for a walk on the heath, perhaps, buy her a puppy . . . impossible! What on earth was Antony asking? No wonder Simon had tried to keep the news of the baby from her, until now. But they were involved and there was no getting out of it.

She knew that Cedric would do anything to refuse the invitation. He said quickly that he was prevented from going by the timing of the event, coming in the middle of the barley harvest which he could not leave. The perfect excuse.

'Ant will understand, he knows all about farming. I would really like to see the old bloke again, Lily, but you know what an ordeal that sort of thing is for me, and going to London and all. You go with Simon and bring me back a full report. Anyway, you don't want me around when you see your old love again.'

He laughed and kissed her kindly on the forehead.

'I got the gem, like my old ma said.'

It was difficult for Lily to take a day away, her hands full with the children, her father, feeding the harvesters, but it was impossible to turn the invitation down. Boring old John who came to see her said she could be a godmother by proxy if she wished, but she didn't wish. She knew it would be excruciating for her: to see his child . . . God knew, she loved her three with all her heart and soul and had never wished her life to be anything different from what it was. Her Antony-life had simply threaded her boring everyday life with a touch of magic – there was no reality to it, never had been, just like the stars in the sky or the whiff of a rose, something untouchable, and she had never wanted it any different.

She had never thought of her love for Antony as carnal, just a dream. But now it was being thrust in her face: *his child!* There was no one she could explain this to. Only Simon could guess what it was doing to her. Everyone else – those who still lived on the scandal of the Sylvester family, which was most the village – thought it a lovely honour: 'How sweet to be remembered by him, dear, after all this time!' Those of the Mrs Carruthers faction thought it shocking for him to sink so low as to ask a servant to be a godparent – 'But of course the boy lost his mind long ago.'

Cedric's sisters thought it a great lark. Amelia and Sarah said they would hold the fort for her at home.

'I bet old Maud hasn't given the idea her blessing! I bet she's gnashing her teeth! I bet she had some snotty solicitor's wife lined up!'

'She won't kiss you, Lily, that's for sure—'

'Thank God for that!'

'Poor old Ant! He was so sweet. We all loved him – those looks! To die for!'

'He wasn't sweet! He was an arrogant bastard.'

'A sweet arrogant bastard.'

'What are you going to wear, Lily? He won't recognize you after all this time. You'll have to make a label.'

'He will recognize her. Lily hasn't changed a bit. No grey hairs, in spite of being married to old Ced. She's not got fat or wrinkly like us.'

'And what's this about old Ced saying he's not going? Because of the harvest? That's just an excuse. He's got to go. He just cannot not go. He's being ridiculous.'

'We'll tell him.'

'He'll hate it!'

'That's not the point. It's his duty. Of course he's got to go. Once in a lifetime, for goodness sake! If just to say goodbye to Ant, if he's as bad as Simon says. You tell him, Lily, he's got to go.'

'He won't take it from me.'

'We'll tell him then. The idiot!'

'I don't think he's ever been to London.'

'Well, it's high time he did! What a bumpkin!'

'He did fly with Ant,' Lily remembered. 'More than Simon and John did.'

'Ma and Pa allowed him, that's why. They thought it was great.'

'Simon and John were forbidden.'

'So would you have been if your old pa had known about it!'

'Yes, well, he didn't.'

Cedric could not hold out against the scorn and insistence of his two sisters, so when the day came, he walked down the drive with Lily in his one and only suit (for funerals) to meet Simon's car, grumbling and groaning all the way.

'You can't feel worse than I do, so just shut up,' Lily snapped at him, in the rare role of nagging wife. If he was only complaining about wearing a suit and going to London, how could he imagine how she felt, screwed up with dread about the day ahead? She wasn't even sure she would carry it through without breaking down completely. Cedric had no idea, but Simon would understand. It was, of course, a beautiful day for this ordeal, so Cedric stopped grumbling and started to guess how long the sunshine would hold out.

'At least you'll be in church, so you can pray for the weather,' Lily snapped.

Simon's car was waiting on the road. He got out as they approached.

'Blimey, Lily, it's only a christening, not a wedding,' he said, but his eyes shone with admiration as he took in her glorious dress and elegant hat. She had put all her skill into making her outfit, thinking ahead of seeing Antony's face when – if? – he recognized her after such a long time. She knew she looked gorgeous, the golden flush of her silk dress bringing out the colour in her still mostly golden hair. She rarely looked in a mirror, her life not requiring it, for she made few clothes for herself, but this time she had surprised herself by seeing a neat, slender and still quite youthful figure, turning this way and that to check on the fit of her dress. She was nearly forty. Three children and the work of a farmer's wife should have coarsened her figure, but it hadn't. She was soothed by Simon's admiration.

'You look fantastic! Poor Ant will fall out of his wheelchair when he sees you.'

To Lily's surprise, Melanie was sitting in the car.

'I asked her to come, for Antony,' Simon explained. 'It's a day out after all. And she was always fond of old Ant, so she agreed.'

'Nice to have a day off from the girls.' Melanie smiled at Lily and said, 'You look gorgeous! I hope you don't mind?'

'No, of course not.'

Lily was pleased to see that there was no bad feeling between Simon and Melanie in spite of the split, and actually felt glad to have the female presence, quite rare in her life. Cedric sat in the front with Simon and talked farming, and Lily felt her nerves quietening as she listened to Melanie's undemanding conversation. Age had mellowed her and her life was no longer easy; Lily got the impression that she regretted leaving Simon.

'But he was away so long. Why on earth did he go, the idiot?'

Lily could have told her, but didn't. She sat watching the endless suburbs slipping past, then the river Thames and Putney bridge and buildings without end. How could all these people live without grass, without space, without cows? She would die.

Simon said, 'Nearly there. We're going to be early. We'll find the church, then park round the corner somewhere and wait for the time.'

Simon was familiar with the area and knew the church nearest to Antony's house, no doubt where Antony visited on Sundays and had been married. It was a hideous Victorian monstrosity, more like a warehouse than a thanksgiving to God, but at least it had a garden round it and there was a small marquee set up on a scrap of lawn.

'Tea and cakes, by Jove!' Simon said. 'They're doing us proud.'

'Should be champagne, surely? We haven't got to hang around though, have we?'

'Cedric, yes, I'm afraid we've got to be polite. We are guests of honour, Lily and I. We have to be congratulated by the famous Aunt Maud.'

Simon parked the car in a side road and they sat waiting. Lily did not join in the desultory conversation. Simon had told her earlier that Aunt Maud was over the moon about the baby and planning the right school already and interviewing nannies and saying she felt ten years younger. Lily wondered how old the old bat really was: she seemed to go on for ever. What joy had come her way getting poor Antony under her thumb, helpless in his wheelchair!

But what would have become of him without her? God moved in mysterious ways, so cruel to Antony, cruel to her own family. Why did they praise God so in church when he was so cruel? She herself was the last person in truth to be a godparent when the service was all about steering the child into godly ways. She had read the service in the church at home, to see what it entailed. She had never thought much about God herself, but had noticed that as people grew near to death they thought more about the whole thing. Perhaps Antony was thinking about God now, but she doubted it. To her God was the clouds and the trees and the lake and the fields of ripe corn rippling in the breeze and the dear cart-horses, which made her catch her breath sometimes at the beauty of them and the feelings they provoked. But she didn't think John would agree that that was religion.

'Time to go, I think,' Simon said.

A few well-dressed elderly people were dribbling towards the church. Lily was glad to move, feeling herself trembling. Oh, for it to be over! Simon, guessing, took her arm firmly.

'We'll stay out of the way,' Melanie said quietly.

'I could wait outside,' Cedric said hopefully.

'You will not!'

Simon walked Lily firmly into the churchyard. People were passing them, going in now. Simon looked inside the church and came back to Lily. 'We'll wait outside. Antony's not here yet. As we're the godparents, it's best to meet him out here, and all go in together.'

'I wish it was over!'

'You're not going to pass out, are you? Pull yourself together, Lily! For heaven's sake!'

She could see that he was genuinely nervous about her, so did her best to calm herself down. It was the approach of Aunt

Maud that helped her, flooding her with the old familiar loathing. For it was obvious that there was no relenting in her attitude to the servant girl Simon had chosen as godparent.

'Nice to see you, Simon. I am glad that you could make it, such a long way to come.' And then the undressing stare for Lily, up and down. 'And you, Lily,' was the best she could come out with.

Lily did not reply. The old bag had not changed, save for an obvious ageing. She walked with a stick more slowly than before, painfully (Lily hoped).

'Will you come in?' She indicated with her stick that they walk before her.

'We're waiting here for Antony.'

'I think you should be at the font.'

'No. We're waiting here.'

Lily saw that Simon had not forgotten how to be an army officer. She almost laughed, seeing the indecision on Aunt Maud's face, totally unused to being disobeyed. What an army officer she would have made!

'Very well.'

The incident had overcome Lily's nerves. As Aunt Maud limped into the church alone, she was able to laugh. 'Oh, Simon, that was magnificent!'

'It got her out of the way. Here comes Antony. Keep smiling, for God's sake.'

Lily turned and saw a wheelchair coming through the gateway. Her heart started to pump so hard she thought she would faint, but Simon swore at her and gave her a shake.

Maureen was pushing the wheelchair and Antony had the baby on his lap.

As they came up Lily saw that Antony was smiling, but he looked so old she hardly recognized him. His black curls were chopped short and turned white; his laughing face was creased with lines of endurance and his eyes were the dim eyes of an old man. But when they saw her, she thought she saw the old gorgeous blue flash of delight. Or was she willing it, the momentary collision of their old selves? She was scarcely coherent.

'Oh, Lily,' he said, 'my lovely Lily, how gorgeous you look! After all this time, you haven't changed.'

She mustn't cry! She could not speak. If only she could say the same! But he was lifting up the bundle in the white lace shawl.

'Here, for you. It's yours.'

She thought the christening gown must once have been Aunt Maud's: it was so incredibly old and fragile, but the little face that peeped out of all the finery was Antony's own, so like that she gasped. A baby Antony, the still faintly unfocused eyes laughing at her. This baby was all fun and jokes, she could see, like the old Antony.

She looked up, still speechless, and saw the stout severe figure of the baby's mother Maureen looking at her with searching pebble-grey eyes.

'A fine likeness, isn't she?'

'Yes, oh yes.'

'She's no trouble, though, not like him.' A slight smile, a hint of friendship. 'You take her now, for the service.'

311

Antony handed her up and Lily took her in her arms. Simon shook Antony's hand and said, 'Good to see you again, mate.' Lily felt so shaky she was afraid she might drop the precious young life, but Simon hissed in her ear, 'Thank God. Old John is waiting for you.'

Maureen pushed the wheelchair forward, with Simon holding the door for her, and then they followed the parents to the font where John was waiting. If that was the old John, Lily hardly took him in. A real droning vicar doing his duty; he, like his father, had never been the right man for the job, she thought, wanting so badly for God to be kind to this little baby girl in her arms, as he had not been kind to her father. John, make it be so!

Aunt Maud stood beside him to make sure he made no mistakes, and a throng of mostly elderly people murmured responses to the prayers which sounded to Lily as if they were all steeped irrevocably in sin. How could it be possible?

Then John was holding out his arms for the baby. He took her rather awkwardly and said, 'Name this child.'

Lily froze. Was she supposed to know? Stupid Ant hadn't told them. Maud something she had always supposed. She opened her mouth to say, 'I don't know the name,' but before she could get the words out Antony said in a clear voice, 'She is to be christened Lily Antonia.'

'Lily Antonia,' repeated John, with more than a hint of surprise in his voice.

And Lily too, astonished, turned to Antony and repeated, 'Lily Antonia?'

She couldn't believe it. And Antony actually laughed and said, 'Yes, she is to be called Lily Antonia.'

And then Lily had to stop herself from laughing out loud at the triumphant grin on Antony's face as he enjoyed her shock. And Simon letting out a guffaw . . . it was almost as if they were children again, saying rude words.

And, looking up, she saw anger flash across Aunt Maud's face, her cheeks turning a dangerous purple colour, her mouth opening and closing in dismay. Of course it should have been Maud something . . . Lily almost said it to John, 'Stop!', thinking it was quite wrong, but Antony said again, as John hesitated, 'She is to be christened Lily Antonia.' And the delight flooded Lily so that she had to stifle her laughter, burying her face in Simon's shoulder, grateful for the strong arm he always seemed to have ready for her at moments of crisis. No doubt everyone thought they were a married couple. She was laughing and crying together and did not hear any-thing of the rest of the service, only surfacing when John thrust the baby back to into her arms.

He too was smiling by then, and said to her, 'How lovely, Lily, you are honoured.'

But Aunt Maud . . . even before they were out of the church she was hissing venomously to Antony, 'Have you gone mad? At the last moment, to come out with that? What were you thinking of?'

'I thought of it long ago. It wasn't at the last moment.'

'We agreed on Maud Victoria. I remember discussing it – that Maud and Maureen didn't sound right together, so Victoria was better, after our wonderful queen.'

'You discussed it with Maureen. I never said a word.'

'Did she know you had changed it?'

'Yes, she agreed, said it was sweet.'

Aunt Maud's colour deepened even more. Maureen took the baby back from Lily with a secret little smile, which made Lily unexpectedly warm to her, and started away down the path, and fortunately John came up at that moment and started to talk to Aunt Maud, then other people came up to chat and Antony was saved from a further diatribe. As they waited for the small crowd to dissipate Antony said, 'Hold on, I want you to meet this gentleman.'

This gentleman was a well-dressed, urbane visitor, approaching cautiously.

'Is this the right moment?' he said to Antony.

'Yes, it is, sir. The perfect moment. We are all together.' He looked up and introduced the gentleman to them all as Sir Richard Margrave. 'He is my lawyer. We need to discuss something rather important, before the tea and cakes. Find Cedric, Simon. We need him too.'

'Shall we go to the vestry?' Sir Richard suggested. 'We need to be private.'

'Yes, of course. About turn, back to the vestry.'

Simon, puzzled, went off to find Cedric and Lily followed Antony, propelling himself, back into the church and down the aisle to the door to the vestry. She supposed that, with a lawyer, this was something technical to do with the christening: she knew so little about lawyerish things (luckily) that she was not curious. She was still trying to recover from the shock of hearing the baby's name: it was the loveliest gift she could imagine, the gift of a lifetime.

She knew people went into the vestry during the wedding to sign things and was not surprised to find a table there, spread with papers. The lawyer sat down as if he knew what to expect and looked around.

'You can tell Lily what this is all about, sir,' Antony said to him. 'Give her time to take it in before Cedric arrives. It's for her to make the decision after all.'

'You haven't given her any warning?' Sir Richard was smiling. He turned to Lily and said, 'Lily Antonia's parents want you to adopt her, to take her for your own.'

Lily did not take this in at once. 'Adopt her?' Was it what she thought it meant?

'Yes, to bring up as your own child. To be yours.'

Antony said, 'Maureen wants it too. We want you to become her legal parents. You and Cedric.'

Lily was speechless. That little thing, the image of Antony, to be her own, the daughter she had always wanted . . .

The door behind them opened and Simon came in with Cedric. They were laughing at something. Lily turned to Cedric and flung herself into his arms, nearly knocking him over.

'Cedric! Cedric! Antony is giving us – he says – Oh, Cedric, it's so lovely! Say yes, you must say yes! He's giving us his baby!'

'What on earth—?'

'Look, it's a terrible shock for you,' Antony said. 'You don't have to make up your mind now, today. We've made the offer – for you to adopt our child, Cedric – and it's only fair that you should think it over calmly. It's a huge commitment, after all. You've already got three children to bring up, I know. If you refuse, we shall quite understand.'

'Blimey!' Cedric said.

'A daughter, Cedric,' Lily said. 'What we've always wanted to make our family complete!'

'A little heifer, eh?' He laughed.

The lawyer said, 'There are quite a lot of things to think about before you are sure. Miss Sylvester hasn't been told of this plan, I understand. She can't stop it happening if it's the parents' wish. But I am sure she will put great objections in the way, which Antony and Maureen will have to face, with my help if it's required.'

'You haven't told her?' Simon asked.

'Not yet. Like we didn't tell her about the name. It's called *fait accompli*, Simon, you surely understand? We don't mind facing the music if it's all wrapped up and legal, but arguing with her beforehand, with her trying to stop it – we just couldn't face it.'

'But does Maureen agree with all this?'

'Yes, a hundred per cent. She never wanted to have the child in the first place but did it for me. It was my stupid idea. I never thought ahead of the poor little thing being brought up by Aunt Maud. It's a fate worse than death, I can vouch for that. Maureen didn't want it either. Maud went berserk when Maureen told her she was pregnant. But she got used to the idea, planning out its life, never consulting us, and now she's taken over completely – we have to do this, do that – the child will have no peace here. We neither of us thought ahead, really, what would happen.'

'If we adopt the baby,' Cedric said hesitantly, 'we won't have her on our backs, I hope?'

'I think the law can deal with that, if necessary,' said Sir Richard.

'You haven't got to say yes immediately,' Antony said. 'It's not fair that you don't have time to consider it and all the implications. Money, for example. I haven't any, only some miserly savings. Maybe the old aunt might leave her some, when she dies. Or my father could resurface? Who knows? But don't count on it.'

Cedric said, 'That doesn't matter. One more mouth on the farm makes little difference. The extra work will be all Lily's. And if Lily agrees —'

'I do. I don't need time to consider it,' Lily said firmly. 'Now that Cedric agrees, it's yes, now.'

The men could do the paperwork. Lily just felt she wanted to fly away somewhere, laughing, crying, overwhelmed. She went out of the vestry and went into a quiet part of the church-yard, away from the tea party, and sat on a gravestone and wept. Tears of joy for herself, grief for Antony – she had no idea, only aware of emotions almost too great to contain. Meeting Aunt Maud again shortly would calm her down.

When the men came out she joined them, composed. Cedric wanted to leave straightaway but was over-ruled.

'For heaven's sake, the godparents have got to put in an appearance! Everyone will be wondering where on earth we've all got to as it is.' Simon was firm, pushing Antony rapidly down the path towards the marquee. 'You're not telling Aunt Maud now!' he said to him.

'No fear! Later, when you've all gone. I don't want to dump you in it. Dynamite, stand clear! Maybe Maureen can do it. I'm a sick man, after all. Mustn't have too much excitement, the doc says.'

The tea party was well underway, Aunt Maud holding the fort beside the christening cake. Maureen came to meet them, carrying the baby.

'God, I thought you were never coming!' she said to Antony. 'Is it—?'

'Yes, yes, it's all agreed!'

'Oh, thank God!'

The guarded face broke into such a smile that the staid, boring nurse for a moment looked like the girl she once had been, like the woman she could have been if life had been kinder to her. Lily warmed to her immediately, holding out her arms for the baby that she was proffering up.

'You are glad for me to have her? I just can't believe it! I am so happy!'

'Yes, I wanted it. I wanted it so much, for the little thing to have a happy future, not with Aunt Maud. We neither of us thought ahead when Antony wanted to have a child, that she would take over. It didn't occur to us. As soon as she is weaned, and the paperwork done, you will have her.'

'It will be terrible when she finds out!'

'Yes, but not today! Don't worry. It'll be bad enough – her anger about the name! And later, we'll get that lawyer to tell her. He's her dear friend, so she tells us, so he can use all his expertise in selling it to her – part of the job. There's nothing she can do to stop it, he assured us, so you don't have anything to worry about.'

'Oh, you are so kind!'

The formalities of the christening party passed Lily by in a dream. The sooty little garden seemed now to be flooded with glorious light. She felt that she was in heaven itself. Seeing the man in the wheelchair, broken and near death, she saw only the old Antony she had loved so dearly, the teasing blue eyes, the tumbled black hair, the cruel tongue that had never professed to love her, but had mocked and laughed and led her on.

The same spirit would live again in her little girl, Lily Antonia. And when he came to lie beside Helena in the village churchyard she would take him flowers with his daughter, picked from the lakeside, and they would lay some too on Barky's grave, and see Uncle Squashy and remember all the fun they had and know that they were the lucky ones, for whom the sun was still shining.

1980s

APRIL, 1983

30

Lily never spoke about the past. Her love for Antony was never to be put into words, only fading gradually during the years into a private, sweet memory, fostered by the presence of the enchanting Antonia. Cedric was an entirely practical man, immune to dreams, wholly taken up, along with his sons, by the running of the farm. He never mentioned nor even thought about the past. He had accepted Antonia as his own daughter and never mentioned otherwise, nor was Antonia ever told otherwise. The boys were the same: she was their sister.

Aunt Maud was dead, no word ever came from Maureen, and there was no one save Lily who remembered the child's real father, though Antonia's looks reminded her everyday: she was his image. Lily wondered sometimes if any of the very old people in the village had noticed, but no one said anything, and now they were all dead.

Life was a throw of the dice, Lily thought, unpredictable, and now she was old she felt surprise at how all the

323

excitements in her life had happened in her youth and since the arrival of Antonia in the family nothing exciting had ever happened again. It was only Antony who had shown her what life could be. And what had happened to him, self-inflicted, was too sad to dwell on.

Life in the farmhouse was quiet. Cedric, now bent and arthritic in his late seventies, was still out on the land all day, working with his two elder sons. Freddie the youngest had eschewed farming and emigrated to Australia, from where he was always writing letters trying to persuade his parents to join him. Cedric threw the letters in the fire with a snort of derision. Lily did not like the sound of Australia, so did not argue. Her horizons, she knew, were pathetically narrow, scarcely ever leaving the Lockwood estate where she had been born, but she had never hankered for other places. She was content, and her main happiness in life had been brought to her by Antonia.

Antonia had spent her childhood just as Lily had, playing round the estate with her brothers and with the children of Lockwood Hall, falling in love with the eldest son and – unlike Lily – marrying him. No cloud had ever drifted across Antonia's sky. Antonia now lived in Lockwood Hall with her husband Peter, her architect father-in-law having built himself a new house in Guildford, and Lily could see her every day if she wished. Antonia had not yet had any children, Lily thought by design, as she and Peter had a very busy social life, travelled abroad a lot and never showed any signs of regret over lack of a family. There were enough grandchildren around as it was, with her boys' children, and Cedric's sisters' children providing enough to make a whole Young Farmers club between them, and Lily got their names muddled up, but always had cake and biscuits at the ready for the frequent visitations.

Lily, heading into the second half of her seventies, was prepared to sink into a contented dotage, feeling her life's work was done. Not that she was incapacitated or ill, just getting a bit tired. She liked to walk down to the lake when she was free and sit by the little inlet where Helena's body had once floated and let her thoughts go back over her strange, beleaguered childhood: the burden of Squashy and her old father and the fun before Helena's death.

She often thought that Antonia should know the truth, but loyalty to Cedric stopped her saying anything. He had been so totally forgiving of all her idiocies and quite happily acknowledged his second place in his wife's affections, a kindness Lily could not despoil. Their marriage had been very successful, no need to stir things. She could keep her fantasies to herself. Her sweetest fantasy was that Antonia had been born to her, not Maureen. Sometimes she could almost believe it, remembering the night she had lain with Antony, even remembering that strange dream in which she had borne the little blonde baby Rose. What had that been all about? But Antonia had no trace of Maureen in her nature. Strangely, Antonia had feelings and character far more in tune with herself than with her birth mother.

Antonia was very kind to her now that she was getting old, and never disparaged her in the way of many young people in their attitude to the elderly. Lily never trespassed on the couple's privacy in their elegant home, but Antonia came across to the farm often with flowers from the restored gardens and tales of their doings. Like his father, Peter was an architect, a large cheerful man with a successful practice, and the pair had many friends from the profession whom they often entertained. Their life was so different from Lily's and Lily, without envy, loved to hear Antonia's stories of domestic life in smart circles, a world away from her own in spite of the fact that scarcely a stone's throw separated the farm from the Hall. Nothing had really changed in the Butterworth kitchen since the days she had helped old Mrs Butterworth – Cedric's mother – when she had been dying. It was still a mess, the same table now, although well-scrubbed, pitted with wear, the same motley dogs wandering through, the same smell of fruit cake baking to stave off the pangs of hunger farmers seemed to suffer from between proper meals.

'I love it in here,' Antonia declared. 'So comfortable. Architects like to impress – it does get boring sometimes.'

'Ah, but your place is beautiful!'

'Yes, but – you know what I mean. No complaints! I just love coming home here.'

Antonia settled herself in Cedric's comfortable chair while Lily put the kettle on. Antonia was approaching her late-thirties and age seemed to have emphasized her beauty rather than detracted, her untamed black curls without yet a hint of grey, the eyes still with the sudden flash of laughing blue that was so reminiscent of her father. It often seemed magical to

Lily that Antonia was so much in the image of Antony, a likeness so rare. None of her own boys were anything as like their father as was Antonia. None of Simon's girls had had a close likeness to either Simon or Melanie. Cedric had remarked once on Antonia's likeness to Antony, but only the once, with no sign of irritation, just mild surprise. Lily thought of it as God's gift to herself, to make up for denying her Antony's love.

He was still there for her, in her head, laughing in Antony's old way.

'Peter said there was a charity stall outside Guildford station last night with some old bat trying to get people to sign up for making a parachute jump for charity. Your friends promise to pay money to this charity if you are brave enough to make the jump. So when lots of people have promised you feel honour-bound to do it, so all that money goes to charity. Peter thought it was a really weird idea. He said he would rather put his head on the railway track than jump out of an aeroplane. A better way to die.'

Lily opened her mouth to make an exclamation of protest, but caught herself up just in time before she said anything stupid. But Antonia's words sent such a sudden frisson of shock and longing through her body that she found it hard to hide her expression, and turned hastily back to the kettle, away from Antonia. Reaching for the teacups she saw that her hands were shaking.

'I told him what a coward he was and he laughed and said, "You do it then!" but I must say it doesn't really appeal. All right floating down perhaps, but the thought of having to make yourself jump – I don't think I could do it.'

It was all Lily could do to stop herself from bursting out with a diatribe on the amazing feelings a parachute jump induced and that it was the most wonderful and marvellous and mind-blowing experience of a lifetime, but her self-control won over her excitement, and she just mumbled something about Peter being quite sensible: it was a bit much a charity asking someone to do such an outrageous thing.

'Yes,' Antonia agreed. 'After all, if your aeroplane is on fire it would be brilliant, but just to do it for fun seems a bit odd. I wonder if they get many takers?'

When she had gone Lily sat down and found herself trembling and close to tears. The memory that she had blocked for so long – of seeing Antony hurtle past her on that last jump – came back to her with such needling pain that she almost cried out. Antonia's careless words had opened a wound so deep that she had forgotten it existed. In the evening, Cedric asked her if she was ill: she was so withdrawn and touchy. It was so unlike him to remark on her demeanour that she said yes, she thought she must be sickening for something – how else could she explain it? – so he made her a hot toddy and tucked her into bed.

But the idea of the parachute jump stayed with her and she made a special visit into Guildford to find out more about the offer. Nobody said you had to be under eighty, only that you had to be over eighteen. The more she thought about it the more enticing the offer became – to do it again! Float down through the sky without any troubles this time, her mind perfectly attuned to absorbing every nuance of the beauty, the silence, the magic that she still remembered – to do it again!

Not to tell anyone. They wouldn't let her. They would say she was an idiot. She could just see the boys jeering, and Antonia shocked and fussing and Cedric . . .

Impossible. But did she have to tell anyone? She came and went as she pleased, after all, and why did she have to tell anyone? She could do it and no one need ever know. She went home with the details and decided to put it out of her mind.

But it wouldn't go.

She decided not to mention it to Cedric, for she thought he would fuss, be bound to tell her she was too old. They rarely had serious conversations, only stuff about cows and the grandchildren and weather. They had grown together, Lily thought, like a pair of old socks, comfortable and hard-wearing. She knew she loved him, even if he had no time for cuddles and sweet words. But she wasn't going to risk telling him about her idea. It was warm and throbbing inside her. She must do it!

The next day she went down to the organizing office in Guildford to sign up, but they said kindly, 'You're too old, dear. No one over sixty, and I think you're older than that.'

'But I'm fit, and I've done it before. You must take me!'

'We can't go against the rules, I'm afraid.'

For some reason it had never occurred to Lily that this might happen. But when they were so adamant she realized that she had been so carried away with the idea that she had not given it a sensible scrutiny. Of course she was too old, that's why she was keeping it a secret from her family.

They would all have said the same. But slowly it occurred to her that she could still do it without the help of the charity people: she had her own money, so she could surely get someone from Brooklands to take her up privately, provide the parachute and help her make the jump?

One day when Cedric had gone to the cattle market she borrowed one of the boys' bikes and cycled to Brooklands. It nearly killed her, never having bicycled further than the village, and she had to go to the cafe for a cup of tea to recover. Although the building had undergone a refurbishment and now looked quite different, it was the same place where, once, Antony had been a waiter, where Clarence had revived her with brandy after that terrible day . . . she found the memories flooding back, shaking her: she almost expected Antony to appear, laughing, undamaged, young, gorgeous . . . oh God, how her hands were shaking! She was crazy to be thinking that she could do this thing.

'Is madam well? Can I help you?'

She looked up to a find a suave young man in a waiter's uniform eyeing her anxiously. She saw herself as he was seeing her: an ignorant, badly-dressed countrywoman having a bad turn, out of her milieu, about to be a nuisance . . . God help us, have hysterics! She took a great breath and eyed him fiercely.

'No. I'm perfectly all right. I'm here to make enquiries about making a parachute jump. Perhaps you can help me with that?'

'For yourself, madam?' And he laughed.

Lily sprang to her feet, eyes blazing. 'Yes, for myself! Before I die! Because I've done it before, several times, and I don't know why you find that so amusing? Why do you laugh? Have you no manners? As you offered to help me, yes, find me someone who can provide the service I'm looking for. For that I shall be much obliged.'

Was this herself talking? She could not believe it. She had leaped off her seat and was standing here feeling about ten feet tall, her lethargy completely dissolved, an amazing resolve flooding her.

The young man stepped back, embarrassed colour flooding his young cheeks. 'Please, I'm sorry! Forgive me. I didn't mean—'

'Well, make amends, and find me someone who knows about parachute jumping.'

'Yes, ma'm, of course. I will make enquiries.'

He hurried away and Lily sat down again, feeling the sparks still jumping in her breast. It was like old times, when the young blood had coursed and thrills had overwhelmed her. Good and bad, she had lived once! So she would again! All her strength seemed to be flooding back, excitement catching hold.

Of course it was not straightforward, but as Lily devoted herself secretly to fulfilling this mad ambition, she did a few days later receive a letter from a pilot from Brooklands who specialized in parachute jumping and was willing to take her up for a jump for a modest sum, modest in respect of her advanced years and his great admiration for her spirit. She read this with amusement. She arranged to meet him (on another cattle market day) to discuss business.

She made another crucifying bicycle ride to Brooklands and was introduced to her saviour by the same young man whom she had so embarrassed on her first visit.

The willing pilot was fiftyish, lithe and personable. He had a slight American accent and said he had been brought up over there.

'They're really keen on it in the States. Big exhibitions, people love it, all clamouring to have a go. It doesn't seem to have taken off here in the same way, but perhaps it's coming.'

'If you've never tried it, I suppose you can't guess.'

'It's something else,' he said simply. 'The feeling. Indescribable.'

'Oh, I know, I know! That's why I want to do it again. One last time! They won't have me on the charity jump – too old, they said. I said I've done it before, I know all about it, but they said it was against the rules.'

'You can't be too old, not for that sort of magic.'

Lily warmed to this new friend. His name was Robert Arnold: he had a very calm demeanour, and eyes that took her in with both amusement and respect.

'Well, I don't make rules, and if you've done it before you know what to expect. When did you jump before?'

'Oh, I was just a kid. Ages ago. Once just with my friend, who was trying it out on me – he wanted to do it himself but had no one else to fly the plane. The next time from here . . .'

She did not want to relive that day.

Robert said, 'My dad worked over here for an American called Clarence something. He told me something about Clarence piloting a plane for some parachute jumpers and it scared him so much that he said he'd rather die than jump himself. Clarence was a lousy pilot himself but mad on flying. He employed my father to fly his plane and thought he might learn from him, but my dad said he never did. Nice chap though, he said, and it was a super job for my dad. He went back to America with him, best of everything, he said. So I grew up with flying in my blood, you could say.'

Lily was shocked to silence by mention of the name Clarence. Of all the people she might have contacted she had come up with a man whose father was an employee of the American whom Lily remembered so well. The parachute jumpers he mentioned were herself and Antony, yet it was clear that Robert did not suspect this. After all, his father had not been on the flight and perhaps had never known what had happened. It was certainly something Clarence would not have wanted anyone to know about if he could help it.

Lily did not want to follow this turn the conversation had taken. It was bad enough this man raking up Clarence – of all the coincidences that his father had worked for him! Lily sat recalling Clarence, and his thousand pounds which had saved her life, and the Van Gogh he had taken, and the other lovely pictures, which they had reluctantly turned over to the powers-that-be to be rehomed in public galleries. All so long ago. She missed the pictures. They had been so lovely. Squashy had cried when they went.

Robert was talking about choosing the right weather, a windless day, and about his aeroplane, which he clearly regarded as most men regarded their girlfriends, and Lily brought herself back from the shock of finding out how his past coincided so eerily with hers and paid attention to what he was saying. The logistics. A parachute . . . transport . . .

She told Robert that the jump was a secret and none of her family must know. It made it very difficult to make arrangements for him to let her know when the moment was ripe. The farm was not on the telephone, although Antonia's residence was and sometimes, on rare occasions – usually to call the vet – she had used it. Lily decided to risk giving Robert Antonia's number.

'Just ask for me to ring you back. You must give me your number. She will come and fetch me if you ask her to. She's only five minutes away. But don't tell her what it's for!'

It was the best she could manage. Robert did not seem to think it was a problem. 'Sure. That should work OK.'

She gave Robert Antonia's telephone number and made to depart.

'Can I give you a lift home?' Robert asked. 'I've got my car right here.'

'I came on a bike. I can't leave it here.'

'We can sling it in the back, not a problem.'

As she might have guessed, the car was an open two-seater sports car and the bike was easily laid behind the two seats. What bliss! Lily did not think she would have made it back to the farm, pedalling all that way again. Luxury was not something she was accustomed to and the ride back with such a personable young man and with the blazing excitement in her brain of a mission accomplished was glorious. But it was over in ten minutes.

'It won't be long to wait?'

'No. The weather is set fair, I think, perhaps in just a day or two if we are lucky.'

It was hard for Lily to maintain her usual composure with the prospect of the jump on her mind. She kept out of Cedric's way, guilty that she was deceiving him. For all she knew he could well have been quite happy about her plan: he had been happy enough flying with Antony when Simon and John were forbidden. But she could not risk it.

The phone call to Antonia came through exactly when Lily was expecting it, seeing the weather so perfect for herself. Robert said he would come and pick her up, and they arranged to meet on the edge of the village, by the cemetery. Lily slipped away in good time to sit by Antony's grave for a few minutes, trying to calm the excitement that was bubbling in her guts: he would be laughing at her, she thought. How he would have enjoyed Robert's company! They were alike in their passions, if not in temperament.

At last the little sports car drew up beside the church. Lily ran to it, gasping.

Robert was laughing, leaning over to open the door. 'Steady on, dear girl! Don't have a heart attack before we've started!'

'Oh, I can't believe it's really happening! I've died of impatience, more like – every day – it's crazy—'

He must think her demented, she thought. He told her he planned to use a small airfield he knew in Middlesex, with plenty of empty fields around it where landing would be safe in all circumstances and there would be complete privacy.

'My mate Tom will come up with us, see you out. He might want to jump too, I don't know. But it will be a fun outing. I'm really pleased to do this for you.'

What more could she ask?

It was the perfect day, cloudless and still. Robert said his plane was at Hendon, not Brooklands, so the drive was unfamiliar, but Lily was wrapped in a cocoon of gorgeous anticipation, no longer fearful, anxious and uncertain, but now perfectly sure that she had made the right decision. And had, amazingly, chosen the perfect partner. Robert wasn't bossy or anxious or patronizing, just a good companion, quietly amused and supportive of her last throw for excitement in her life.

The aeroplane was a neat little monoplane tucked discreetly into a quiet corner of the busy commercial aerodrome. Robert parked his car nearby and his mate Tom was waiting there with the gear for Lily.

Tom was young, full of enthusiasm and admiration for

Lily. 'I'll tell my old gran tonight,' he said. 'She'll throw a fit.'

'Nobody knows,' Lily said. 'My family wouldn't have it, I'm sure.'

Their confidence was balm. It hadn't been at all like that before: fear had been the overriding emotion, fear and confusion. But so many years had passed since then. She was smiling now with happiness.

They fixed her parachute and she was bunked up through the plane's door. Tom was fixed up with a parachute too, to follow her down and see her right.

'In case you land in a cowpat.'

'He'll see you back to the plane,' Robert said. 'In case you don't land near.'

The roar of the engine, the old familiar smell, brought the old days back to Lily with a jolt. The excitement boiled up inside her – at last, after all her weeks of shilly-shallying, doubting, longing, it was going to happen!

The little plane tore along the runway, so fast after Antony's machine, that she was amazed, looking down to see the ground shrinking so rapidly below her, nothing like their old plane's labouring ascent to clear the boundary trees. How Antony would have loved it! Heading south and already climbing steadily, it passed over the western edge of London; she could make out the Thames and Richmond Park and realized that they could well pass over their own farm but, so high now, it was impossible to see the detail. The earth was a green blur, the sky enlarging all around her, taking her up into its arms, it seemed, until the land seemed almost to have disappeared.

She had told Robert high, and they were already far, far higher than she had been before. There was only the sky, all around, above and below: they were an infinitesimal dot in the universe, completely detached from the earth. To jump from here was going to be like launching into pure space. Lily felt her breath quickening, beginning to feel frightened: what had she been thinking of, to do this again?

Then Tom was beside her, grinning, giving her a thumbs up. He was so near and real and laughing: 'Bit of fun, eh? Ready to go? Just wait for Rob's signal, any minute now. And I'll be right behind you.'

She stood up frantically, and Tom slid the door open. The wind roared and the plane tilted, tipping Lily forward. She clung to the doorway and Tom roared, 'Jump!' in her ear and she let go and fell. A moment of panic, and then an amazing silence, only the wind whistling in her ears. She pulled the ripcord, and then came the stomach-turning lurch, bringing her up short, the first unnerving swings and then – oh bliss! – the pure beauty of the sky, silence, peace . . . hanging there so gently, not seeming to move at all, alone in the great blue world. She could scarcely see the ground yet, scarcely breathe, the air so thin, scarcely remember any of the stupid tangles her brain had got into planning this jump, but just gently swing with the beautiful silk canopy above holding her like some benign sky mother.

She wished Antony was with her. In a sense he was, because none of this would have happened without him. She would never have felt the joy that now flooded her, the indescribable sense of the whole world slowly revolving below her, the promise of the kind land beneath her dangling feet that she belonged to and was returning to, to all its riches and loving beings and eternal pleasures: the sense of being alive more acute than ever she could remember.

Never to forget.

AN INTERVIEW WITH
K. M. PEYTON

You had your first novel published at the age of just 15, and have since written over 70 books!
Did writing *Wild Lily* feel any different from your first book all those years ago?

Not in the sense that I had a strong desire to put down the story in my head. I don't write if I haven't a good plot that is asking to be written. The first one was written out of frustration that I wasn't able to have a pony of my own and I longed for one so badly, so it helped to write my dreams down. I met someone many years later who sat on her local beach waiting for a horse to walk up out of the sea (as happens in my first book) and of course it never happened and I felt very guilty about her disappointment. Writing *Wild Lily* was easier on a computer than my first book in pen and ink.

Wild Lily is set in the roaring 20s – what is it about this era that drew you to it?

The era was dictated by the plot: the story couldn't be set today, as no boy could just go and fly an aeroplane with so little paperwork – a little earlier you could just go and buy an aeroplane and fly it away without even proving you could fly. No wonder the death rate was so enormous! And the period I chose is just when parachuting was no longer just an escape apparatus, but something that could be fun.

Can you tell us where you got your inspiration for *Wild Lily?*

My inspiration for *Wild Lily* I suppose came from Painshill Park in Cobham and its grotto in the lake, which I once explored many years ago. The house is purely imaginary and so are the surroundings. I also went to Brooklands recently and that set me off on the flying and parachuting angle. As a child my parents took me there when they went to watch the motor racing, but I hadn't been back since. I have always loved aeroplanes (why? perhaps my passion for Biggles books as a child). My bedroom has very high windows and I lie in bed in the mornings and watch the aeroplanes coming over, very high, often with white streamers, and wonder where they have come from, who is up there and going where and why. It is the flight path to Heathrow from Germany, Hamburg

I think, or Amsterdam. I love seeing a summer sky streaked with the white paths of high aeroplanes, too high to hear; on the other hand I wouldn't want to live close under the flight path near Heathrow, too much of a good thing.

Tell us about your writing process – how you plan, where you write, any essential snacks?!

I plan my books in quite a lot of detail a long time before I start writing. I know the beginning and the end and quite a lot of the middle, although that is the part that is most likely to change and hopefully develop as I go along. I don't take notes, except names and dates, etc., and what the dog is called, that sort of thing, nothing else. It is all in my head. I only make one draft, unless I am forced by my editor, David Fickling, to write some more. I do trust David, but someone said the other day, "David isn't always right.". I rather think he is. I write on a computer mostly in the mornings for two or three hours, no longer. I am very slow. A thousand words is an excellent day. I work for longer if it is rushing along, an easy, active bit, not very often. My planning is done all the time, a lot of it when I am in bed and not sleeping or in the bath or on a train (not when driving the car – dangerous!). I drink coffee when I write. I don't bother ordinarily.

Which character did you find easiest
to write/relate to the most?

I found Antony difficult. Some way through the book my critical daughter said Antony wasn't much good as a character as you didn't know where you were with him and Eureka! the penny dropped – that was his character. He was ineffectual, no hero, just useless. Everything he did proved wrong. Poor old Ant.

We were blown away by that parachuting scene!
Have you ever experienced jumping out of a
plane yourself? If not – do you wish you had?

No. No desire to do it whatever. But if I did I know it would be mind-blowing.

Which books have changed your life?

As far as I know, no books have changed my life. I have been very moved by some. One that comes to mind is *Testament of Youth* by Vera Brittain, which I read when I was eighteen or so. I have a large library of climbing books. Also horse racing and thoroughbred breeding, masses of old pony books, music books, and books on my heroes: Chopin, Elvis Presley, Dougal Haston, Fred Archer, José Mourinho, Mummery, Dickie Lee DSO, DFC, etc..

What has been your proudest moment?

There are lots! I think my proudest moment was when I went to court, and won, in order to get a disused railway line near where I live turned into a bridleway. Also we have planted a five-acre wood next to our house and it is so beautiful it makes me very proud when I walk through it.

Other proud moments include when our dear race horse came fourth in the four-mile chase at the Cheltenham Festival. Only once removed from the winners' enclosure! Oh, the glory! Out of twenty-three runners, no less. No, he never won the Grand National, but it was as good as.

I was awarded an MBE in 2014. Surprise was more my reaction, but I suppose I have to admit that yes, it made me proud. I have completely forgotten it now and never add it to my name. It is such an unfair thing: wonderful people who deserve it never get near it. I have never found out who put my name forward, none of my publishers or literary friends. Who?

Do you have a motto?

No I haven't a motto, but if I had it would be 'Persevere'. Don't give up.